ROSES
&
VIOLETS

THE ROSENHOLM TRILOGY
VOLUME 1

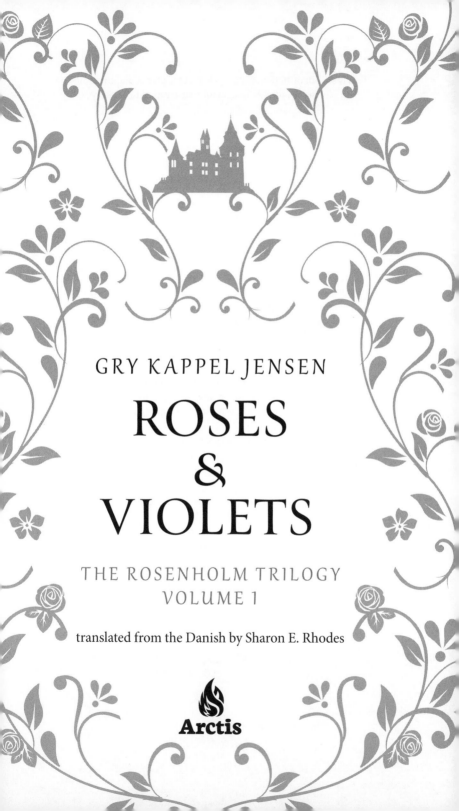

GRY KAPPEL JENSEN

ROSES & VIOLETS

THE ROSENHOLM TRILOGY
VOLUME 1

translated from the Danish by Sharon E. Rhodes

Arctis

This is a work of fiction. Names, characters, places, and incidents are from the author's imagination or are used fictitiously.

W1-Media, Inc.
Arctis Books USA
Stamford, CT, USA

Copyright © 2023 by W1-Media Inc. for this edition
ROSER OG VIOLER © Gry Kappel Jensen og Turbine, 2019
Published by agreement with Babel-Bridge Literary Agency
First hardcover English edition published by W1-Media Inc. /
Arctis Books USA 2023

Visit our website at www.arctis-books.com

1 3 5 7 9 8 6 4 2

The Library of Congress Control Number: 2022951140

ISBN 978-1-64690-012-1
eBook ISBN 978-1-64690-612-3

English translation copyright © Sharon E. Rhodes, 2023

Printed in China

PROLOGUE

He lays me down in the grass. The sky spins above me, like when my sister and I played as small children. We spun and spun with our faces toward the sky, arms spread, our dresses forming perfect circles around us.

He repositions my arms, arranges my legs, spreads out my hair. He strokes my cheek, his mouth is very close to my ear, his breath is warm. He sings for me, he tells me that I am beautiful, that he loves me.

He bends over me, a dark figure, a shadow against the swirling spiral of the sky. I know who he is, but I cannot see his face. I want to scream, but I cannot. The rustling of the silver poplars vies with the sound of my pulse whooshing in my ears, the violets bloom around me and the sky goes black.

PART 1
SUMMER

Roses are red
Violets are blue
Strawberries are sweet
And so are you

Traditional love poem,
often used in 19th-century
autograph books

JULY 6ᵀᴴ
3:45 P.M.

Kirstine

Kirstine listened. It was silent in the house. She forced herself to take a deep breath.

Relax. It's not the same as stealing.

The letter *was* hers, after all. It just happened to be lying in the top drawer of the large, oak writing desk. The drawer where her father kept their passports and baptismal certificates and that sort of thing. The drawer that could be locked.

Her sweaty fingers clutched the small, gold key she'd taken from the back corner of the china cabinet, where it was always kept.

"Kirstine, do you want some coffee? There's still a bit of cake from yesterday."

The sound of her mother's voice from out in the garden made her jump.

"No thanks!" She closed the door into the living room and attempted to ignore the small crucifix hanging over the writing desk. Jesus looked down at her reprovingly. The key turned easily, but the drawer stuck. She had to yank it open. It was sitting on top—she recognized it immediately. The thick, white envelope. A stamp with a postmark indicating that the letter was sent

9

several weeks ago. And her name on the front. *Kirstine Marie Jensen*. Despite this, it was locked away in a drawer. And despite this, someone had opened the envelope and read it. She grabbed the letter and put it in her pocket.

Footsteps on the kitchen floor, someone opening the door to the living room. She hastily shoved the drawer closed.

"Are you in here? Don't you want to get outside now that the sun's finally shining?" Her mother briefly scanned Kirstine's face and body. Was she looking for something? Had she seen something? Kirstine's heart pounded.

"No. I mean yes. I think I'll go for a bike ride."

"Oh, okay. But be sure to get home by dinner time . . ."

Kirstine nodded and edged around her mother. Her hand still clutched around the key, and she could clearly feel the letter in her pocket as she unlocked her bike. She would have to put both the letter and the key back again tonight, after her parents had gone to bed.

Kirstine had just pushed her bike out through the gate when she saw her mother standing in the street, waiting for her. She must have gone through the front door.

"Did you take something from your father's desk?"

Kirstine

The westerly wind whipped in her face. She pedaled so hard that her thighs burned and her knees ached.

She'd screamed at her mother. Loud enough that the neighbors must have heard. It wasn't like her, but it was *her* letter, they had no right to hide it from her. And now she was running away from it all.

Kirstine swung her bike to the right, toward the forest. She stood up on the pedals for the last stretch and then threw the bike against the ancient, moss-covered stone wall encircling the small, white church. Then she walked past the church and into the forest. The wind made the treetops sigh, but it was quiet among the trunks. The air smelled of pine needles, dead leaves, moss, water, earth. She followed the path a short way, but then turned in among the trees to follow her own route, the one the mushroom pickers didn't know about. It had been a rainy summer, but today the sky was clear and the sun shone through the deep-green branches. She felt the water rising up through the thick layer of moss with each step, her sandals getting wet in the process. She stopped, pulled the sandals off, and continued barefoot. It was a strange feeling, walking through the moss of the forest floor as the ice-cold rainwater rose up between her bare toes. Her mother had looked alarmed when Kirstine began shouting at her. *No, not alarmed. Afraid.*

There was a small hill in the middle of the clearing where the heather was in bloom and chanterelles grew in late summer. At the top of the hill were five large stones, some of which had fallen over hundreds of years ago, and no one now living knew their original purpose. Kirstine sat on the largest stone—it lay on its side and had almost disappeared into the heather and grass. She pulled out the envelope. She'd first seen the letter on the kitchen counter alongside brochures and the local paper one afternoon a few weeks ago. She hadn't thought anything of it until her mother hurriedly swept it away and took the stack of mail with her into the living room. That's when she'd gotten the feeling that the letter was for her. She finally opened the envelope and unfolded the letter. It was printed on thick paper with a grooved texture she could feel between her fingers, and there was an embossed logo of a rose at the top of the paper. In gold letters, the envelope read: *Rosenholm Academy.*

June 17*th*
Rosenholm Academy

Dear Kirstine Marie Jensen,

The faculty of Rosenholm Academy for gifted and exceptionally talented youth invites you to an informational meeting to tell you more about Rosenholm's program and, potentially, admit you to the first-year class this fall.

Rosenholm Academy is located on Zealand and surrounded by natural beauty. We have a long, glorious history specializing in the education and molding of young people possessed of rare and special talents. Rosenholm Academy comprises approximately three hundred students, all of whom live at the school for the duration of our three-year program. The course of study corresponds to the final years of traditional secondary education and is tuition-free.

We hope to see you at the informational meeting on July 7*th* at 10:00 a.m. Please note that the meeting is only for prospective students—parents are not welcome.

The enclosed information sheet includes the school's address as well as options for traveling to the school via public transportation.

We look forward to meeting you.

With best wishes,

Birgit Lund

Birgit Lund
Headmistress

It took her a long time to work her way through the letter. She let her eyes scan the words again . . . *gifted and exceptionally talented* . . . Uh, what? If there was one thing Kirstine was sure of, it was that she did *not* fit that description. That much she had gathered after years of failing school. Special instruction, school psychologists, discussions, reading programs—nothing had helped, and in the end, everyone around her had apparently given up. After a disastrous attempt to finish high school, she'd stopped going to school altogether, and now she only left home to go to her cleaning job at the assisted living facility. And the church functions her parents were always dragging her to. In short, she'd just turned eighteen and had no idea what to do with herself.

Kirstine let her fingers run over the envelope's beautiful gold embossing. If she hadn't been sure no one would bother going to so much trouble to trick her, she would have thought it was a prank. But no . . . She'd perfected the art of making herself invisible. She wasn't bullied, just overlooked.

She checked the date again. The meeting was tomorrow. *Forget it. It's never going to happen.*

Her parents would never, ever give her permission. She'd never even been allowed to go to the parties held by her classmates. So going all the way across Funen to some strange school on Zealand? *No way.* It was just as well they'd hidden the letter in the first place.

Kirstine lay on the ground at the center of the circle of stones. She stayed there until she felt the tingling sensation she always felt when she lay there long enough. A prickling heat that spread through her body until she almost felt as if she was lifting from the ground and rising up toward the white clouds drifting across the blue summer sky. A feeling of strength and energy filled her body, driving out the anger. Although she'd never told them about her experiences in the forest, she was sure her parents would not approve. *Where do you get this stuff, Kirstine! Stop this nonsense . . .* But she didn't care. When she felt like this, it almost felt as if she could go wherever she wanted, and she just let her body rest against the forest floor like an empty vessel.

Her thoughts swirled around the mysterious letter. Maybe she could tell her parents how she actually felt, what she did and thought about, was afraid of, wished for. Simply explain it all until they understood and supported her and would see her off on the train, rejoicing over the fact that she could stand on her own two feet. Yes, that's exactly what she would do—except for the part about telling them anything.

Kirstine breathed deeply until she felt she'd fully returned to her body. Then she pulled out her phone and typed the school's address into Google Maps.

Victoria

See me . . .

"No!"

Victoria gasped for air. *It was only a dream, only a dream. Breathe . . .*

She sat straight up in bed and wrapped her arms around herself. Slowly, she regained control of her breathing, but the anxiety left her shivering. The moon sent a diffuse light through the white curtains fluttering in the breeze from the open windows, and the dreamcatcher over her bed spun around slowly. She let her eyes follow its movement. It was there to protect her.

She'd dreamed about the white shadows again, but this time was different. One of them had come up close, had practically bent over her. *Way too close.*

She wrapped herself up in her comforter, but the cold wouldn't loosen its grip. She was still shivering when she went downstairs to make a cup of tea. The large house was silent. The twins slept further down the hall. Despite the many bedrooms, they insisted on sleeping in the same room. Their au pair had her room in the basement, and her parents' bedroom was at the opposite end of the house. *There's no one here, there's no danger.*

Victoria turned on the light in the kitchen and, as always, avoided looking at the windows when it was dark outside. She didn't want to see her own image reflected in the glass. She poured water from the instant hot water tap directly over the teabag and counted the seconds as the tea steeped. *No one's trying to hurt you.*

It startled her when, inevitably, she did make eye contact with her pale reflection in the windowpane. The white shadow was clearly visible behind her. She closed her eyes. *Face your fears . . .*

Victoria turned around slowly but kept her eyes closed a moment longer. Then she forced herself to open them. *There's no one else here, you're alone.* Or at least that's what she tried to tell herself. But Victoria was never truly alone.

Kirstine

It was getting light outside the train's windows. Kirstine imagined the birds competing in song outside, but inside the train you could only hear the monotonous rattling of the motor and the metallic clang of the rails. Her stomach was in knots, and it was impossible to breathe normally, even when she really tried. What was she was doing? Running away in the middle of the night—who does that? She did. Obviously.

There weren't many people on the train. Diagonally opposite her seat was a young man, asleep with his head leaned back against the seat. His reddish hair lay sprawled over his forehead. His skin was fair with small freckles strewn over his cheeks and the bridge of his nose. He was older than her, but she wasn't sure how much older. Somewhere, as the train worked its way through Jutland, he'd gotten on board, chosen a seat, thrown himself down, and immediately fallen asleep. But she couldn't sleep. The young man shifted in his sleep, and she realized she'd been staring at him. She turned her face toward the window instead and pressed her forehead into the cold glass. It was almost light now.

Almost twenty minutes before they reached Sorø, Kirstine put on her jacket, zipped her bag shut, and sat with it in her lap. She'd read the directions again and again until she knew the stations by heart in case the loudspeaker system was down and she had to read the flickering names of stations and cities flashing past on the information display at the top of the train compartment.

"Next station Sorø."

She jumped up and edged carefully out between the legs of the people who had boarded as the train crossed Funen. The young man was still asleep as she went past. Just then the train took a turn, and her leg bumped into his knee.

"Wha—?" he blurted out, looking up blearily, as if he had no idea where he was. "Is this Sorø?"

She couldn't get a word out, but luckily she managed to nod.

"Oh, thanks," he said. He ran a hand through his already tousled hair before grabbing his jacket and springing out of his seat toward the doors that had only just opened onto the platform.

"Wait!" Her voice stuck in her throat, and it was impossible for her to shout louder. "Your bag!"

Out on the platform she finally caught up with the young man as he walked away from the train determinedly.

"Your bag!" Shyly, she handed him a brown, leather shoulder bag. "You left it on the train."

"Aww shit, did I? Thanks a million." He smiled, looking simultaneously happy and embarrassed. He looked a bit older now that he was awake. "Really, thank you," he said with a crooked grin. "And you were getting off at Sorø too?

"Yes," she said, trying to force her voice to a normal volume. "I mean, I'm continuing on by bus."

"Me too. The busses leave from over there." He vaguely indicated the direction with a careless movement of his arm. The sun was up now, and the birds were singing in the early morning.

"Which bus are you taking?" he asked when they'd reached the row of blue bus signs.

"Number 14, I think," she said. But she didn't *think*, she was absolutely certain that she would remember the bus number to her dying day after having studied the route so many times.

"Number 14? Huh, that's funny. Me too. Then again, maybe it's not so strange. I doubt anyone takes the train to Sorø at this time of day, unless . . . May I ask if you're on your way to Rosenholm?"

Kirstine nodded. "Yes, for a meeting."

The young man's eyes scanned her face as if he was searching for something.

"Yes, well, I know they need people. But I should introduce myself: Jakob." He extended his hand and gave hers a firm squeeze. "I've got Norse Studies there."

She settled for nodding again. He said it as if it was self-explanatory, and she had no intention of exposing her ignorance by asking what that meant.

"You know it's only half past six, and the bus doesn't leave until eight," said Jakob, studying the old, scratched watch on his wrist. "We might as well sit down." He pointed at a shelter about thirty feet away from the bus stop. The bus station was desolate. There was just a solitary bus with the motor running and the text *Not in service* glowing in yellow above the windshield. Kirstine couldn't remember ever having been on Zealand before, but this was pretty similar to what she was used to at home. Maybe that's what gave her the courage to start a conversation. Or maybe it was because Jakob didn't seem nearly as intimidating as he would have if she hadn't seen him sitting and sleeping and running away from his bag.

"Do you live in Jutland?" she asked.

"No, but my parents live in Skanderborg. The options for getting here are awful, aren't they? It takes almost an entire night."

"This is the first time I've made the trip," she said as they sat down in the small shelter.

Jakob turned his face toward her in surprise. "Is that right? You've never been to Rosenholm before?"

Kirstine shook her head. Had she just said something stupid after all?

"Did you go to school abroad then?"

"No, only in Thy."

The remark made him chuckle, and she laughed too, even though she hadn't said it to be funny.

"Well, there you go," he said, and he didn't seem to think she was stupid, just that she'd told a joke.

They sat there without saying anything for a few minutes. The air was chilly and nipped at her cheeks. They hadn't seen too many cloud-free skies this summer, but on this cold July morning there wasn't a cloud in sight. She shivered in her thin summer jacket, regretting that she hadn't worn more layers.

"Just a minute," Jakob bent forward and unzipped his bag. "I think I have it with me."

He handed her a wool scarf with a checkered pattern.

"What a summer," he said, as he invited her to take the scarf with a nod. He was wearing a short, dark wool coat, even though it was, theoretically, the height of summer. She took the scarf and wrapped it carefully around her neck. It smelled faintly of woods and wood smoke. The bus, which had kept its motor running, had changed its *Not in service* out for a number and rolled slowly over to one of the other bus bays.

"You shouldn't be nervous about today," Jakob said, as he followed the bus with his eyes. "They're really nice at Rosenholm. A little old-fashioned, maybe. Birgit, the headmistress, you know? She seems a bit stern, but she's super fair. She's helped me out a lot. And you really don't need to worry about your age and all that," he said, casting a quick glance her way so that the heat rose to her cheeks.

Embarrassing! Of course, he'd noticed that she was too old to still be in high school.

"Hey," he said, as if he sensed her embarrassment, "they took me, right?" He winked at her, and she felt herself begin to smile. If she had dared, she would have asked which year he was in. But he was right, he seemed older than a typical student, even if he was in his final year.

The bus gave up on waiting for passengers and drove away empty.

"Pretty quiet, huh?" she asked, not actually expecting an answer.

"Quiet? It's absolutely dead. Totally dead." Jakob's voice had taken on an apocalyptic tone, which again made her smile.

"It doesn't really bother me, I'm used to it," Kirstine said.

"You still live at home? In Thy or wherever it was?" he asked.

She nodded.

"What then, your parents are sitting at home, cheering you on from afar?"

"No, they don't even know I'm here."

"What? Huh," Jakob said.

"It's a little complicated. They're pretty strange. It's because . . . we—my family—we're very Christian," she stammered, blushing over the words. What was happening to her? Why was she sitting here and telling this to a complete stranger?

"Okay, shit, like some kind of cult or what?" Jakob asked, looking at her with concern.

"No," Kirstine started to laugh. "Inner Mission, if you know what that is?"

"No, not at all. No one in my family has followed the Christian faith exactly. But . . . it must be a lot to deal with, right?" He laughed as if he couldn't quite wrap his head around all the implications of what she'd just told him.

She shrugged. "Well, I never really thought about it when I was a kid."

"Nah, of course not. Listen, you know, there used to be a vending machine that sold plastic cups of really, really awful coffee. Should we see if still works? That is—if can you even drink coffee when you're from some scary cult up in Thy?"

Kirstine laughed and stood up to go with him. *You have no idea.*

Chamomile

Chamomile's mother had, for once, gotten up before her. She could hear her mother rattling around out in the kitchen. She heard the sound of stirring, in at least one bowl, something falling, her mother cursing, and a pan spluttering on the gas burner. *As long as she doesn't set herself on fire in there.*

Chamomile tiptoed from her room out to the bathroom. The floor was cold against her bare toes. It might be summer, but it was still cold inside the old house.

After showering, she wrapped a towel around herself and went back to her room. Judging from the noise, her mother was still busy with something in the kitchen, and now she could hear sounds coming from the living room too.

Chamomile opened the old wardrobe with the creaking door and looked inside. She didn't want to look too fancy, but it was still a special day. A summer dress, maybe? It *was* summer, even if they hadn't felt it much. She grabbed two hangers and went out to the living room.

"Mom, which one?"

Her mother stood in the living room, putting a bouquet of garden roses into a vase. She had gathered her red hair into a messy knot on top of her head and was wearing pajama pants, an oversized wool sweater, and an apron. The woodstove was lit, and tea lights stood on the little table set for two.

"Oh, this is nice. But aren't you going a bit overboard?" Chamomile said.

"Not at all. Now just you wait, I'm making pancakes with loads of syrup. And wear the green dress, it's such a nice cut for you."

Chamomile shrugged and threw on the green dress.

"Look at you," said her mother, zipping the dress up in the back. "What a figure you have. Classic hourglass, I tell you. Marilyn Monroe, go home!"

Chamomile rolled her eyes. What her mother called an hourglass figure was what the meanest of the girls in her old class had called fat. But if today went well, she didn't need to worry about them anymore. She'd get a whole new set of classmates. *Nice classmates, hopefully!*

"Let me look at you," said Chamomile's mother, spinning her daughter a half-turn around. "You are so beautiful, my girl. Shall I braid your hair? Come and sit down. I've made you a special cup of tea. Perfect for today." Her mother went out into the little kitchen and came back with a steaming cup the size of a small washbasin.

"Here you are. Lemon balm, which is good for restlessness and nerves, and sage, which counteracts indigestion and gas. On a day like this you'd rather not sit down and . . . *pfft!*" Her mother made a very true-to-nature fart sound with her mouth.

"Mom," she groaned, but she couldn't help laughing all the same.

"And then, of course, there's lots and lots of chamomile. And honey, plenty of that too."

"Then it can't be too bad. Thanks, Mom."

She let herself be pushed down into a chair as her mother brushed her red hair until it had almost dried in the heat from the woodstove. She enjoyed her mother's firm yet gentle grip with the hairbrush. She had always brushed Chamomile's hair like that. Every so often a creaking sound came from inside the woodstove, and the living room was delightfully scented with the woodsmoke and the various bunches of herbs hanging from the ceiling to dry.

"Are you doing a French braid?" she asked.

"Mmm," answered her mother, concentrating. "Sit still."

When the braid was finished, her mother brought in a towering heap of mismatched pancakes.

"Here, have them with the dandelion syrup."

"Aren't you having any?"

"Yes, but later. Just now I want to sit and gaze at my big girl. Where have the years gone? You're all grown up."

"What's going on with you?" asked Chamomile, her mouth full of pancakes. "It's not as though I'm moving out today. And, by the way, there's no guarantee they'll even want me."

"Of course they will, Mile-Mouse," said her mother, planting a kiss on her forehead. "I've never had the least bit of doubt that you have what it takes."

"Thanks, but take it easy. You're a little bit . . . a little much with things like this."

"Much?"

"Yes, like when you threw a first menstruation party for me and invited all the girls in my class."

"What?" Chamomile's mother said, looking both surprised and offended.

"Ugh, Mom, stop. You remember."

Of the many, many embarrassing experiences of Chamomile's life to date, the menstruation party took the cake. Her mother had invited eight girls from her class to celebrate the fact that Chamomile had gotten her first period. She'd covered the floor of the living room with a thick rag rug because the table wasn't big enough for everyone, and then she served red soda (unfortunate coloring), chocolate cake, and herbal tea, which was supposed to be good for bloating and menstrual cramps.

None of the other girls had gotten their periods yet and they sat quiet as mice on the rug, staring at Chamomile's mother with large, round eyes. Her mother had worn a long sunshine-yellow dress with a fluttering skirt for the occasion. She gave a solemn speech about the moon's phases and woman's cycle before pulling out a drum and singing an Indian hymn in praise of woman and nature. Chamomile had truly believed she would die of embarrassment right there on the rug.

"The other parents called and complained afterward. My classmates weren't allowed to come over anymore."

Her mother threw her head back and laughed so hard her belly shook. "You know it was only one of the girls who couldn't come over anymore. The one with the thin hair. It's all because I'm just so proud of you," her mother said.

"Yeah, well, we'll have to see how it goes," Chamomile said. "I really wish I could've prepared better. Can't you just tell me a little bit about what will happen today?"

"Unfortunately, that is against the rules," her mother said, clamping her lips together. "And anyway, things have probably changed a bit since I was there. Eat up, we'll have to leave soon."

Chamomile sighed deeply and got up to pack her bag. It was no use badgering her mother; it didn't affect her anyway. The woman was stubborn as a mule.

"Here, put on my good cardigan, it's cold outside. The one grandma knitted, with the silver buttons."

She took the sweater. Chamomile's mother was wearing a wool poncho over her sweater and had stuck her bare feet into a pair of green, glow-in-the-dark plastic clogs. "You've got your bag? Then we're ready."

The fastest route to the main road ran along the edge of the field and past the old burial mound, but that trip was best made in rubber boots, especially when it had rained as much as it had lately, so today they would go by the gravel road.

"Parents aren't allowed to come, it said so in the letter," Chamomile said.

"I know, darling, I'm just taking you down to the bus. Don't you worry. I won't do anything to embarrass you," she said, winking as she tucked a loose wisp of hair behind her ear. There were streaks of gray in her mother's red hair. It was true enough that time was passing.

They walked out through the kitchen door and, even though neither of them was particularly tall, they had to duck to keep from knocking into the top of the doorframe. It was an old stable door, and the lock didn't work properly. "It doesn't matter," Chamomile's mother always said, "after all, anyone who comes all the way out here has always been invited first."

Chamomile stood a moment and let her eyes wander over the old half-timbered house where she'd lived her whole life. The thatch roof needed replacing. There were several bare patches where the straw had fallen out.

"Come on." Chamomile's mother stuck her arm through hers, and in that fashion they walked across the yard as an orange cat meowed at them reproachfully. "You'll just have to wait, Mismis," her mother called. "We have a bus to catch."

They walked along the gravel road and turned onto the slightly larger paved road. It cut straight across the landscape so that it rose and fell with the rolling hills. The sun had yet to gain much strength, and in all the low points a mist hung over the road like a magic veil hiding mysterious secrets. From the road, they could see the large burial mound over which five mighty and ancient oak trees had reigned in safety from the hundreds of farmers that had plowed the field around the mound since they'd first sprouted.

Once they reached the main road, they waited at the edge. There was no official bus stop, but the driver always pulled over if he saw them standing there. As they waited, the sun crept farther up in the sky, heating the earth so that it steamed around them.

"Good luck today," her mother said when the bus finally came. She squeezed Chamomile's hands and suddenly looked serious. "Chamomile? Take care of yourself, okay?"

"Of course," she said, giving her one last squeeze. "Take it easy, Mom, it's just a school. What's the worst that could happen?"

Her mother nodded and quickly dried her eyes as she attempted a smile, but, when Chamomile had found a seat on the bus and waved goodbye to the small, round lady in the glow-in-the-dark clogs, she got the sense that there was something important her mother had not told her about Rosenholm Academy.

Kirstine

Jakob breathed heavily; he must have been deeply asleep. Kirstine could feel his breath against her neck. The feeling filled her body with a dizzying lightness. She couldn't possibly sleep. She sat with her face pressed against the glass, gazing out at the landscape. The sun shone on the waving fields, dotted with more burial mounds than she remembered ever having seen in all her childhood. The earth must be rich here.

They drank bad coffee and talked while they waited for the bus. Jakob had told her about his parents—he'd just been visiting them. She didn't understand half of what he said, but she had just nodded and let him talk. There was something about their having had completely different expectations for him, that they didn't support his choice, and it all had something to do with Rosenholm, though she did not understand how exactly. He'd spoken to her as if she was a completely normal person and not a weirdo. As if she was a grown-up and not little Kirstine who never understood anything.

That Kirstine was in the past now. She could feel it. This here was *The New Kirstine*. The girl who laughed out loud without being embarrassed. The girl who listened with interest and produced small, understanding comments along the way so you felt like entrusting her with all your worries. The girl who sat with a handsome young man's head on her shoulder.

"Rosenholm," said the driver, and Jakob sat up with a start and dragged a hand over his face.

They stepped out into the most delightful sunshine. It was still morning, but no longer cold, and Jakob stopped to take off his coat. A lark swooped high above them, trilling its notes.

"We only have to walk a little ways. Once we round that bend, you'll be able to see the school," Jakob said, pointing.

Rosenholm—it sounded fancy, and yet she didn't really know what she'd expected. *Not this.* Rosenholm was practically a castle. A small white castle with ancient red tiles on the roof, four small towers—one in each corner—and a small suspension bridge leading over a moat. A long avenue of old, knotted chestnut trees led up to the school, but first you had to walk through a large park filled with, among other shrubs and trees, mighty rhododendrons, tall silver poplars, an ancient magnolia tree, and a gigantic copper beech.

"Oh wow," she said.

"Yeah, it's nice, right?" Jakob smiled, looking as proud as if he had built it himself.

They walked over the small wooden bridge and the gravel crunched under their feet as they approached the gate into the inner courtyard. An impressively large, antique-pink climbing rose grew up the wall in front of them, sprinkling its petals over the courtyard's cobblestones. A clock on the wall above them said it was almost nine.

"I wasn't supposed to get here until ten," she said. "Maybe I should just wait out here."

"No, come on. I'll introduce you to Birgit and show you around a bit." He opened a large, ancient door into a great hall where a wide staircase led further up. Inside the hall it seemed very dark, especially after they'd walked through the sun-filled park. There were tall wooden panels along the walls and up under the ceiling were four words written in large, cursive letters. *Earth, Growth, Blood, Death*, she read.

"I can even put in a good word for you," Jakob smiled, winking as if they had concocted some sinister plan together.

"Jakob Engholm!"

Kirstine flinched at the sound of the sharp voice that echoed in the great hall. At the top of the staircase stood a tall woman with short, gray hair and distinctive black glasses.

"Birgit, good morning, here's someone you have to meet," Jakob said, taking the stairs two steps at a time. "This is Kirstine," he said, gesturing toward her as she lagged behind.

The headmistress didn't even glance in her direction but stared fixedly at Jakob.

"What's going on? Teachers are to have absolutely no contact with prospective students except as part of the official program."

"But . . . what? Aren't you here for a job interview?" Jakob stared at her in confusion.

Job interview? No, he had it all wrong. Kirstine wanted to say something, but the severe-looking woman made the words stick in her throat. Her head just shook faintly from side to side.

"We have no job interviews today," the headmistress said. "We are, however, holding an informational meeting for prospective students, and you would know that if you'd bothered to empty your faculty mailbox or take part in the meetings with the rest of the faculty."

She turned away from Jakob and looked at Kirstine. "Am I correct in assuming that you received a letter about an informational meeting?"

She nodded.

"Oh, shit, that's . . . why didn't you say so?" Jakob said.

Kirstine just shook her head again. Jakob had actually believed she was here for an interview? And he was a teacher?

"I must have misunderstood, my apologies," mumbled Jakob, avoiding Kirstine's eyes. "Good luck today," he added, and then he turned away without another word.

The headmistress sighed disapprovingly before turning back to Kirstine. "You'd better wait outside," she said. "Once the others have arrived, you'll all be shown into the room where the meeting will be held."

Kirstine nodded and walked down the stairs like a guest who had been turned away at the door. It wasn't until she was standing in the small, sunny courtyard that she realized she still had Jakob's scarf around her neck. *So much for The New Kirstine.*

Malou

Towers, spire, a goddamned moat . . .

As soon as Malou saw Rosenholm, she was sure of two things. The first was that it looked like the sort of place that was absolutely not tuition-free—it oozed wealth and power. And the second was that, if it was against-all-odds free to attend, then she would do everything in her power to get in. This was most certainly a place for the elite.

She tightened her high ponytail and smoothed the blond hair with her hand before walking the last stretch down to the school. She preferred to not walk with anyone else and made an effort to lag behind the girls who'd arrived on the same bus, but it wasn't easy. The girl in front of her slowly ambled along as if she had all the time in the world. She was tall and slender and wearing a simple white oxford with the sleeves pushed up to reveal her golden arms. Her hair was dark and cut short and she wore leather sandals and had a leather bag over her shoulder. The whole ensemble was strikingly simple, but she was sure the shirt alone cost more than Malou's entire outfit put together.

Malou pulled her top down a bit; the white fabric against her tanned skin looked good. The sun was shining today for a change, and she already felt hot in her blazer. Yesterday she'd spent the whole evening removing all the labels so no one would ever guess it came from H&M.

She frowned. There was sure to be a brand-new MacBook in the girl's bag. The dark-haired girl looked like someone who belonged at an elite boarding school. The opposite of Malou. But were her grades good? Not too many people had grades as good as Malou's. Girls like her, who had never learned to fight for anything, got everything handed to them. Malou ate those sorts of girls for breakfast.

She sighed impatiently and overtook the dark-haired girl before walking over the moat and into the small, shaded courtyard. There was a large group. *Only girls. Aren't there any boys at this school?*

At that moment, the clock on the opposite wall struck ten and a large door opened. A woman in her fifties stepped out. Her hair was short and steel-gray, she was dressed all in black, and her large glasses created a sharp border around her eyes. Everyone turned toward her, and the scattered murmuring among the girls was silenced.

"Welcome to Rosenholm," the woman said, her voice echoing around the courtyard. "I am the headmistress. My name is Birgit Lund. On behalf of the faculty, I bid you all welcome. We'll begin in the school's great hall."

The great hall really *was* a great hall; Malou guessed it could easily accommodate five hundred. A pair of enormous chandeliers, the sort of things usually only seen in old churches, hung from the high ceiling. There was a picture of a Viking-like figure on the wall, another depicted a beautiful woman in a forest with a wreath of leaves in her blond hair. Above them were two more pictures. In one a young man was cutting the palm of his hand with a dagger, while in the other painting a pale woman held a skull in one hand, extending it toward the viewer. *Freaky decor choice.*

In the middle of the great hall stood a row of tables, and along one wall another table was set with coffee urns, various juices in tall glass carafes, buns and rolls in large baskets, various cheeses, fruits, preserves, and something that looked like homemade Nutella. She realized with a pang how hungry she was. There were small name cards on the long tables and Malou found her seat next to two dark-haired girls, who were apparently sisters, and diagonally across from the dark-haired girl in the expensive white shirt.

When everyone had been to the breakfast buffet and the majority of plates were empty, Birgit tapped the edge of a slim glass apparently filled with blood-orange juice.

"Now I hope you're all fed and feeling comfortable," she said, clearly not struggling to make herself heard in the massive hall. "We'll begin the day with an entrance exam or, more precisely, a *series* of exams."

A collective groan ran through the hall. *Entrance exams?* She smiled for a moment. *Makes sense.* This wasn't the sort of place to let just anyone in. Of course you'd have to prove that you were capable of something. She straightened up in her chair and looked around. Many of the girls suddenly looked nervous, but Malou's mood had lifted. If admission was based on merit—rather than your parents' wallets and connections—then she had a real chance.

"You will be divided into groups that will then circulate to the various exams. After these exams everyone will reassemble in the great hall for the last exam, the written test. And please pay

36

attention now." Birgit paused to underscore the importance of what she was about to say. "There are no right or wrong answers today. These exams are very different from the sort of testing to which you're most likely accustomed. You will not fully comprehend everything, but do your best to respond honestly. The tests will sketch an outline of each of you to give us the best and most accurate idea of who you are. When the last test is over, I'll explain everything you need to know."

Malou looked around. A small woman with beautiful brown skin, dark eyes, and a long, black braid over one shoulder was now standing at the end of their table. It was difficult to guess how old she was.

"Follow me," she said, her smile reaching all the way to her black-lined eyes.

Suddenly the great hall was filled with the din of chairs being pushed back and confused and excited murmuring. Without waiting for them, the black-haired woman began to walk away, and they had to hurry to keep up. The woman led them down to the end of the great hall, where a double door led out to a small stairwell. The woman sprang up the steps with impressive agility as they raced after her. Malou lost track of how far up they had gone. *Third floor, maybe?* The woman opened a new door and now they found themselves in a long hallway with large windows on one side and all sorts of old paintings on the other.

"This is the gallery," the woman said when the last girl had walked through the door. "And my name is Lisa. Your first exam will take place in the room next door. You will go in one at a time."

Malou raised her eyebrows. An oral exam without any time to prepare? And they didn't even know the subject. *Okay, this is not going to be easy.*

Lisa put on a pair of reading glasses and pulled out a piece of paper.

"Will Anne please come with me?"

A girl with a blond bob stepped forward shyly. "That's me," she said.

"Come along," Lisa said, walking off without looking to see if the girl was following.

"Good luck!" a red-haired girl said.

One by one they were led into a room while the rest passed the time in the long hallway, the sun's light pouring in through the tall windows and illuminating the old paintings. Lisa had asked them not to talk to each other and, especially, not to discuss the test with each other, so there was plenty of time to study the paintings. Malou concluded that they depicted the passage of the seasons.

Now another girl was coming out. She was tall but walked strangely hunched over, as if she was trying to hide. Her light brown hair was parted on the side and gathered in a low ponytail. The girl looked utterly horrified and was clutching her right hand against her chest. *How bad could this test be?*

"Malou," called Lisa, "please come with me."

It was dark in the room. The curtains were drawn, and her eyes struggled to adjust to the low light. In the middle of the room a large man sat at a table with his back toward the door. His hair was gathered in a long braid and his back was so broad that she found herself wondering how he'd gotten through the narrow stairwell.

"Please, have a seat." The voice was deep but gentle, and she walked around to the other side of the table and sat across from the man. He had a bushy blond beard and friendly eyes.

"Under this cloth," he gestured, and now she could see that a thick piece of fabric was spread over the tabletop, "are a variety of objects. I want you to take them in hand, one by one, and tell me if you can sense or feel anything as you hold the object."

"Seriously?"

That was the test? It reminded her of a game they played in her after-school program when she was little. The grownups put cold spaghetti or some other slimy thing in a cardboard box with holes cut in and made them guess what it was by feeling it.

She was about to comment on the ridiculousness of the task but hesitated a moment. Maybe she understood the point of this after all. Something their homeroom teacher had done with them came to mind. The teacher had brought in a large bag of buttons—some of the buttons were black, others were white. Each student got a button and was told to put it in their mouth. *Pretty gross when you thought about it. They were certainly neither the first nor the last class to suck on the buttons.* The teacher told them that she'd dipped some of the buttons in licorice. Everyone who could taste licorice should raise their hand. After that, she told them she had dipped some of the buttons in vanilla. More children raised their hands. Malou had eventually gotten super stressed out that the other children could taste licorice and vanilla and lemon and salt and when the teacher said that she had dipped some of them in sugar, she thought that she sensed sweetness in her mouth and had raised her hand. Of course, none of the buttons had been dipped in anything but other children's saliva, and Malou remembered how annoyed she'd been that she'd succumbed to the pressure and had raised her hand. The teacher revealed that it hadn't been a test of their tastebuds at all. They were actually meant to learn something about how easily the brain can be tricked. It was the concept of placebo. Like when sick people felt they were getting better from taking medication that was really just sugar pills. Maybe the goal of this test might be to determine if they had a strong personality or if they were the type to try to satisfy a teacher by inventing feelings and sensations.

"Okay," she said.

"Start at this end," said the large man. He was silent as Malou slowly felt around under the thick, heavy fabric. The first few objects seemed to be different kinds of stone. Some were polished, others jagged. She held each in her hand for a moment before either shaking her head or saying: "Nothing." After the stones were a number of metal objects, a staff of some sort, a bulky pendant on a cord, possibly made of leather, a small bowl, and something that felt like a polished stick. None of it gave her any special sensations. But when she put her fingers on the last object, she felt a sort of jolt. It was a knife, and she'd picked it up by the blade. She fumbled for the handle. It felt significantly colder than the other objects, maybe because it was made of steel. She gripped it for a slightly longer period of time before setting it down again.

"Unfortunately, nothing," she said.

"Thank you," said the man, "you may go out to the others."

His tone of voice was unsuggestive, but Malou caught a glimpse of disappointment in his friendly eyes.

Damn! Why hadn't she said the knife felt cold?

Chamomile

Okay, apparently there was a lot that her mother hadn't told her about Rosenholm.

Chamomile shut the door after meeting with the enormous man.

"Wow, how weird was that!"

A few of the girls smiled and nodded, but Lisa raised an eyebrow and looked at her sternly. "Please do not discuss the tests," she said.

Chamomile did not want to be on the receiving end of another disapproving look from the woman with the black eyes, so she held her tongue and followed along in silence when Lisa led them back down the stairs. She sympathized with the other girls. Her mother may have refused to reveal what the tests involved, but at least Chamomile had known there would be tests. All in all, she thought the first test had gone pretty well.

This time the black-haired woman led them outside and behind the castle where the grounds seemed wilder and more overgrown than in the park they had passed through on their way up to the castle. They followed a graveled path to a circle of flagstones surrounded by trees.

"Welcome!"

Chamomile was startled when a man's voice broke the silence. A thickset man in his fifties stepped forward from among the birch trees that encircled the small, circular terrace. His face was weathered and sunburned, his hair was silver-gray and short, and he was dressed all in black. He wasn't especially tall, but his charisma immediately drew everyone's attention. The man asked them to stand, hand-in-hand, in a circle around some sort of large, stone block in the middle of the clearing. The stone was about three feet tall, and when she got closer, she could see that there was a water-filled depression in the middle, like an over-sized birdbath or a baptismal font. The man took a small bottle out of his jacket pocket.

"I'll call on you each, one at a time, to approach the stone while the rest of you remain standing in the circle. Focus your attention on the basin; it will help the girl gazing into the water see more clearly. Will you begin?" he asked, looking at Chamomile. His expression was both friendly and intense.

She stepped hesitantly into the middle of the circle formed by the other girls. This test seemed somewhat more serious than the first, but definitely less mysterious.

"Good luck," someone whispered as she walked toward the teacher.

"Concentrate on looking into the water. Try to keep your eyes open, and reject nothing that comes to you," he said, speaking at such a low volume that the others heard nothing. "If you see something, it's fine. If you see nothing, it's fine. Whatever you see, whisper it to me, understood?"

Chamomile nodded. She'd seen her mother do something similar once. The man unscrewed the top of the small bottle and let a few drops of black, viscous liquid fall into the water. She bent over the water-mirror and concentrated.

At first, the blackness just spread, as you would expect, but, slowly, it began to move. That was the best way she could describe it. Although the surface of the water remained still, the black whirled around to form various patterns from the shadows in the water. Now and then she thought she almost recognized a shape, but then it changed before she could make out what it was. Then—suddenly—the shadows gathered into a fixed shape, a branch or a root maybe. It twisted around itself, grew, and momentarily unfurled like a leaf or a flower before curling up again.

"A plant sprouting," she whispered. "See!"

But the man did not bend over the water. Instead, he simply nodded and jotted something down on a little pad he'd pulled out of his pocket.

"That's fine, you may return to the circle now."

One by one, each girl took her turn. Some stood looking down into the water for a long time. The blond girl with the tight ponytail stood there with a frustrated look on her face for a quite a while, concentrating, keeping her gaze directed at the water-mirror. Suddenly she took a startled step back.

"It turned red!" she said, completely forgetting to whisper.

A pair of sisters with long, dark hair, Sara and Sofie—one was a year older than the other—saw nothing at all, or at least they whispered nothing to the man. After them came a tall girl with a serious expression on her face. When she bent over the water, Chamomile noticed the small gold cross that hung around her neck. The girl looked down into the water with an expression of terror and blushed all the way up to her hairline as she whispered what she had seen.

Finally, the girl with the short, dark hair took her turn. But she had only just begun to look when the man, with a firm movement, pulled her away from the depression in the stone and said, "Thank you."

The girls looked nervously at each other. *What did the dark-haired girl see in the water?*

Lisa nodded to the man standing in the mysterious circle. "We'll continue inside. This way."

Chamomile joined the other girls as they walked back down the path. This time she felt no need to remark on what they'd just experienced.

Malou

Malou tightened her ponytail and tried to psych herself up while waiting for her turn. The self-confidence she'd felt earlier in the day had almost completely evaporated. What were they looking for at this school?

"Here you are, have a seat," said the man sitting in the room into which Lisa had shown her. She detected a slight accent in his voice. He was at least in his thirties, tall and sinewy. Indian or Roma, perhaps. His skin was brown, his eyes black, and his long, gleaming hair was black too, and tied up in a knot on top of his head. He smiled at her, but she wasn't sure if the smile was friendly or simply mocking. Unlike the large, kindly man from the first test, she felt like she shouldn't let her guard down around him.

"The test is simple," the man said. "Hold my hands and look into my eyes. Say nothing, just relax. And do not look away before I say so, okay?"

He put his hands on the table, palms up, and nodded. Malou hesitated for a moment, but then she shrugged. She sat in the chair, put both of her hands in his and lifted her gaze.

It was very uncomfortable to sit like this with a strange man, and she immediately felt an urge to tear herself away from his dark eyes and intense stare. *What the hell was this test supposed to reveal?*

The man still had a bit of a smile on his mouth, and his smile broadened as she grew more and more uncomfortable. She was no longer unsure: The smile was mocking, condescending. As if he was laughing at her. She stared back angrily and refused to let her gaze drop first, but the angrier she became the more the man seemed amused. *Must be some sort of pervert who enjoys holding hands with all the young girls. But he won't get the better of me.*

She unconsciously tried to pull her hands away, but the man tightened his grip and slowly shook his head, all the while smiling his irritating smile. She could hear her pulse beating in her ears, and her anger flared. *Freak! Who the hell does he think he is?*

And then he suddenly let go of her hands.

"Thank you, that was very good," he said calmly. "There's just one thing, may I see your arms?"

"What?" Malou was completely taken aback by the strange request. "Why?"

"Just the left, if you'll roll up your sleeve." He looked at her so intently that she felt naked. She yanked up her sleeve and showed him her wrist and the inside of her arm.

"There's nothing, okay? Are we done?"

"The whole arm," he said simply.

"Forget it," she said, and she would have pulled her jacket sleeve back down, but the man was faster. With one hand he grabbed her wrist, holding it in an iron grip, and with the other he pushed the jacket up so that the bandage came into view.

"Let go!" she shouted. She writhed as she tried to pull her arm away, but he was too strong.

"And what's that? Nothing?" he said, as if he found it all quite entertaining. He ripped off the bandage. Malou froze. The man's eyes shone with curiosity as he studied the strange character she'd cut into her upper arm.

"Yes," he said, letting go. "That's all, you may go."

Victoria

Face your fears . . .

She was up next. Victoria ran a hand through her short, dark hair and deliberately avoided looking around at the other girls. She already felt them all too clearly. All their emotions—anxiety, ambition, curiosity—made the low-ceilinged hallway feel cramped, and she had an uncomfortable rushing sensation in her ears. *It's just a basement.*

"Malou hasn't come back?" Lisa looked around the group of girls. They shook their heads. The blond girl had stormed off after the last test, and they hadn't seen her since. Victoria had noticed her on the walk from the bus up to the castle. Her energy was strong, but her anger and jealous gaze had made Victoria shiver even despite the warm sunshine. What would the girl have said if Victoria had turned around and told her she had absolutely nothing to be jealous of?

"Okay, Victoria, you're the last one then," Lisa said after opening the basement door for the red-haired girl. Chamomile shrugged her shoulders as if she hadn't understood this test. *See, nothing to be afraid of.*

She felt her heart pounding as she walked through the door

48

and took a few steps down into the large, old-fashioned basement. Once Lisa shut the door behind her the silence was deafening. The basement was much larger than she'd imagined. It had raw brick walls and sandstone pillars, and the vaulted ceiling was astonishingly high. But there were no windows—the space was lit only by old-fashioned oil lamps—and the air was cool. Back in the day they must have stored food in the cold basement under the castle, but now it was empty, apart from some boxes stacked at the far end.

She breathed in deeply and tried to calm her heart rate. What was the point of shutting them up in a dark basement? What was expected of her? She walked slowly along the wall, letting her fingers glide over the old, rough bricks that had been shaped by hand hundreds of years ago. *22, 23, 24 . . .* She counted her steps; there was something soothing about the rhythm. *56, 57, 58 . . .*

She stopped when she got to the far wall. Her fingertips had caught an irregularity in one of the bricks, a scratch in the surface that felt sharper, more distinct, maybe purposeful. And then she noticed it. The smell. *Heavy, sweet . . . a flower maybe.* It got stronger and stronger, and she almost felt she could hear something too. *A whisper, no, someone singing.* A children's song, but she couldn't quite grasp the words. Instead, she focused on sensing the emotion that was suddenly palpable to her own ice-cold anxiety. She felt it in her own body. *Curious, eager . . . insistent.* The song was getting louder. At first it sounded cheerful but then the tone changed, became lamenting, hoarse, labored . . . And the feelings shifted. They felt intrusive, uncomfortable, almost desperate. There was something important, something she needed to understand . . .

Slowly, she turned and let her eyes follow her arm. Her white shirt was all but glowing in the murky darkness, her fingers pale against the dark bricks. The nail on her index finger rested in the scratch cut into the old wall. It was a letter. A message had been etched into the bricks.

SEE
ME

Victoria pulled her hand back as if she she'd been burned. She wanted out, but suddenly the air around her was freezing cold, and she struggled to breathe the icy air into her lungs. It stabbed like knives. She gasped, she was suffocating. Instinctively, she raised both hands to her neck to protect it.

"Victoria? Victoria?" Lisa shook her arm. Victoria hadn't heard her approach. "Breathe," Lisa urged, and her breath hovered as a cloud in the ice-cold room. With a deep gasp, Victoria inhaled.

"Come on," Lisa said, putting an arm around her. "We've got to get you out of here, now!"

Lisa pulled her out of the room while softly murmuring something Victoria couldn't quite make out. Their steps crackled in the thin layer of frost suddenly covering the basement's floor.

Malou

Damn! This school is a frickin' labyrinth. It was impossible to get out. Malou was completely disoriented, but she'd rather end her days in a deserted stairwell than go back and pass by that flock of girls again. *To hell with them. And to hell with this school.*

She didn't have to put up with this. She could report him to the police if she wanted. You couldn't do that to a student, she was sure of that. What the hell was it to him? *And how the hell did he know?*

Malou found a new staircase. If she was lucky, it would lead her down and out into the little courtyard. But these stairs only led down to the next level then stopped. Maybe they'd been blocked off by a remodeling project at some point, or maybe they'd always been like this. Stuck on that level, she walked down a long hallway entirely devoid of either windows or doors. She had no idea where she was going. A long series of photographs— class portraits—hung on the wall. The oldest were old, yellowed images in which any student who hadn't been able to sit still— for the full length of time it took to take the photograph—had been rendered as strange, faded shadows. As she moved down the hallway, the portraits seemed, more and more, to come from her own time.

At the end of the hallway there was a large door. *Please let this take me to a stairwell!* But instead of revealing a way down to the ground floor, the large door opened onto a high-ceilinged room, or rather, a series of interconnected spaces. Bookshelves covered the walls from floor to ceiling, and deep armchairs stood grouped around low, round tables. A library. She looked around. Maybe she should go all the way back and risk running into the others. She walked hesitantly through the large, beautiful room.

"Hey, what are you doing here!"

Malou turned at the sound of the voice. There was a boy with a trolley full of books standing in the niche to her left.

"You're not supposed to be here. Are you lost?"

He was a few years older than her, and she couldn't help but notice that he was unusually good-looking, even if he wasn't terribly polite.

"I'm looking for the exit. How do I get out, I mean all the way out?"

"Aren't you here for the entrance exams?" he asked curiously, obviously studying her.

"Uh, I don't think this school is for me. Do you know the way out or not?"

He laughed and pushed his dark hair out of his face. "And you know that after having been here all of two hours?"

"Oh, hello, do we have guests?" Another boy emerged from behind a bookshelf further several yards away. He was tall, thin, and had curly, blond hair surrounding his face, vaguely surfer style.

"Yeah, this girl . . . what's your name?"

"Malou."

"Good afternoon, Malou, I'm Benjamin, and this here is Vitus," the dark-haired boy said. Turning to his comrade he said, "Malou here's been spooked by one of the exams."

"I was not *spooked*," snapped Malou, "I just don't think that a school with psychopathic teachers who perform sick tests on the students is the place for me."

"Whoa!" Vitus smiled at Benjamin. "Who would you guess she's just seen?"

"Hmm . . . it could be any number of our dear teachers. All of them, actually. There's nothing but psychopathic teachers here, come to think of it," Benjamin said.

Malou rolled her eyes and started to leave. They were clearly intent on messing with her.

"Hey, wait, Malou. It was Malou, right?" Vitus, the blond-haired boy, was following her. "Wait a minute. You're talking to two of the school's most experienced students. And we can assure you that even if everything seems a little . . . screwed up, this actually is a pretty okay place. Ish. And things will make sense eventually. More or less. Anyway, it's a bit shortsighted to not even give it a chance."

Malou stopped and sighed deeply. He was right, and she knew it. Her temper was always getting the best of her. She shouldn't give up her chance to get into a prestigious school just because she'd met a single jerk.

"In any case, you won't find your way out that way," said Benjamin.

Malou turned toward them. "If you're students here, why aren't you on summer vacation?"

Vitus laughed and laid a hand on Benjamin's shoulder.

"Someone seemed to think we'd enjoy having summer jobs. Funnily enough, there were no other applicants, and I don't actually remember applying myself. But it's absolutely lovely to have something to do when you would otherwise just have loads of leisure time."

"In other words, it's not recommended," Benjamin added. "You'd better hurry out the same way you came in and find your group."

He said it with a matter-of-factness that made Malou think he was the sort of person who was used to being obeyed by others.

"Gee, thanks for all your help," she said sarcastically as she turned.

"No problem—and Malou?" Benjamin called after her. "Maybe don't mention to anyone that you chatted with us. Birgit will have a cow if she hears about it."

Malou turned in the doorway. "Are students not allowed to talk to each other at Rosenholm?"

"Hmm . . . yes and no," Benjamin said.

"It's complicated!" added Vitus, raising his eyebrows as he gave his friend a shrewd look.

"Oh, shut up," Malou said to herself as she slammed the door and left the two grinning boys to themselves.

Hi Mile-Mouse. You probably don't have time to answer but just wanted to say break a leg darling. Looking forward to hearing all about it when you get home. Am SO proud of you! Making lasagna.
♡ Mom

Hi from Mismis.
She misses you.

Kirstine

Kirstine looked for the card with her name. Down in the great hall, the long tables they'd sat at that morning had been replaced with individual desks, and each was set with paper, a pencil, a pencil sharpener, and an eraser. The written exam. Why was she putting herself through this?

Kirstine found her desk. To her right sat a girl she thought must be Malou. The blond girl had rejoined them without saying a word to anyone; she sat up straight and self-assured in her chair. Apparently, a written exam was nothing to worry about in her world. The dark-haired Victoria sat to her left. She looked pale and tired, but even so she gave Kirstine a small, encouraging smile. She didn't want to appear rude, but unfortunately, Kirstine could not return the smile—the knot in her stomach made smiling impossible.

"The exam will begin now," the headmistress announced without further instruction. "You have one hour."

Kirstine stared helplessly at the white sheet of paper. The girl in front of her had already bent over her paper and started writing. But what were you supposed to write? She felt the sweat soaking through the armholes of her blouse. She would never be able to hide the disgusting sweat spots. She looked around desperately. Malou's pencil raced across the paper as a slight smile played on her mouth.

"Turn the paper over," Victoria whispered. Kirstine turned and saw that she was gesturing to Kirstine to flip over the paper lying in front of her. *Perfect, Kirstine! Again, you have proven yourself to be a complete idiot.*

The paper turned out to be a small booklet with written questions and space in which to record her answers. Some were multiple choice; others had a few lines for longer written responses. She slogged through the first few questions, but she didn't really understand the context. Was it some sort of history test? There were questions about witch-burning, petroglyphs, and Nordic mythology. But there were also questions about plants and a part that seemed pretty personal, such as: *What would you do if you discovered that your best friend was sick and you could cure the disease by harming your enemy?*

She didn't know how much time had passed, but Malou had already turned several pages while Kirstine was still on the first page. She decided to skip the historical questions and answer only the more personal questions—and only the personal questions with multiple choice. Even so, she had only gotten to page two when Birgit told them time was up and to set their pencils down and leave the booklets on their desks.

"I didn't get to the last page," she heard the red-haired girl whisper in frustration a few desks away. Kirstine hurried to turn her booklet over. At least only the teachers would see her bumbling attempt to answer the questions.

"You can relax: The exams are now over. Well done, everyone," the headmistress announced. "The informational meeting will begin shortly, but first coffee, tea, and cake will be served in the library. Thorbjørn will take you there."

The giant man with the beard, the one who had conducted the first test, stepped forward so that everyone could see him.

"This way," he growled. As she followed the stream of students up yet another staircase, Kirstine thought that if, against all probability, she got into this school, she'd be perpetually lost in this maze of a castle.

The library was warm and cozy, with a fire in an open fireplace at one end and deep leather armchairs set around circular tables. Most of the girls spread out among the tables, set with trays of cakes and carafes of coffee and tea, but Kirstine didn't feel like sitting down among crowd of girls now chattering freely. It was as if they'd known each other their whole lives. Instead, she sat by one of the tall windows on a cushioned window seat. Several of the other girls were calling home to say they would be late, and Kirstine pushed the thought of her parents as far away as possible. She didn't want to think about that now. She'd left a note telling them not to worry, but she hadn't said where she was going. Who knows what they would say when she finally got home.

Chamomile

Click, clack, click, clack . . .

Chamomile followed the blond girl with her eyes as she paced restlessly up and down along the bookshelves. Her high-heeled sandals beat a frenzied rhythm against the old floors.

The rhythm of Malou's pacing basically matched Chamomile's heartrate. She hadn't finished the entire written exam, but she felt like most of the oral exams had gone alright. Had the teachers seen what they were looking for in her?

Chamomile had been so happy when her mother told her about Rosenholm. "A school where people are like you," she'd said. But what if she was wrong? What if Chamomile didn't have what it took? What if she didn't fit in anywhere, not even at Rosenholm? The thought gave her an unpleasant sinking feeling in her stomach, and she tried to put it out of her mind. Suddenly the chattering fell away: Birgit had walked into the library. She held a list in her hand.

"Will the following girls please come with me," she said. She had instantly gotten everyone's attention. "Emma, Julie, Nicoline . . ."

Chamomile looked around. What did it mean if your name was announced—was that good or bad? She held her breath as Birgit continued reading the names aloud. Eventually she stopped, and a dozen or so girls got up to follow her. Her name hadn't been on the list.

After a few moments that felt like hours, Birgit returned to the library. "Now the rest of you may come with me," she said.

They were once again led down to the great hall where the long tables had reappeared. This time, however, there were no assigned seats; they could sit wherever they wanted. Chamomile sat on the edge of her chair.

"Thank you for your patience," the headmistress began. "I know it's been a long, hard, and probably confusing day. However, over the course of the exams, we have had the opportunity to observe you and test your abilities. I'm sure you all did your best."

There was dead silence in the large hall. *Please, come on . . .*

"And I am very pleased to announce that each of you has been admitted to Rosenholm Academy."

Yes! Chamomile felt the blood surge through her body. She'd done it. She'd actually gotten in! Applause broke out, scattered at first, but then it spread. Birgit smiled and nodded.

"Yes, congratulations, you've all done very well," she said as the girls fell silent. "And now I'm sure you're curious to hear more about the school. As you probably noticed, Rosenholm is a special school, and that is because our students are special. You are special." She looked out over them, and Chamomile got the feeling that Birgit was letting her eyes rest briefly on each and every student.

"Rosenholm," she said, having assured herself that she had everyone's attention before going on, "is a school that engages with what some call the supernatural. Here, we most often use the term *magic*." Birgit paused again before going on. "Actually, we do not speak of the 'supernatural' at all. What concerns us is, in fact, completely natural. 'Magic' comes from the word "*magh-,' meaning 'power' in the oldest languages. And magic, at its core, is about having the power to direct the energies and forces that surround us in a specific direction. Focusing these forces, using them consciously. You who sit here all have the potential to learn to channel these forces to achieve the greatest benefit. You all have the potential to become mages."

There was dead silence in the hall. Some looked surprised, others alarmed. Chamomile suddenly felt sorry for them again. *What a shock.* Victoria nodded thoughtfully in front of her, the sisters Sara and Sofie held each other's hands without saying a word, Malou frowned as if she couldn't believe what she'd just heard, and Kirstine stared stiffly ahead of her, clutching the cross she wore around her neck. She looked like she'd just come face to face with her worst nightmare. Their lives would be forever changed after this moment. Chamomile's life would be changed too. At least, she hoped it would be.

I watch them as they leave the school in the evening. The path meanders between the hills and out toward the road. The sun, sitting low in the sky, casts an orange light over them and creates long dark-blue shadows in the form of trees or bushes or young women on their way home.

Some of them walk in small groups, others walk two by two, some walk alone. They do not see me; I do not catch their eye. But I see them. I see each and every one of them. I memorize their faces. Who to choose is of paramount importance. You might say it's a question of life or death.

Dear Malou Nielsen,

I am hereby pleased to inform you that you have been admitted to Rosenholm Academy.

The school year starts on the 3rd of September. Upon arrival you will be assigned a room in the girls' wing. At Rosenholm Academy, boys and girls live and attend classes separately, and romantic relationships of any kind are forbidden.

The school's rules are included with this letter; please read them thoroughly before the start of term.

With best regards,

Birgit Lund

Birgit Lund
Headmistress

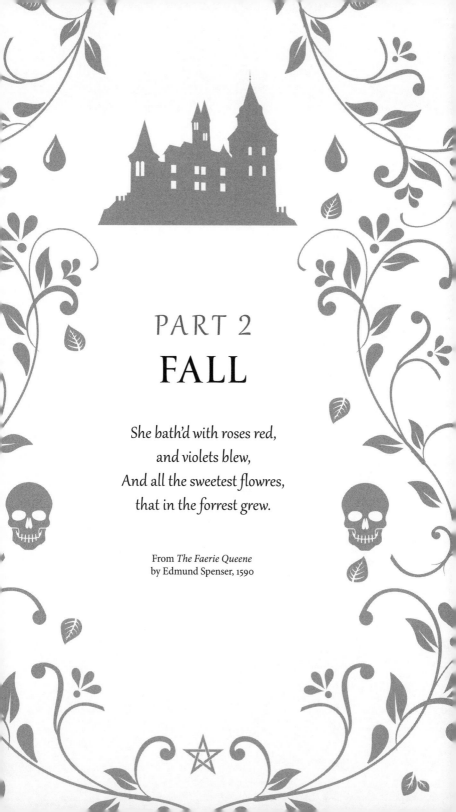

PART 2
FALL

She bath'd with roses red,
and violets blew,
And all the sweetest flowres,
that in the forrest grew.

From *The Faerie Queene*
by Edmund Spenser, 1590

Rules and Regulations
of Rosenholm Academy

1. Students are strictly prohibited from discussing magic in general and the curriculum at Rosenholm Academy in particular with those not already acquainted with it.

Chamomile

Chamomile dropped the overfilled duffel bag in the cobble-stoned courtyard and stretched her aching back. The sun shone from a bright blue September sky, and the temperature felt more like summer than summer had. She looked around. She had no intention of dragging the heavy duffel bag up the school's steep stairs when she didn't even know where she was going. *Where is everyone?* She decided to check the great hall first, and there she saw, to her great relief, a bunch of other girls surrounded by enormous suitcases and overfilled duffel bags. She recognized the sisters, Sara and Sofie. She saw Malou too, though she didn't notice Chamomile.

"Hey, I was just starting to get scared I'd made a mistake," she said, dragging the duffel bag inside. "Where's everyone else?"

"Oh, hey. They've gone up to find their rooms. They won't take you up until your roommate has arrived, so they don't have to make the trek so many times," Sara said, wrapping a comforting arm around her sister. That's when Chamomile noticed Sofie was crying.

"We're not going to be in the same room," Sara explained.

70

"Oh, that's too bad," Chamomile said. "Maybe one of you will room with me?"

"No," Sara shook her head, "I'm with someone named Yasmin. I think she was in our group for the entrance exams too. And Sofie is going to live with someone named Anne."

"That was the girl with the bob? The petite one? She was really nice," Chamomile said, hoping to comfort Sofie. But the younger sister had dissolved into tears, and whenever she tried to say something, it was swallowed by a sob. Chamomile saw, out of the corner of her eye, that Malou was rolling her eyes at the crying girl and looking around impatiently. Just then the door opened and a girl with long, dark dreadlocks, black eyeliner, and a single silver ring in her nose walked in.

"Heyo! Have any more roomies found each other?" The girl smiled at Chamomile and extended her hand. "Hi, I'm Molly. I'm a third year and I'll be your official mentor, kind of a guide—some say *babysitter*. I'm here to help you adjust to life at Rosenholm."

"I've been waiting almost forty-five minutes already. Can't you just show me where my room is?" Malou interrupted impatiently.

"What's your roomie's name?" Molly asked.

"Camilla or something," Malou answered, turning toward a notice posted on the wall. "Here it is: Chamomila L. Ingemann."

"Chamomile," said Chamomile. "My name is Chamomile with an *e* at the end—like the tea."

"Finally. Why didn't you say anything? We're ready," Malou said, addressing Molly as she hoisted an old brown suitcase held together with duct tape.

"Nice to meet you too, roomie," Chamomile whispered to herself as she slung her duffel bag over her shoulder and followed Malou and Molly up the stairs.

Molly chattered the whole way up and didn't seem to notice that neither Malou nor Chamomile had breath to respond as they struggled up the stairs with their luggage.

"I'm the mentor for your cluster. Your class lucked out— all the first years are going to live on the top floor."

"Cluster? What's that?" Chamomile groaned.

"Oh yeah, I always forget to explain. Each incoming class is divided into clusters. Your cluster lives in a suite consisting of two rooms—that makes four girls per cluster because you live two to a room. And each suite shares a bathroom and a kitchenette. We're almost there now, just wait, your room's really nice."

The room really *was* nice, with tons of natural light and high ceilings, though it wasn't particularly large. A tall window with sunshine-yellow curtains and a deep windowsill looked out toward a forest-like garden behind the castle. The walls were white, and the floor was made of old, planed planks that creaked with every step. There was a white, wooden bed frame with a carved headboard, comforter, and pillow on either side of the room, each with a small nightstand. And there was a large, elaborately carved wooden wardrobe on one wall.

"This *is* nice," Chamomile agreed, leaning against the wall to catch her breath.

"Is there only the one wardrobe?" Malou asked.

"Yes," Molly said. "But it's gigantic, just look," she said, throwing open the old doors. "You can easily fit all your things in here."

Malou eyed Chamomile's duffel bag. "I have a lot of clothes that need to hang on hangers," she said.

"Fine, I'll take the drawers then," Chamomile said.

"I'll take the bed on the right," Malou added, flinging the large, old suitcase up on the bed. "What about sheets?"

"Yeah, if you haven't brought any from home you can borrow some from the school. They're super stiff, though," said Molly.

"I'd like to borrow some," Malou said, looking at Molly imperiously.

"Uh . . . sure, I'll find some for you," she answered, but she turned around in the doorway. "Oh, I forgot to tell you the best part: Your room has a view of the boys' side of the park—I'm totally jealous!"

"Is the park divided too? Why can't girls and boys have anything to do with each other at this school? It's so old-fashioned," Chamomile said.

"I know, right? The teachers say it's for our own safety. Falling in love and sex release enormous amounts of energy, and when you combine that with the forces at work in a young, untrained mage it's like pouring gasoline on a bonfire. At least, that's what they tell us."

"What, so boys and girls have nothing to do with each other?" asked Malou.

"Not if you follow the rules," Molly replied, winking. "But there's no rule against looking. And here comes a taste!"

Chamomile looked out the window. The park behind the castle was wilder and more overgrown. There were larger trees and more meandering paths than in the more manicured park in front of the castle. She could see a boy walking down a path between a few old birch trees.

"Who's that?" Malou asked, looking toward Molly over her shoulder.

"Ah, yes, that's Benjamin," Molly said, smiling deviously. "According to most of the sillier girls at Rosenholm, he is the school's tastiest guy. And I get it too. He's super cute and a little mysterious, but I like a guy named Vitus better. That's Benjamin's best friend; a lot of people don't really notice him because he always goes around with Benjamin, and Benjamin totally outshines him."

"What makes this Benjamin so mysterious?" Malou asked.

"Oh, there are tons of rumors running around this school," Molly said, waving her hand as if to wipe the subject off the board. But Malou didn't give up.

"Come on, tell us!"

"Yeah, you can't just leave it at that!" Chamomile chimed in.

"Okay, okay," Molly laughed. "You should probably discount at least half of this, but I've heard that Benjamin is gay, that his father is in prison, and that he's been caught playing with dark magic. And some people say he's a shapeshifter. That he can change himself into an animal."

"Seriously? No one actually believes that, right?" said Malou.

"They exist," Molly said. "But they're super rare. And Benjamin is almost certainly not one of them."

"Right."

"Open your minds, ladies," Molly smiled. "The world is much larger than you might think. And now I'll go grab those sheets."

Malou remained by the window, watching the dark-haired boy while Chamomile started making her bed. She'd just finished when another girl appeared in the doorway and knocked on the frame.

"Can I come in? I'm Victoria. We're neighbors."

"Hi. I'm Chamomile. I remember you from the exams."

The dark-haired girl was wearing a light-gray T-shirt and tight black jeans. Her pretty face with its large brown eyes and delicate features reminded Chamomile of a French actress.

"Oh, what a lovely room," she said, sitting on a corner of Chamomile's bed.

"Who's your roomie?" Chamomile asked. She found herself wishing she was sharing a room with Victoria instead of Malou, who still hadn't turned around to greet their guest.

"The noticeboard said Kirstine. But she hasn't come yet, and they're not sure she'll come at all. So, for the time being, I live alone."

"What? You don't have to share your room with anyone?" Malou finally pulled herself away from the window. "That's totally unfair if you get a single."

"Maybe," said Victoria. "But I hope she comes. I think I'll like having a roommate."

"Okay, but if she doesn't come then let us know. Maybe we can swap," Malou said before she resumed staring out the window.

"Has the school heard from her at all?" Chamomile asked, trying to ignore the insult in Malou's suggestion.

"They probably wouldn't tell me if they have. Maybe she's having problems with her family. Saying goodbye isn't always easy."

"Tell me about it," Chamomile said, throwing herself onto the bed so that Victoria was nearly catapulted off of it. "Oops, sorry."

"My mother squeezed my hand so hard the whole bus ride here that I was afraid I'd have to have it amputated afterward."

"Your mother came with you?" Malou asked, throwing a look of utter condescension Chamomile's way.

"Yeah, I couldn't talk her out of it. But not the whole way, you know? Even though she wanted to see the school again."

"Your mother went here?" Chamomile suddenly had Malou's full attention.

"Yes, but she told me almost nothing about it. Not even about the tests. She didn't even have a guilty conscience about having sent me off for all that crazy stuff they put us through in total ignorance. She said it was because of the rules, but that would have to be the first time my mother worried about following the rules."

"Still, it's really nice for you that your mother understands this whole world," Victoria said.

"Yeah, you've got a major advantage," Malou said acidly. "She can give you all kinds of important information. And she probably has connections."

"Ha! You clearly don't know my mother," Chamomile laughed. "She doesn't care about that sort of thing. I don't actually think she knows any other mages. And the most valuable information I've gotten from her about Rosenholm is that the floor gets cold in the castle, so it's a good idea to bring wool socks."

"That's *very* important information," Victoria said. "I hate having cold feet."

"Did you always know your mother had . . . you know, magical powers?" Malou asked.

"Hmm . . . yeah, I guess I did. I mean, she didn't really talk about magic, but the supernatural was always part of life at home. My mother works as a wise woman."

"What's that?"

"She helps people. They come to her to have their fortunes told, like if they want to hear if they'll meet a lover soon, or if they're wondering if they should sell their house. Or they'll ask for an herbal blend for constipation. Or one for their husband if he can't get it up . . ."

"Really?" Victoria laughed.

"Okay, well that isn't exactly what I dreamed about using this for," Malou said as she began unpacking the rest of her things.

Boy is she a pill. Maybe it wouldn't be so bad if Kirstine didn't show up? Then Chamomile could move in with Victoria, and Malou could have the whole room and the whole wardrobe to herself.

"And your dad? Is he a mage too?" Victoria asked.

"Never met him, so I don't know," Chamomile replied. "But I think maybe my mother met him here at school. At least, she had me not long after she graduated from Rosenholm. But the woman refuses to tell me anything else about him, so I don't know..."

Chamomile stopped abruptly. *Cool it, missy!* She didn't even know these people, and now she was telling them all her secrets? Hopefully she hadn't already scared them away. "What about your family? Any mages?" she hurried to ask Victoria.

"Unfortunately, not," Victoria answered. "They all seem very normal."

"Normal actually sounds pretty nice," Chamomile laughed. "But what about you? Did you know that you were different than the rest of your family?"

"Yeah, I guess I knew, but I didn't know . . . this," Victoria said, indicating the school as a whole with a wave of her hand. Chamomile understood what she meant perfectly. It was all pretty overwhelming.

"So can you do anything magical yet?" Malou asked. She still had her back to them, but Chamomile got the feeling that she was very interested in the answer.

Victoria thought for a moment.

"Yes, I think so. I can often sense things that others can't."

"Things?"

"Hmm . . . sometimes I can tell what other people are feeling. Other times I can sense something in the room that others can't see or feel."

"Uhh . . . okaay . . ."

"I know it sounds weird," Victoria added quickly.

Chamomile tried to look unfazed. "No, no, of course it doesn't sound weird," she said, as Malou's skeptical glare bored into the pathetic lie. *No, not weird at all—just super creepy.*

"So, can you read our thoughts or what?" Malou raised a perfectly plucked eyebrow and crossed her arms over her chest.

"No," Victoria said, "not at all. But I might be able to feel some of your emotions."

"Try it!" Chamomile sat up. "That's fun. What do you feel?"

"You want me to try? Okay. I've got to close my eyes." Victoria sat quietly and unmoving for a minute. Malou sighed audibly and rolled her eyes as she resumed unpacking, but Chamomile sat there studying Victoria's face as she alternately squeezed her eyes shut tighter or pursed her lips without making a sound.

"It's a little confusing. There's a good deal of noise, but beneath it all I feel loneliness. Yes, I believe it's loneliness I feel most strongly."

"From whom?" whispered Chamomile.

". . . from all of us," Victoria answered hesitantly. "All four . . ."

"We're only three," Malou snapped. "Sorry, fortune teller, but I want my money back."

"No," Victoria said. She still had her eyes closed, and she was now frowning as if listening for a very faint sound. "No, there's one more."

"What do you mean?" Chamomile asked. "You mean like a . . . a spirit or something?"

Victoria opened her eyes. "Yes, maybe."

"Come on, she's messing with you," Malou sighed.

"I wasn't trying to scare you," Victoria said.

"Easy for you to say!" Chamomile exclaimed. "You've just told us there's a ghost in our room!"

"No, I don't think it lives here. Actually, I think it's me they're following. It's like they want me to do something, but I don't know what."

Chamomile couldn't stop staring at the other girl. Maybe it was just as well that she wasn't rooming with Victoria. It was one thing to share a room with someone who's perpetually pissed off, but a ghost? She'd rather avoid that.

Victoria

Victoria sat up in bed. The moon shone through the tower window in the large, round room, and everything lay bathed in a piercing white light. She thought she heard footsteps approaching. And whispering voices. Someone was at the door. She groped for the lamp on her nightstand, but couldn't remember how to turn it on.

"Here it is," a voice whispered as the door slowly opened and a strip of light fell on the old, wooden floor. "Try and get a little sleep; Molly will help you get settled in in the morning."

A figure crept into the room and the door was carefully closed again. Finally, Victoria found the switch, turned on the bedside lamp and revealed Kirstine as she awkwardly crept through the room.

"Oh," she said, turning, startled, toward Victoria. "Sorry, I didn't mean to wake you up."

"I wasn't asleep, so no worries," she said, throwing off the comforter. "Welcome to our room, I'm Victoria."

"Kirstine."

"Your bed's over there. I took this one, if that's okay with you. I would have waited for you to come, but . . ."

"Oh, no, that's fine," Kirstine said, letting herself sink onto the unoccupied bed. Their room was in one of the castle's towers. It was pretty big, and the ceilings were unusually high, but the round walls made the space a little difficult to use and the old wooden furniture was arranged somewhat haphazardly.

Victoria took a good look at Kirstine. She was pale and looked defeated. Victoria could feel her insecurity like a cold mist hitting her in the face, but she had no idea how to comfort the miserable girl.

"Can I warm up some soup for you?" she asked. "We had tomato soup for dinner, and we saved some in case you turned up."

Kirstine just shook her head.

"Was it a difficult trip?" Victoria sat down beside her, but once more Kirstine nodded without saying a word. Then her face crumpled, and she burst into tears.

"Oh, it'll be alright," Victoria tried to comfort her, but Kirstine seemed completely inconsolable and continue weeping into her hands. What should she do? Luckily there was a knock at the door; Victoria got up to open it.

"Sorry to bother you, but are you okay?" Chamomile stood outside the door wearing an oversized T-shirt with a sunflower over her belly. "It sounded like someone was crying."

"Kirstine's just gotten here. She's a little upset."

"It looks like she's *very* upset," Chamomile said as she walked decisively over to the crying girl and gave her a firm hug.

"I know just what you need. A good strong cup of my mother's fall-down tea. Wait here," she said, even though Kirstine seemed to have no intention of going anywhere.

They listened as Chamomile slammed cupboard doors and rattled around with the electric kettle in the kitchen, and then there was another knock at the door. This time it was Malou; she wore a white satin nightshirt. Her hair was gathered in a messy knot and her face was devoid of makeup. She looked younger, Victoria thought.

"What's going on? Why is Chamomile making such a racket? She said Kirstine's here, but that she's having a nervous break-down or something?"

Victoria didn't answer. She just opened the door wider so that Malou could come in and see for herself.

"What's wrong with her?" she asked Victoria, who shrugged her shoulders.

"I don't know."

"Here we are," Chamomile said as she came back into the room with a large, steaming mug in her hand. "I couldn't find any honey, but there's sugar in it. Here, drink, it works every time."

Chamomile pushed the mug into Kirstine's hands, and she sipped at the tea. Gradually, she stopped crying, but her breath-ing was still ragged.

"What did you give her?" Malou asked skeptically.

"Fall-down tea. My mother always makes it when I'm upset. Valerian and lemon balm. It's impossible to stay awake after a cup, if it's strong enough. Don't worry, it won't knock you out," she added when she saw Kirstine's startled look. "Are you homesick?"

Malou snorted. "Homesick? She just got here."

"It can be hard to say goodbye," Chamomile said. "But don't worry; you can go home for fall break in just a few weeks."

Kirstine shook her head and the tears started streaming down her cheeks again.

"I can't go home," she hiccupped. "Never again. My parents don't want to see me again."

"What?" exclaimed Chamomile. "Why not?"

"Because I chose to go to this school. They didn't want me to. But Birgit said they couldn't stop me because I'm already eighteen and a legal adult." Kirstine looked as if she was overwhelmed by the quantity of words she'd suddenly managed to produce.

"That's because they're Christian, right? They think Rosenholm is a school for satanists or something?" Malou had her arms crossed over her chest and was frowning disapprovingly. "I assumed there was a reason you wore that big cross."

Kirstine shook her head and grabbed her necklace with the gold cross as if to shield it from Malou's merciless glare. "They don't actually know what kind of school this is. Birgit said I didn't need to tell them anything. But they didn't want me to move away to go to a school with boys and alcohol and . . ."

"Valerian tea?" Malou suggested. "Listen, your parents sound like assholes, forget them. And please be quiet. Some of us want to sleep for a few more hours before getting up again." With those words, she marched out of the room.

Victoria gently closed the door behind her. She still had no idea what to do.

"Don't mind her," Chamomile said, patting Kirstine's hand, "she's full of it."

"They're not really . . . assholes," Kirstine sobbed. "They just don't understand."

"Of course not, you'll see. It'll work itself out."

But Kirstine just shook her head, and Chamomile urged her to drink the rest of the tea. Whether it was the tea or good old-fashioned exhaustion is hard to say, but eventually she calmed down.

"I've got an extra set of sheets you can borrow," Victoria said finally. "How about I make your bed while Chamomile shows you where the bathroom is."

At long last they could all relax. Kirstine had gratefully allowed herself to be put to bed, and now they could tell from her deep breathing that she'd fallen asleep. The sound was soothing to Victoria, and all the nervous energy that had been flitting around the tower room settled down again, quiet and calm.

But Victoria still couldn't sleep. Or maybe she didn't want to. She was sure she would dream tonight.

Notice for All First-Year Students

The initiation ceremony will take
place tomorrow evening.
Thereafter, new students will be
officially matriculated at Rosenholm.
At the initiation ceremony,
all first-year students will be informed
of the branch of magic to which they belong:
Earth, Growth, Blood, or Death.

The ceremony will commence
at 11:30 p.m.
New students must wear
the robes provided.

Chamomile

The line of students in white robes meandered over the meadow like a glowing ribbon. The long grass was wet, and her feet were bare, but Chamomile barely noticed. Her cheeks burned, even though her hair was damp and cold, and fog blanketed the landscape.

The group continued into the forest and the darkness seemed to concentrate. Only the sound of feet, occasionally snapping fallen sticks, could be heard. They walked a long way, deeper and deeper into the forest; there was no real path to follow, only old deer trails winding among the old trunks and fallen giants. Then they were there. At first Chamomile thought they were alone, but then she realized the rest of the school's students were standing at the edge of the clearing. Dressed in black cloaks, they were nearly invisible in the dark forest. A giant oak tree, knotted and scarred as an old man, was enthroned in the center of the clearing. No one knew how old the tree was, but it had probably stood in that forest for more than a thousand years. Chamomile studied it. The oak's rough trunk split into four large branches supporting its enormous crown of tangled twigs and leaves. It was here that the ceremony was to take place.

Suddenly the black-clad students and teachers began chanting. The strange, monotonous melody swelled around them and lifted toward the sky. And as their voices rose, the oak tree seemed to come to life. It glowed, first faintly, then more strongly, and the light pulsed as if the oak tree had its own heartbeat. It was as if everyone knew what they were supposed to do without being told: all the white-clad students took each other's hands, forming a circle around the old tree. The voices continued chanting the same verses over and over again, and Chamomile focused on trying to understand the strange words.

Earth is magic's first branch.
The forefathers' crumbling bones.
Millenia's relics buried.
History is your source of power.

Growth is magic's second branch.
Growth in flora and fauna.
Everywhere in nature around us.
Life is your source of power.

Blood is magic's third branch.
Warm and red. Given or taken.
It flows through man and beast.
Sacrifice is your source of power.

Death is magic's fourth branch.
Those who live no more,
Remembered or forgotten.
Departed souls are your source of power.

Suddenly they stopped chanting and the forest fell silent once more. A movement caught her eye, and she realized there was a woman leaning against the trunk of the old oak tree. Her hair was loose and long. She wore a wreath of branches and leaves in her hair like a crown, but otherwise she was naked, and in the darkness her body blended in with the tree's bark. It wasn't until she spoke that Chamomile recognized Lisa.

"The first branch of magic is Earth, and the Earth's source of power is History." Lisa's voice was clear and crisp, like that of a very young woman, but also warm and resonant, like that of an affectionate grandmother. As she spoke, one of the four large branches of the old oak tree glowed brightly in the night. "The crumbling bones of our forefathers, who left behind settlements and middens, cities and tombs, these are the traces left to us by generations and generations, it is the power of the earth we walk on."

Leaves began to fall from the glowing branch, and the shining, silver leaves drifted to the forest floor. They whirled around and shone as if made of light. The leaves morphed into images of people and then primitive houses arose and disappeared, grave mounds arose around them, only to fade away again, a glowing person walked behind a plow drawn by some kind of oxen, a Viking ship slid over a glowing sea of withered silver leaves, and then it too faded away. And all the while, as the centuries passed before their eyes, more and more leaves gathered.

It was beautiful.

Lisa spoke again: "The second branch is Growth, and its source is Life, the power of Growth is found in every living thing, in the plants and the animals and the natural world."

And the tree's second branch began to glow instead. A tremor ran through it, and out of the branch sprang glowing flowers that turned into large, apple-like fruits. The fruits swelled and matured and eventually fell from the branch. Some fell to the earth where they transformed into rabbits and foxes and deer that, dazed, sprang to their feet and bounded away into the forest, or birds that soared upward and became glowing dots in the sky before disappearing.

"The third branch is Blood and its source is Sacrifice," Lisa said. And the fruits and animals faded and disappeared. With a quick movement, her hand sliced through the air, wielding a sharp weapon, and the movement left a deep gash in the now-glowing third branch. The tree's sap slowly filled the gash in the silver branch, overflowed, and began dripping, red, down to the forest floor.

"We sacrifice blood, hot and vital, to make contact with our innermost powers and the powers around us."

A shiver ran through Chamomile's body. She knew what the fourth branch of magic was, because the words appeared on so many of the walls of Rosenholm.

"The fourth branch is Death, and its source are the Souls of the Departed," Lisa said as the last branch of the tree began to glow. It writhed as if in pain, and the leaves shriveled and disappeared until the whole branch was twisted and withered, a shadow of itself. "The souls of those who are no longer in this life yet still possess great power and wisdom and energy."

A silvery, shining mist seeped from the tree's fourth branch and slowly coalesced into human forms that floated out among the students and left the air around them ice cold.

When the last luminous souls had disappeared, the fourth branch of the tree dimmed and smoldered faintly in the clearing.

Lisa stepped down between the many gnarled roots and walked along the line of students, meeting each with her gaze. She stopped when she came to Chamomile.

"Come."

Chamomile's legs shook as she walked the few steps to the tree and leaned her forehead against its trunk. It felt as if the branches and roots wound in and out and around her body, wrapping around her organs, filling her ears with strange, clicking sounds. Then the tree released her and she looked toward the enormous crown of the tree to see which branch was glowing.

"Welcome," Lisa said. She smiled and handed Chamomile a necklace. She closed her hand around it and felt the pendant against her skin. It wasn't until she had resumed her place in the circle that she looked at what lay in her palm. A small, silver leaf. She'd seen it before. Thousands of times. The same pendant hung from her mother's neck too. *The symbol of Growth.*

I let my eyes wander over the white-clad girls in the clearing. They are all worthy, the tree never makes a mistake. But which girl should I choose? Which girl is the right one? Should she be pretty, wise, talented, funny, or serious? Curious? Shy?

Earth. Blood. Growth. Or Death?

Malou

Malou squeezed the teardrop-shaped pendant. There had been a mistake and she would just have to explain it to the instructor. Birgit hadn't wanted to talk about it; she'd simply told Malou to take it up with the Blood Magic teacher. Ever since the ceremony, the other girls had talked about nothing but the branch of magic to which they belonged. Kirstine and Anne had gotten Earth, probably the best branch you could get. Or at least it was the branch that derived abilities from Nordic Studies, and everyone seemed to think that was oh-so-important. Chamomile had gotten Growth, and that was all well and good. She seemed happy. Both of the sisters, Sara and Sofie, had gotten Growth too, and they'd been ecstatic. Even Victoria, who'd gotten Death, put the chain with the little silver skull around her neck. But Malou had gotten Blood.

Ever since she saw that totally sick picture down in the great hall, the painting of a pasty loser cutting his own hand, she'd gotten the sense—and a conversation with Molly had only strengthened her foreboding—that Blood mages were the freaks of magic. They were rare, but not in a good way. Blood magic was about sacrifice, just like the students sang in those crazy gibberish verses around the old oak tree, but Malou was no victim, refused to be a victim. Was she actually supposed to spend her time at Rosenholm walking around sacrificing herself for others? No, she was here because she wanted to be someone. Being a mage had sounded pretty cool. And Birgit had said magic meant power, but if her power consisted of sacrificing herself all the time then what was the point. *Oh hell no.*

She looked at her phone. It was twenty minutes to eight. She'd found the classroom and was hoping to catch the teacher before their first Blood Magic class began. She knocked—three loud knocks.

"Come in." It sounded like she was in luck.

Or not. It was the black-haired man. Of course it was him. The man who'd grabbed her arm on the day of the entrance exams. *Shit!* He was sitting at a desk with a pile of papers in front of him. He raised his head and looked at her appraisingly. "Yes?"

"Is this Blood Magic?" she asked, hoping he would say no.

"It is, but you're early."

"I know. I wanted to talk to you about something. You teach Blood Magic?"

"I do," he nodded, a slight glint playing in his black eyes. Just like the first time they met, he seemed to be amused at her expense. "I remember you. Come in."

"There's been a mistake," she said, holding out the necklace with the teardrop-shaped pendant. "I got Blood magic, but it's really not for me."

"But the tree chose Blood magic for you, no?"

"Yes, but . . ."

"Then there's been no mistake." He turned back to his papers.

"Could you just listen!" She wouldn't let him think she could be brushed off. "I'm not the sort of submissive person who walks around sacrificing myself all the time. I'm not. I'm here for *me*. There must have been a mistake with the test results. Just let me take the test again."

He looked at her a moment, as if he was legitimately perplexed by what she'd said. Then he threw his head back and his booming laughter echoed around the room.

"Now you listen to me—it's Malou, right?" His accent made her name sound foreign. She nodded. "I don't need to see your test results to know that you're a Blood mage," he continued. "You were a Blood mage before you started here. You cut yourself, no?"

She felt herself reddening with anger. *What the hell is he talking about?* It wasn't like *that*.

"Do you know what the symbol you cut on yourself means?" he asked. "It was two runes, braided together. The aurochs rune, *Uruz*, which symbolizes the primordial creative forces, the will to live, and the survival instinct. Used properly it can heal both sorrow and illness. And *Naudiz*, the need rune, which can protect against attacks, bind negative energy, and make an opponent's actions ineffective. I'd never seen them blended like that way before, but I imagine it was pretty effective. Surprising really, given your overwhelming ignorance."

Malou narrowed her eyes.

"What do you mean? Are you calling me stupid?"

"You've yet to attend a single class on blood magic, and yet you think you know what it's all about. Let's just be honest—that's pretty stupid. Being a Blood mage has nothing to do with being a pathetic victim, running around and turning the other cheek.

94

Do I look like a victim to you?" The black-haired teacher stood up from his chair so that she could see him at his full height. He wasn't laughing any more. Instead, his face was twisted into an angry grimace. "A Blood mage sacrifices their own blood to achieve what they want. Much as a wolf bites her own paw to escape a trap. Just as *you* sacrificed your own blood to protect yourself again that which wanted to harm *you*. You have the ability to sacrifice. You have what it takes to achieve what you desire. The only question is what you want." He raised his eyebrows questioningly. Malou suddenly had nothing more to say. Then he sat back down at his desk and returned to the papers in front of him.

"And now stop wasting my time. Sit down. The other students will arrive shortly."

She let herself drop, shocked, into a chair as her thoughts whirled around until she almost felt dizzy. With her right hand she rubbed her arm in the spot where the thin lines of the symbol she had cut into herself were still faintly visible. Had she really made rune symbols without knowing it?

Soon the rest of the students began filtering into the room. Sara and Sofie gave each other knowing looks when they saw the black-haired man sitting at the desk, and Kirstine looked outright horrified. After they'd all taken their seats, he stood.

"Welcome to Blood Magic. My name is Zlavko, and I am your instructor. The majority of you belong to other branches of magic, but all mages should receive training in all four branches. And that's lucky for you; Blood magic is the most beautiful, strongest, and most dangerous form of magic there is. It can do good—and it can do great harm if someone wishes. What is Blood magic? What does it look like? It looks like this."

Zlavko stood so that everyone could see him. His long, black hair was gathered in a tight braid at the crown of his head. Then he grabbed the sweater he was wearing and slipped it over his head so that he stood naked from the waist up.

A gasp escaped several girls, and the devious glint in Zlavko's eyes indicated that that was precisely the reaction he'd expected. There were scars all over his sinewy upper body. They twisted in and out among each other, wound across his ribcage, over his shoulders and out onto his arms where they formed strange patterns. Slowly, he turned around so that they could see that his back was just as scarred. Some were old and faded, some shallow, others deep and gnarled. A single wound was still glistening with blood. It was a star.

"I've studied Blood magic all over the world, as you can see. Chinese characters, Arabic characters, Sanskrit, the magic of indigenous peoples, runes, and symbols. Blood magic is difficult to grasp. Even the most skilled can never be entirely sure of the results and whether they may be exposing themselves to danger by practicing it. In my classes you will learn a small fraction of this beautiful branch of magic, and those of you who possess the requisite abilities will, perhaps, be so lucky as to learn more than a small fraction." The teacher smiled his wolf's smile and Malou felt his black eyes burning into her.

Kill. Me. Now.

SEPTEMBER 12TH
8:07 A.M.

Kirstine

"Welcome to your first class in Norse Studies. My name is Thorbjørn, and I teach Norse magic and history here at Rosenholm."

Kirstine studied the giant man with long hair and a bushy beard; they'd met him during the entrance exams over the summer. As he stood by the blackboard, she was reminded of an animal trapped in a cage. The room, at first glance, looked like a perfectly normal classroom with two-person desks and chairs, but when you looked closer, there were plenty of things you would not find in a typical classroom. A poster of the runic alphabet hung next to the chalkboard, and just beneath the ceiling there were illustrated portraits of the Norse gods. She recognized Thor with his hammer and the one-eyed Odin, but there were many others she didn't recognize at all. Two stuffed ravens sat on top of a cabinet, and behind them was a black-and-white illustration of various types of Viking ships. She'd found a seat at the back where she could let her eyes rove among the various objects without it being too obvious that she wasn't focusing exclusively on Thorbjørn's words.

"Norse Studies is the study of our Nordic history, mythology, and the magic that our forefathers practiced. Those of you

97

associated with Earth magic will most often show abilities within Norse magic because it is part of our history, but the subject is important for every student at Rosenholm."

Kirstine realized she was fingering the new silver pendant of the necklace she was now wearing in addition to her gold cross. At first, she'd thought it was some kind of strange knife, but it turned out to be a primitive plow, an *ard*, the symbol of Earth.

"It is for that reason that Norse magic constitutes a significant portion of the first-year curriculum," Thorbjørn continued. "However, I will not have you for the majority of your classes; instead, most of your lessons in first-year Norse Studies will be taught by our teaching assistant, an instructor in training. Actually, he ought to be here now . . ."

Please, say it isn't true. She had begun to feel more or less safe with the nice, calm teacher, but suddenly her heart began to race.

Thorbjørn stood there scratching at his beard for a moment, as if he wasn't sure what to do with himself. "Well, we can start by enumerating some of the subjects you'll studying." He turned toward the board and began writing in large, blocky letters: *Rune magic*.

"We use rune magic for divination. And later you'll also learn to utilize runes as spells to provide protection or execute an attack," explained Thorbjørn, turning back to the board to write another word. "Portents," he read aloud. "Through portents we derive warnings from nature. You will also become acquainted with seid," he continued, writing the word on the board. "When you practice seid, you assume a type of ecstatic state in which you're able to perform magic and predict the future. Finally, you will learn Nordic mythology and the history of the Vikings. Yes, that about sums it up . . . Any questions?"

No one raised their hand or said anything.

Thorbjørn squinted discreetly at the clock hanging over the door. "Yes, well, then we can review the four branches of magic, which is one of the first things you should learn when you begin your studies at Rosenholm. Ahem . . ." He cleared his throat again and began droning the same words the students had chanted at the induction ceremony. Kirstine was clearly not the only one who had not thought to practice the verses, because none of the other students chimed in as Thorbjørn mumbled his way through the words. Halfway through the last verse, the door swung open and a young man with reddish hair all but fell into the room with a giant stack of books in his arms. When he realized that Thorbjørn was in the middle of something, he sat down and nodded for the man to continue. Thorbjørn hastily rattled off the last few words.

"This is your Norse Studies instructor. Jakob, will you introduce yourself?" Thorbjørn said as he cast a sidelong glance at the wobbling stack of books Jakob had set on the desk.

"Of course, and my apologies for being late, I had trouble finding the books down in storage. My name is Jakob Engholm. I'm training as a teacher in Norse Studies, and as a part of my training I will be teaching you for the next year."

Great, just great. She'd involuntarily slumped down in her chair in the attempt to make herself as small as possible. Most of the other girls at the back of the room did the opposite, straining their necks or shifting in their chairs to get a better view of their instructor. While no one would question a giant man with a large beard like Thorbjørn teaching a subject involving Vikings, Jakob seemed like a far less obvious candidate. He was tall, but rather scrawny, not broad and burly like Thorbjørn. With his tousled reddish hair, the freckles over the bridge of his nose and his crooked smile made him look more like a schoolboy than a Viking warrior.

"I think we'll start with the runes," continued Jakob, "Once you know them, you can read Viking-age inscriptions. And rune magic is an important part of Norse magic. You can read more about all of this in these. They might look old and boring, but the contents are incredibly exciting," he said, patting the stack of books so that it collapsed and the books scattered over the floor.

"Ahem!" Malou said. She was sitting in the first row with a finger in the air, but she didn't wait for permission to speak. "If I could just ask something. How can you ensure the quality of the instruction when our teacher isn't fully trained? I'd assumed that all the teachers would be fully qualified to teach their respective subjects."

Jakob, who'd gotten down on his hands and knees to pick up the books, looked up to see who had spoken.

"What? Your education? You don't need to worry about that, you'll learn everything you need and then some!" he said as he heaved the last few books back onto the desk in a messy pile.

"But how can you guarantee that?" Malou asked, looking at Thorbjørn and completely ignoring Jakob. "The school must have guidelines in place for when someone without the required training is responsible for our lessons. Will the classes be supervised? And who will be grading our written assignments?"

"Uh . . ." Thorbjørn, who'd stepped into the corner after Jakob took the floor, seemed to want to throw the door open and run away. "I'm not entirely sure if there are any official rules . . .

uh . . . but we can look into that. In any case, Jakob is fully capable of handling this course, so you can rest assured . . . yes."

"Yes, of course," Jakob said, winking at the class. "You can trust me."

With a slightly nervous laugh, Thorbjørn said goodbye and left.

Kirstine sighed. Why couldn't Thorbjørn be their teacher? It'd been painfully awkward on the day of the entrance exams when Birgit sent Kirstine outside like a naughty student who couldn't sit still. And now Jakob was going to be reading their essays and everything . . .

"Now," said Jakob, rummaging in his bag, "I've printed out your syllabi as well as some book lists, if I can find them . . ."

"How old are you anyway?" It was Malou again, this time she hadn't even raised her hand.

Jakob lifted his head; he wasn't smiling any more. "What's your name?"

"Malou."

"Okay, Malou, in my classes you raise your hand if you have a question. Understood? And the answer to your question is: old enough."

He reached an arm toward the desk and said something Kirstine couldn't quite make out. A gust of wind ran through the room and swept all the books off the desk with a bang. She flinched. *How did he do that?*

"That was the hail rune Hagalaz. As you can see, rune magic is powerful. But we'll get to that. Here they are!" He pulled a stack of papers out of his bag. "Malou, please pick up the books and hand them out to the class."

Malou scowled but got up all the same. Kirstine hid a small smile behind her hand. *You brought this on yourself, Malou.*

"Great. Meanwhile I'll pass these out," Jakob said, apparently in a good mood again. "I don't know your names yet, so please raise your hand when I read your name. We'll start with Anne..."

Oh no...

"Chamomile?"

She briefly considered running away, but she might as well get it over with.

"Kirstine?"

She raised her hand. Jakob's flustered expression as he handed her the syllabus and booklist told her two things: He had not forgotten meeting her over the summer. And he had not known that she was sitting in the class he was going to be teaching. She almost didn't dare look up, but she did it anyway, and their eyes met briefly. He looked confused and a little annoyed. Was having her in his class really that irritating?

Kirstine flipped through the syllabus without seeing what was on the pages. Her heart was hammering away, and she wasn't entirely sure it was purely from nerves.

Mama—we have to write an essay on plants. Do you have any tips on what you can use raspberries for?

Hi honey—how exciting. The leaves can be dried and used in a tea for stomach pain or intestinal issues. Good luck with the essay! Call when you have a minute—so excited to hear how it's going . . .

Perfect!
Thanks mom

SEPTEMBER 14ᵀᴴ
7:15 A.M.

Victoria

See me . . .
Who killed me?
See . . .

The dream's strange whispering merged with the sound of the alarm as it gradually grew louder. Victoria fumbled for her phone and pressed snooze. How long had it been going off?

She let herself fall back onto the bed. *The white shadows always came back.*

Victoria looked at the clock. She'd only gotten a few hours' sleep, but she had to get up now.

The tower room was filled with all sorts of stuff that still felt foreign and odd. Books on herbal remedies, runes, Norse gods, and the religions of indigenous peoples lay spread over the table and in stacks on the floor. There was also a pot and the strange beaker she'd been given in Nature Magic on top of the table, and next to those was a basket with various plant parts she had to write an essay on for Tuesday. And for Norse Studies, they had an essay on the runic alphabet and the Vikings' written language due on Thursday. If they got homework in Spirit Magic, which they were going to have for the first time today, then there'd be precious little free time this weekend. Victoria touched the little silver skull that hung from her necklace. Spirit magic was an especially important subject for her.

She gave up on the idea of showering, pulled a sweatshirt over her head, and trudged downstairs for breakfast. The girls' dining hall was a cozy space with little flowers painted on the ochre-yellow walls and white curtains that flowed all the way down to the old wooden floors. Victoria grabbed a bowl of yogurt and granola and joined the other girls from her cluster.

"Good morning," Kirstine said as she sat down.

"Did you get any sleep?" Chamomile drained her glass of juice and set it on the table.

"Not much," Victoria admitted.

"Is it that spirit again?" Chamomile whispered. She'd been asking about the spirit ever since Victoria had told her about it.

"Argh, not again with the spirit," Malou said, examining her nails. "Why don't we have a seance? The spirit in the glass or whatever it's called. Then we can ask it what it wants from you?"

"Oh no, I don't think we should do that," Kirstine said, startled.

"Well, we could ask the teachers for permission," Malou said. "I mean, I don't care, I'm not the one it's bothering."

The poisonous tone in Malou's voice gave Victoria a bad taste in her mouth, and she gave up on breakfast. Was Malou right? Would she be free of the spirit if she just found out what it wanted from her? She almost felt ready to try anything if it meant she could sleep through a single night. The white shadows had always been there, but they'd never plagued her like this before.

After they'd finished breakfast, Molly led them up to their classroom. Lost in her own thoughts, Victoria followed the others, but she was ripped back to reality by a cloud of flickering energy and the sound of a group of girls suddenly giggling and whispering, like a wind rising on an otherwise still summer day. Further on, as they were passing through the gallery, there was another class—a boy's class. The air trembled. Someone whistled, there were several cheers, and they laughed and pushed each other.

"Behave yourselves, boys," Molly said as they went past. She shook her head. "You'd think they'd never seen a group of girls before. Just move over so we can get by, thanks!"

But the boys didn't move. In fact, it seemed like they had purposefully arranged themselves to hinder the girls. One of the boys even stood directly in Molly's way and put a hand on her shoulder. He had dark, shoulder-length hair, blue eyes, and a beautiful face.

"Hey there, Molly! Where are you rushing off to? Why don't you just tell us who it is you have here?"

"Let go, Benjamin," Molly said, shaking off his hand. "These are my first years. And you'd better leave them alone if you don't want to be sent packing."

"Whoa, easy. I just wanted to be polite and say hi." He held his hands up in front of him and took a step back. "Just relax, Molly, you can trust me. I'm innocence incarnate—just like you, so I hear." His smile was simultaneously charming and infuriating. A boy with blond curls laughed and shook his head at Benjamin's remark.

Molly reddened.

"Shut up!" she said, marching on with the group of girls behind her. From that vantage she didn't notice Benjamin bending forward to study Malou from behind.

After meeting the third-year boys, the girls' whispering and giggling swelled into a storm that continued even after they got to their classroom. Victoria felt a crushing headache pounding in her temples.

Bang.

The door to the room flew open, and the compact, thickset man they'd met at the mysterious water basin on the day of the entrance exams walked in. He tossed his bag on the table with a clunk and clapped his hands. The room fell silent instantly, and Victoria felt their new teacher's energy fill the whole room, practically compelling everyone to direct their eyes to him. As on the day of the entrance exams, he was dressed all in black, and he looked around the class with a curious and energetic expression.

"Many thanks for your attention," he said. His voice was deep and pleasant. "My name is Jens Andersen, and I teach Spirit Magic. Does anyone know what spirit magic is?"

Sara tentatively raised her hand. "Talking to the dead?"

"Yes and no. People consist of flesh and blood, our physical bodies, but we also all have souls. When the body dies, the soul continues to exist. We can make contact with some souls—or spirits—through spirit magic. The spirits can help us and guide us or even show us visions. We can achieve the ability to see what is happening somewhere far away—what we call *tele-vision*, and I'm not talking about Saturday morning cartoons or cable news—or we may be able to see into the future. What we call *clairvoyance*." He turned and wrote the two terms on the board behind him before continuing.

"But spirit magic is also concerned with the study of human nature—or perhaps we should say *spirit nature* in this context.

Learning to recognize the intentions hiding behind actions. To see the writing on the wall, so to speak. This comes with experience. And that is one thing none of you have. It comes with age, like backaches and reading glasses. You see—and this is very important—many people mistakenly believe that spirits are omniscient. That they're merciful. That they're good and only wish us well. Many believe they're like the angels, as represented in God's great book. But that is grossly incorrect. Spirits are souls, and souls were once humans, and humans are not all-knowing or universally merciful or universally good. People can be greedy and covetous and jealous and vengeful. Accordingly, it can be dangerous to trust what a spirit tells you. You must always keep your wits about you, just like when you meet a stranger. Does that make sense?"

Several of the girls nodded. The man in black had everyone's undivided attention. This speech was both exciting and unsettling.

"In these classes we will learn about spirit magic, what it can be used for, the different types of spirits there are, and how to make contact with them. In the practical subject of clairvoyance—which I also teach—we will attempt to make contact with the spirits. However, you must be properly prepared first, so we won't take the first steps into clairvoyance until after the holidays, and then only if I'm completely comfortable letting you make the attempt, okay? We'll start slowly, and, if anything in my classes makes you uncomfortable, please let me know. Is everyone okay with that?"

They all nodded.

"Again, spirit magic can be dangerous. That is why it's strictly forbidden to practice on your own. If we discover students performing spirit magic or any other form of magic without permission, you risk being expelled immediately." He looked at them all for a moment.

"Good, then that's settled," Jens said, clapping his hands again. "Let's get started."

When the hour was over, Jens gave them each yet another stack of heavy books. Before they'd left the room, he said, "Victoria, could you stay back a moment?"

Chamomile gave her a questioning look, but she just shrugged. She didn't know what the Spirit Magic teacher wanted. Maybe he'd be having a chat with everyone that got a silver skull at the induction ceremony.

Jens leaned against the desk and studied her for a moment, but not in a creepy way. His energy felt friendly and strong, and again she felt it fill the classroom.

"I received a message from Lisa. She said you had an unpleasant experience in the basement during the entrance exams."

She nodded.

"Have you had other experiences since you've been here at Rosenholm?"

"Not in the same way, but there is something that won't leave me alone. And then there are all the others . . ." She nodded toward the empty chairs. "And the dreams at night, of course."

"What do you dream about?"

"I don't know what they're usually called, but I call them the white shadows."

"Ah, yes, those are spirits. Souls of the departed trying to make contact with you. It's quite normal for spirit mages, though it can be rather unpleasant. But I'm surprised to hear that you feel a presence when you're awake too? That's more unusual, especially in someone so young."

He looked as if he was considering something. "Hmm . . . may I try holding your hand for a moment? Just relax and breathe calmly. Close your eyes if you like."

Jens took one of her hands and held it in both of his. Victoria closed her eyes. She felt a warm tingling from Jens's hands almost immediately; it traveled up her arm and spread through the rest of her body. His calm was contagious, and she felt safe and warm and worry-free.

After a few moments, he slowly released her hand.

"I couldn't detect any spirit in your vicinity. But it's not surprising that it would scamper off as soon as it senses I'm after it," he smiled at her reassuringly. "But I can tell that you're very, very receptive. All your sensors are vibrating, and your channels are wide open, so to speak. That won't do. From time to time, we'll see a spirit select a victim from among the students and latch on. Especially if it can feel that the student is receptive and hasn't yet learned to shield him or herself."

"Why would a spirit do that?" she asked.

"Well, it might be looking for sympathy or attention or it might just want to absorb your energy. Sometimes the spirit is trying to torment the student—poltergeists and wights do that. The student becomes the victim of a sort of bullying from the spirit and it can be pretty difficult to break that pattern. But no need to worry. We'll make sure that doesn't happen. I think we should start with extra lessons. You need to learn to shield yourself a bit so that you don't have to deal with the emotions of everyone around you, living or dead. That can drive anyone mad."

Victoria nodded. That was exactly what she was afraid of. That she'd just lose her grip and go completely nuts.

Jens pulled his reading glasses out of his shirt pocket and took an old-fashioned planner out of his bag. "Shall we say Monday afternoons at 2:30?"

Kirstine

Hagalaz, the hail rune, Laguz, the water rune, Kaun, the torch rune.

Kirstine had read the same lines five times without knowing what they said. She looked out the window and decided to put her books down and go for a walk. Before she crept out of the tower room and down the stairs, she remembered to text Chamomile.

> Happy sweet 16, Chamomile

She stood there wondering if she should write more. Would it seem strange if she left it at that? Should it be more personal? Then again, Chamomile was probably busy with her guests and her party and didn't care.

> Hope you have a good day and loads of lovely presents

That would have to be good enough, she thought, leaving the suite. It was so quiet everywhere. After the first few weeks, the students had finally gotten a chance to go home for fall break, and, as far as she knew, all the girls from the first year had left. Some of the older students might still be around, but they were probably taking advantage of the chance to sleep late.

Kirstine walked through the girls' park, as it was generally called. It was incredibly windy outside, almost like home. She missed home almost more than she missed her parents. The rugged wilderness, the horizon, the trees blowing in the wind and the heather that might still be in bloom. And the air was crisp and sweet, not heavy and damp like usual. After having wandered around aimlessly, she reached the sheltered east side of the castle. The sun had found its way through the clouds now, and she sat on a bench against the wall. A large bird of prey hovered high above her, an osprey maybe. She turned her face toward the light and closed her eyes.

"Hello." The figure of a man was silhouetted in front of her. She hadn't heard him coming. Maybe she'd dozed off.

"I thought I'd be alone out here. Mind if I sit?" Jakob gestured toward the bench.

"Oh, sure," she stammered, suddenly conscious of the fact that the scarf around her neck was the one Jakob had loaned her when they first met. Why on earth had she worn it?

"I was just walking by and saw you sitting here. This is the teachers' residence," he explained, nodding toward the windows behind them.

"Oh," was the only thing she could think to say. *Great, Kirstine.* One word. Consisting of two letters. It was the best she could do. It hadn't even occurred to her that of course the teachers would have to live somewhere at the school. Even if they probably didn't share their rooms with anyone.

"You didn't go home for the break?"

She just shook her head.

"I would think a Thy-dweller would be hurrying home to Jutland," he said, casting a sidelong glance and a crooked smile in her direction.

Kirstine stared at her hands. She didn't want to cry. She thought she was done with that, but now the tears were coming again. She let her hair hang down around her face so that he wouldn't see. *Doesn't he have anywhere else to be?*

"Um . . . are you okay?"

She quickly dried her face.

"I'm just having some issues . . . with my family."

"Yes, I remember talking about that . . . that day. They're really Christian, right? So, it probably isn't easy, coming out as a Valkyrie all of a sudden . . ."

"No," she laughed even though she was still crying. She couldn't help feeling a little flattered that he remembered what she'd told him about her family that summer's day. Summer felt about a hundred years ago. Maybe that's what gave her the courage to say what she'd wanted to say to him ever since.

"That day . . . over the summer. I didn't know you thought I was coming for a job interview. I wasn't trying to trick you or anything . . ."

"What? No, no, I'm well aware of that. I was just being an idiot." He made a face as if the memory of it was painful. The wind ran through his reddish hair and ruffled it up. "You just seemed so grown up, much more sensible than first-year girls usually are. So I just assumed we were roughly the same age. That you were a young teacher. Like me. Probably wishful thinking. It was stupid of me, telling you all about my family . . ."

"Why was that stupid?"

Jakob turned toward her. "Do you know what the craziest part was? I felt so . . . understood. But, in reality, you didn't understand anything at all. You didn't know what I was talking about. Why didn't you say something?"

"I . . . sorry . . ." she said, feeling like she might start crying again. "You were being so friendly, and I didn't want to ruin it. And . . . and suddenly it had gone on too long and then I couldn't begin to say that I had no idea what you were talking about. Anyway, it's not true that I didn't understand any of it. I didn't understand *why* your parents were disappointed and angry, but I know how it feels . . ." Now she was crying again, and it was impossible to get another word out. Suddenly she felt Jakob put his arm around her. He didn't do anything else, didn't say anything else. Just held her until she got control of the tears again.

"Maybe we should walk a bit?" he said at last. "A little away from the windows."

She was suddenly conscious of the fact that anyone on the teaching staff could look out the window and see them sitting on the bench together. She nodded.

They walked into the forest. "Are they completely freaked out, your parents?" Jakob asked once they were far enough away from the school that no one could see them.

"They don't want anything to do with me," she said. "Not as long as I'm going to this school."

"They'll come around. Give them some time," Jakob said.

"I really don't know. Sometimes I think I might as well give up on Rosenholm and move back home. It's not as if school's going well—but you already know that, of course." She hated all the written assignments, but the worst were the ones she had to turn in for Norse Studies. It was mortifying to think of Jakob sitting there and correcting her attempts to express herself in writing.

"What? No, you can't give up. Is it that you're dyslexic?"

Kirstine froze. She hated that word. But Jakob had said it as an observation, not as a taunt. "I'm just not good at school. Reading, writing, I've never been good at it."

"But what about the classes?"

"They're interesting enough, but I have a hard time keeping up when I can't read aloud."

Jakob sprang ahead of her and turned to walk backward.

"Hey, I have an idea!" He smiled his boyish grin. The wind had reddened his cheeks. "I can give you extra lessons. Orally. It could be an overview of what we'll be working on. That way you'll be as prepared for class as everyone else, and you won't have to read nearly as much. At least not for Norse Studies, and your abilities are in Earth too, right?

She nodded again. "Yeah, but . . ."

"Perfect. Norse is the subject you should concentrate on most anyway," Jakob said, walking beside her again.

"But . . . why would you do that? Is it normal for teachers to give extra lessons?"

"Nah, not really. Maybe it's just because I'm such a nice guy?" He spread his arms as if to indicate that this was self-explanatory. "And maybe it's a little bit because it can be kinda lonely here. The other teachers are all nice enough, sure, but they're a lot older than me. We don't really have much in common."

"How old are you anyway?"

He turned his head and looked her in the eye.

"Twenty-four."

"Whoa, you *are* old."

"What!" Jakob stopped dead in the middle of the path. "Here I am trying to do a good deed, and you go and insult your poor, old teacher with his age. That's just cold."

She laughed. "I didn't mean it like that."

"Yeah you did," he said, poking her in the shoulder. "But watch out, I assign your grades, you know. Better be nice."

"I promise not to call you old again," she said, adopting an innocent expression. "From now on I'll just say *older*." She smiled broadly. She wasn't going to let him think he was the only one capable of teasing.

They continued along the small path, their hands swinging in sync and so close to each other it almost felt like they were holding hands.

"Hey, what's that?" Jakob pointed at something lying on the path up ahead.

An animal. It was dead.

"Oh," Kirstine exclaimed, "what happened?"

It was a fox. It lay on its back in the middle of the path, the fore and hind legs spread to either side, the head bent back. There was a large bloody wound from the throat to the groin.

"Who did this?"

"A dog, maybe? Or another fox?" Jakob suggested.

"But look at the way it's lying? It's in the shape of a five-pointed star with the paws and the head, what's it called again . . . ?"

"A pentagram," Jakob observed. "Yeah, if you're looking for it, you could say that it forms a star, but I think that's just coincidence."

She frowned. "I see dead animals all the time when I'm hiking. But I've never seen anything like that."

"Maybe the predators are just more sophisticated here on Zealand?" Jakob joked. "Come on, let's head back. You look cold."

Kirstine suddenly realized she was shivering. Still, she hesitated before tearing her eyes away from the fox. She couldn't help feeling there was something strange about the way the dead fox was lying there.

**Rules and Regulations
of Rosenholm Academy**

2. Students are strictly prohibited
from performing unauthorized magic.

Chamomile

"How does it manifest when the soul of a departed wants to tell us something in our dreams?"

Jens looked around the class. Chamomile slouched in her chair. She hadn't gotten a chance to read for Friday's class in Spirit Magic. Luckily Jens answered his own question. "When we sleep, we're vulnerable, and the mind is open. Accordingly, those who cannot make contact with spirits in a waking state may be able to do so in dreams. However, this makes it still more difficult to decipher a potential message. Sometimes the spirit speaks to us through sensory impressions—usually sounds and smells—which may be felt far more strongly than they normally do in dreams. Other times we may dream of symbols we must properly interpret before we can comprehend the message, and other times still we dream the same dream over and over again. That's the spirit's way of trying to communicate that it wants to make contact."

Spirit magic sounded exciting, but they hadn't been allowed to do much magic in Jens Andersen's class yet. The first lesson had been thrilling, but since then it'd pretty much been pure theory. And they'd worked through a massive, century-old book on necromancy that wasn't nearly as exciting as you'd expect.

"I'll give you a little extra assignment for the weekend," said Jens, clapping his hands as if he'd just announced a special treat.

Several people in the class groaned. They already had an essay about the Norse gods due next week.

"Before you go to sleep tonight, be sure to have pencil and paper nearby. If you wake up during the night or when you wake up in the morning, write down whatever you dreamed. Tonight, especially, there is a good possibility that a spirit will try to make contact with you. Who can tell me why?"

No one raised a hand. Now it was Jens who sighed, and Chamomile thought he was looking a little TGIF-tired too.

"Tonight is All Hallows Eve. In the Christian tradition this is the night we remember our dead. Some families set candles on grave sites, and the names of those who have passed away over the course of the year are read aloud in churches. And, for a long time before Christianity's dominance, people solemnly celebrated Halloween, or *Allehelgen*, as it is called in Danish. The Celts in Ireland and on the British Isles celebrated a great feast— *Samhain*—over the course of several days around the first of November. They were celebrating the harvest and marking the summer's end and the coming of a new year. Like many other European peoples, the Celts believed that those who had died in the preceding year would, at this point between the old and new year, travel to the kingdom of the dead. The dead were particularly active and moved among the living as spirits on this day. Among other practices, people lit bonfires to ward off evil spirits. Over time these bonfires were replaced by jack-o'-lanterns as we know them today."

Malou sat with her hand in the air.

"Yes?"

"If it's such an optimal time to make contact with a departed soul just now, why aren't we trying? I mean for real, not just in dreams."

Chamomile straightened up. Now it was getting interesting.

"We don't do that with the first-year students," Jens said bluntly. "But tonight I'll be conducting a seance with the third-year students."

"How does a seance work?" Malou asked.

"There are many ways to do such a thing. The most important part is to focus the energy and keep the mind open. And that is precisely what you should do tonight before you go to sleep. I look forward to reading about the exciting things you experience on All Hallows Eve."

In honor of All Hallows, there were decorations all over the school, like the thousands of little jack-o'-lanterns carved out of root vegetables. That was the way you traditionally made lanterns for All Hallows, but Chamomile spotted a few carved pumpkins too. Birgit probably wasn't crazy about that—she wanted to stick to the old ways and almost certainly wouldn't approve of the impishly grinning, American-style jack-o'-lanterns.

After dinner, which had culminated in a cloyingly sweet pumpkin tart to mark the occasion, Chamomile walked up to the tower room with Victoria and Kirstine to have tea. When they were all seated with their steaming mugs, Malou burst into the room.

"Trick or treat! Or should I say: Trick or RUM! I think I've finally figured out how to make that herbal garbage go down a bit easier!" Malou waved a green bottle.

"What's that?" asked Chamomile.

"Rum, my friend," Malou said, pulling out the cork. "Come on, it's Friday! We can sit around and be bored any old night." She poured a serious splash of rum into Chamomile's mug before she could react. Chamomile sipped cautiously.

"Hmm, it wouldn't be half bad with a little extra sugar," she observed.

"That's the spirit!" Malou said, sounding downright cheerful. "Kirstine?"

"Oh, I don't usually drink alcohol . . ."

"Usual is dead. A little drop never hurt anyone," Malou said as she poured rum into Kirstine's tea. "Give me yours, Victoria."

"No thanks, I shouldn't have any."

"Stop being such a party pooper," Malou protested. "You can sleep late tomorrow."

"I'm not trying to ruin the party, but I really don't want any."

"Are you sick?" Malou looked at her appraisingly.

Victoria did look a little ill. She was very pale and had dark circles under her eyes, and she'd been very quiet all evening. Actually, she'd been very quiet all week.

"I'm just so tired . . ." her voice broke.

"Victoria, are you okay? Is there something we can do?" Chamomile laid her hand on Victoria's.

"I just need sleep . . ." Her voice sounded hoarse.

"Is it the spirit?"

She nodded.

"Forget the damned spirit. Drink a little rum, it'll help," Malou insisted.

"But that's just it . . . I can't forget it. It's always there. Every time I close my eyes . . ." Now she was crying.

"Oh, honey," Chamomile said, stroking Victoria's arm.

"If it won't leave you alone, then confront it," Malou reasoned. "Go on the offensive. That's the only thing to do if you've got someone at your throat."

"Have you ever tried it?" Kirstine asked.

"Not with spirits, but I've got some experience with people," Malou said. "Let's try to do a seance! I read about them in the book on spirit magic, there are supposed to be four of you, so this is perfect. And you heard Jens yourselves, there's no better time than right now."

"How much have you had to drink, Malou?" Chamomile asked. "We could get kicked out of school!"

"Only if it someone finds out. And who would snitch? Victoria, believe me, you'll have to look your tormentor in the eye sooner or later."

No one said anything. Chamomile took a large swig of her tea and started coughing.

"How strong is this?"

"Eighty percent. It's good, right? Drink up, then we can have another round."

"Are you sure this is a good idea?" Kirstine said, pushing her untouched mug toward the center of the table. "With the spirit . . ."

Victoria wiped her eyes with her sweater. "I just want to know what it wants from me. It's as if it has a message for me, but every time I'm about to grasp it, it dissolves into mist . . . if you would help me, then I think . . ."

"So, you're in? Great!" Malou said.

"But only if you all want to, of course," Victoria hurried to add.

Chamomile's eyes met Kirstine's. It was almost as if she could see the battle playing out inside her. On the one hand, Kirstine definitely wanted to help Victoria, but, on the other, she was the one with the most to lose if they got caught. If she was kicked out, she'd have nowhere to go.

Kirstine turned toward Victoria. "If you want to, I'm in." Her voice was barely more than a whisper. Chamomile felt everyone's eyes turn toward her.

"It'll only work if we're all in," said Malou. "It said you needed four people . . ."

Chamomile took her cup, drained it, and set it down hard on the table.

"Okay, I'm in."

"That's the spirit! Finally we're going to see some action!" Malou cheered.

"We're doing this to help Victoria," Chamomile said.

"Absolutely. We'll need a candle. I'll grab one from the kitchen."

They lit the candle, turned off the lamps and brought in four chairs from the kitchen. They arranged the chairs around the candle in the middle of the room. Then they sat holding each other's hands.

"Okay, now what?" Chamomile asked. "You're the expert, Malou."

"Are you ready?" Malou said. "I think we should start by welcoming the spirit."

"We could offer it a drop of rum," Chamomile said.

"This is serious," Malou scolded. She made her voice deep and solemn. "On this All Hallows Eve, we bid the spirits speak to us."

Chamomile looked around at the other girls. Victoria stared straight ahead, Kirstine was staring at the floor, and Malou had her eyes squeezed shut, as if she was gassy. Maybe it was the rum, but Chamomile couldn't help thinking it was all a little funny.

Come on, this is too stupid. We clearly have no idea what we're doing.

"Victoria's spirit! Speak to us!" Malou bellowed.

Chamomile started giggling.

"Hey, stop that. You're ruining it!"

"Sorry! It's just your voice . . ."

"Okay, we'll just sit without saying anything. Close your eyes, open your mind, and concentrate."

Chamomile closed her eyes and fought the urge to open them again to see if the others were still concentrating. She took a deep breath in and tried to gather her thoughts. They all sat still for a long time. Chamomile registered each and every sound. She heard a slight rustling in the trees from outside.

"Hrrrrrrg!"

She jumped, her eyes sprang open, and her heart raced. The strange sound was coming from Victoria. She sat in an unnatural position with her head bent way back. She was still holding Malou and Chamomile's hands, but her arms were stretched straight out and rigid. Chamomile momentarily wondered if they were teasing her, but then she noticed the candle was flickering wildly, despite the total lack of wind.

"The spirit is here!" Malou whispered, her eyes wide. When she spoke, her breath rose in a small cloud. The room had suddenly become ice cold.

"Hhhaaarrr!" Victoria took a deep breath and slowly bent her head forward, toward them. Her eyes were wide open and the brown of her irises had disappeared.

Damn, that's so creepy! Chamomile had to concentrate to keep from letting go of Kirstine's and Victoria's hands in sheer terror.

Kirstine gasped.

"*See me . . . I am here now,*" Victoria said, but the voice was not her own. It sounded simultaneously hoarse and childish.

"What is your name?" Malou whispered.

"*My name is Trine.*"

They exchanged glances, and Malou looked at her encouragingly, but Chamomile just shrugged, her face was full of fear. She had no idea how to commune with a spirit.

"Who are you?" Malou asked.

"*Trine.*" Victoria sat rigidly, and her empty eyes stared straight ahead.

"Where are you from?"

"*Here.*"

"The school?" Malou suggested.

"*Yes, Rosenholm,*" Victoria said in the strangely hoarse yet light voice.

"I don't like this!" Kirstine whimpered. "Shouldn't we stop?"

Malou shook her head.

"What do you want from Victoria?" she asked.

"*Warning!*" The voice was suddenly so loud it made them all jump.

"A warning about what?" Malou asked in a low voice.

Victoria became uneasy and moved around on her chair, shaking her head.

"*I can . . . not . . .*"

Malou swallowed.

Victoria began to lean her head back, her body trembled and spasmed.

"Malou," Chamomile said. "That's enough. We have to make it to stop."

Victoria groaned as if the words were stuck in her throat.

"He . . . killed . . . me," the voice gasped.

"Who?"

Victoria shook her head violently, her body arching backwards in the chair. "Who? Who killed me! Who killed me?!" she babbled. She'd let go of their hands and was now desperately holding onto the seat of the chair as she moaned the same words over and over.

"Malou, make it stop!" Chamomile shouted.

"Trine, answer one last question," Malou said. "How did you die?"

Victoria stopped shaking her head, her blank eyes still wide open. Then she suddenly threw herself back so that the chair fell over and she lay convulsing on the floor. Her whole body was taut like a bow, her arms lay rigidly alongside her body, her jaw tensed.

"Victoria!" Chamomile screamed. "She's not breathing! Do something!"

"Victoria!" Malou knelt by her and pulled down the collar of her shirt. "She's suffocating, look at her neck!"

To her horror, Chamomile saw red splotches emerging on Victoria's throat, as if invisible hands were choking her.

"Make it stop!" Kirstine shouted.

"Breathe, Victoria, you can do it, come on!" Malou tried.

"It's not working, her lips are blue!"

Victoria was pale as a sheet, her lips were indeed turning blue, her mouth frothing. The red splotches on her neck were spreading.

"Let her go!" screamed Chamomile. "Let her go, Trine!"

Victoria sat up suddenly, like a mechanical doll triggered by a spring. She was no longer convulsing, her eyes still blank and wide. Slowly, she turned to face them.

"*Promise me. Promise me you'll find out who killed me.*"

"We promise," Chamomile cried. "We promise!"

As soon as Chamomile had spoken those words, Victoria collapsed.

The sudden silence in the room almost felt more terrifying.

"It's gone," Chamomile whispered. "The spirit is gone."

"But she's not breathing," Kirstine cried. "She's dying!"

"Oh, hell no!" Malou shouted as she sprang to her feet. She ran to the kitchen frantically, ripped open a drawer, and rummaged around until she found what she was looking for. With a large chef's knife, she cut a gash across her own palm so that the blood immediately streamed out. She cupped her hands and caught the blood before sitting astride Victoria. Malou put both of her hands on Victoria's throat, over the red patches.

"Breathe, breathe, breathe," she chanted as if it was a prayer.

"Malou?" Chamomile whispered. "What are you doing?" But Malou just shook her head and continued chanting.

"Help her!" Kirstine sat beside them and laid her hands over Malou's. In a steady voice, she too began to chant. At first Chamomile didn't understand what she was saying, but then it dawned on her that Kirstine was pronouncing the name of the need rune, *Naudiz*, over and over again as she rocked back and forth. Hesitantly, Chamomile placed her hand over the others' and attempted to think about life, about life-giving breath, about air filling Victoria's lungs. Slowly she began to feel vibrations in her hands.

Then two things happened at once: Victoria took a deep, rasping breath, and Malou collapsed.

Victoria

Victoria was awoken by clattering sounds and whispering voices. For a moment she thought she was at home in Frederiksberg and that one of her little brothers was wanting to get in her bed after a bad dream. She fumbled for her phone on the nightstand, but it wasn't there. Then it all came flooding back to her, and an icy sensation flooded her body. She'd let one of the white shadows get way too close. It had almost cost her her life.

Victoria breathed deeply. The anxiety left a metallic taste in her mouth, but she reminded herself that she was safe here.

"We have a student here already, but you can take the other bed." It was the school's healer, Ingrid, speaking in the consultation room on the other side of the door.

"No need. You can just give me a bandage. Do you have any more of that salve Lisa made?" The voice belonged to a boy and sounded somewhat familiar, but she couldn't place it.

"No, unfortunately I'm out of it. Shall I wake her?"

"No, no, it's fine. Just a bandage."

"I cannot understand why they can't figure out how to take better care of you. This is going to sting; I have to clean the wound."

Victoria heard the boy groan as Ingrid murmured healing charms.

"The wound won't close, it keeps bleeding," she said, frustrated. "This isn't exactly a normal scratch. You'll need to spend the night here, even though I already have a girl here. I want to keep an eye on you. I don't know what they were thinking. Sit still."

Victoria was wide awake when the door slid open, and a bright strip of light fell into the room. Ingrid was wearing a robe over flowery pajamas, and her blond hair was disheveled. Victoria guessed she was in her early forties. It was the second time that night she'd been woken up by injured students, and she seemed tired and grumpy. But it was the student Victoria was most interested in. As the light fell on his face, she recognized him. It was Benjamin, the third-year boy, the one they'd met in the hallway with Molly. The one they often watched from their tower windows. He was wearing tight, black jeans, but his upper body was bare. There was a bandage around his chest.

"Shh, don't wake her. I'll be right next door if you need anything. And Benjamin? There's no need to speak to my other patient."

Ingrid crept out as quietly as she could so as to not disturb the students and closed the door so that there was complete darkness.

Victoria no longer felt at all tired. Benjamin's energy filled the room. It felt restless and unfamiliar, but not unpleasant.

Victoria turned over, trying not to rustle the covers. She could hear Benjamin turning over. *Why on earth does he have to spend the night here too?*

"Are you asleep?" he whispered softly. Maybe so Ingrid wouldn't hear. Maybe to avoid waking her if she actually was asleep.

"No," whispered Victoria. Her throat hurt when she spoke.

"Then I'm going to get a little water. I'm nearly dying of thirst." He turned on the lamp above the bed, carefully swung his legs over the side, and walked over to the sink on the opposite wall. Victoria sat up and watched as he bent over the sink and greedily gulped water straight from the tap. He paused for a moment and then moaned in pain when he stood back up. It was a low, deep sound.

"What happened?" she whispered.

"Just an accident." He walked back to his bed and sat down slowly. "What about you?"

"Just an accident," she echoed.

An accident that must not be repeated. From now on she would do everything she could to keep the white shadows away.

Benjamin turned toward her. Studied her. Then smiled crookedly. "What's your name?"

"Victoria."

"First year? I don't think I've seen you before."

She nodded. His energy felt so massive when he looked at her like that. *Self-assured, strong, clear.*

"Listen, Victoria, can we make a deal? Lots of rumors run around at a school like this. Too many. Half of them are lies. Student rule number 1: Do not believe all the gossip you hear. Something like this quickly turns into gossip. So, if you won't say anything about seeing me here, then I won't saying anything about seeing you."

"Okay," Victoria whispered. "Deal." She couldn't help noticing that Benjamin had asked her name but hadn't introduced himself. He must have assumed she already knew who he was. And she did.

"Good," he said, laying back in the bed. The lamp illuminated half of his face and left the other half in shadow. "Then it's our little secret."

He smiled amiably before shutting off the light.

Malou

Damn. Her throbbing head was killing her. Malou was going crazy just sitting there, waiting. Did they all have to wait for Victoria like some kind of depressing welcome committee?

"Maybe I should make some tea?" Chamomile took a step toward the kitchen counter.

Malou shrugged and picked at the bandage Ingrid had put on her hand. The school's healer had done it without questioning the vague explanation Malou gave about an accident with a knife and Victoria fainting at the sight of the blood. But she hadn't exactly looked convinced.

"Hello! Tea or what?" Chamomile asked.

"Yes, but it has to be Earl Grey," Kirstine said. She was doodling aimlessly on a scrap of paper while anxiously rocking back and forth. "Victoria likes the normal stuff best."

"Does she?" asked Chamomile.

"Seriously, no one can stand that herbal garbage," Malou said. The pounding in her temples was hell. Was it an aftereffect of the blood magic she'd performed? Or was it just the rum?

"Are you sure you're okay? You look terrible," Chamomile remarked as she filled the electric kettle.

"I'm doing fine thanks," Malou said. *If "fine" meant "like hell."*

"Shouldn't she be back by now?" Kirstine asked. "What if something serious happened to her?"

"I honestly thought we'd lost her," Chamomile said as she took out four cups. "It seemed like she was completely gone . . ."

"Uh, Chamomile?" Malou gave her a warning look.

Chamomile turned around. Victoria stood in the door to the kitchen. She was pale and had dark circles under her eyes, but somehow they made her look even more beautiful. Malou felt her eyes travel over Victoria's face and down her throat. There was no trace of the red marks they'd seen the day before. Instead, her gaze landed on the necklace around Victoria's throat. And the little silver skull.

"Victoria, come sit down." Chamomile gave her a hug. She looked like she was trying to guess how much Victoria might have heard of their conversation. "How are you?"

"I'm okay, better than yesterday," she said with the hint of a smile.

"What the hell happened?" Malou asked.

"Let's just let Victoria have some tea first," Chamomile said as she poured a cup for Victoria. "And something to eat. I could butter a roll?"

"That's okay," Victoria said, moving her hand as if she wanted to wave away Chamomile's attempts to take care of her. Malou almost felt sorry for her. Chamomile really needed to ease up with all this mother-hen fussing.

"I don't know why the spirit suddenly turned on me," Victoria said.

"You didn't say anything, right?" Malou tried to make her voice sound relaxed but was entirely unsuccessful. If the teachers found out what they'd done, there was a serious risk they'd be sent home. And they would start with her. It had been her idea. But she could *not* go home.

Victoria shook her head. "No, I didn't say anything. And I just want to forget it ever happened. I don't want anything to do with that spirit ever again. I'm done playing necromancer."

Chamomile's eyes darted around, Kirstine clenched. *Oh, crap.*

"Uh, so you don't remember what happened?" Chamomile asked.

"What do you mean?"

"At the end, where . . . I mean . . ."

"We promised to find out who killed the damned spirit, okay?" Malou interrupted. "And you have to help us because you're like the only one who can talk to it."

"What?!"

"It wouldn't have let go of you unless we promised," Chamomile said. "It was killing you. We didn't know what else to do!"

"Tell me this isn't true."

"I'm sorry . . ." Kirstine whispered.

Victoria hid her face in her hands. "And what if we can't figure it out?"

"Hey, we *will* figure it out. Right?" Chamomile rubbed Victoria's back and looked encouragingly at Malou. "Right?"

"Of course we'll figure it out," Malou said.

"If we just help each other, it'll be fine," Chamomile added. "One for all and all for one and all that. Don't be afraid. It's all going to be fine."

Malou continued sitting in the kitchen after the others had gone to bed that night. Her thoughts were still racing. She really wanted Chamomile to be right. That there was nothing to fear. Unfortunately, all signs pointed to the idea that they had a very good reason to be afraid.

The days are growing shorter, the time approaches, but there is still time. Time to find her. Time to bind her to me. For eternity.

PART 3
WINTER

For roses and violets
can never be parted

From *Far Away on Norway's Shores,*
Sea Shanty, 1800s

Malou

Malou slammed the yearbook shut and put it back on the shelf. Nothing in the class of 1999. She crossed out 1999 on her list. So far they'd found three former students named Trine, but it hadn't been difficult to figure out that they were all alive and well. Malou pulled out her phone; she only had to type a few letters. The phone remembered her latest searches and suggested different combinations.

Trine killed
Trine Rosenholm Academy
Death Rosenholm Trine
Trine murder Rosenholm

Nothing. Still, she tried a few extra searches by combining the terms in new ways. It didn't help. Maybe the murder had happened so long ago that there was nothing to find online. For all they knew Trine had been murdered a hundred years ago. They needed a new plan.

Malou got up. She would just be able to grab some dinner before the kitchen closed. The whole school was decorated with pine boughs, Christmas hearts, and little lanterns, and outside the frost-covered grass crunched like broken glass underfoot. But Malou was not in a Christmassy mood. And the fact that "Last Christmas" was playing in the dining hall didn't help.

"What's up, did you find anything?" Chamomile was almost done with her meatballs in curry when Malou sat down.

"No, nothing."

Chamomile looked disappointed. "Okay, well, we'll just have to keep trying. I can try tomorrow. I'm almost done with the assignment for Nature Magic."

"We need a new strategy," said Malou. "This is too slow. Who can we ask who knows anything about the school's history?"

"What about Birgit?" Kirstine asked tentatively.

"She'll ask too many questions," Malou said. "Birgit isn't stupid, she'll get suspicious immediately."

"The same goes for Jens," Victoria said.

"What about Jakob?" Chamomile asked.

"That's an idea," Malou said. "You could probably convince him it's for an assignment or something. Maybe the teachers have access to old archives he could search for us."

"I know who should ask him!" Chamomile said eagerly. "I just happen to know his favorite student." She gave Kirstine an exaggerated wink.

"What do you mean?" Kirstine turned chalk white at first, but then a blush spread over her face.

"Chamomile just means you're the best in the class for Norse Studies," Victoria said.

"But . . ."

"We'll need to be a little sneaky so he doesn't get suspicious," Chamomile continued.

"What if Kirstine waits until the Yule celebration to ask?" Malou said, emptying her water glass. "Molly says the teachers really cut loose and drink a ton. It's always easier to get the truth out of drunk people."

"But . . ."

"Just relax, you can do it," Chamomile said, patting Kirstine on the back.

Malou frowned. *Kirstine coax information out of a teacher? Yeah right.*

See you at the Yule celebration, Beautiful?

Will you please stop calling me that?

OOOOOKAYYYY . . .
But see you there?

. . . Sweetheart?

Maybe. I'm not crazy about parties.
And please—no sweetheart

Kirstine

"I'll make two braids and wrap them over your head, okay?" Kirstine nodded and tried to sit still as Chamomile fussed with her hair.

"Honestly, what are you supposed to wear to something like this?" Malou was standing with her head inside the large wooden wardrobe. Chamomile had also been graciously allowed to braid Malou's blond hair, which hung down her back in a beautiful, tight fishtail. "It's a party, sure, but it's outside and it's December. This is just impossible to dress for."

The end of the semester was to be celebrated traditionally. And *traditional* here at Rosenholm meant Viking-style. Accordingly, for the students who would be staying at school all break, there would also be a more modern Christmas celebration on the 24ᵗʰ. *A party for those of us with nowhere else to be.* Kirstine sighed at the thought.

Victoria walked in. She was dressed in black velour pants and a black turtleneck sweater. It looked expensive and stylish.

"Wow, cashmere?" Malou asked, completely failing to conceal her jealousy.

"I think so. I thought I'd better go with something warm."

"I'm wearing my red dress," Chamomile said, her lips pressed tightly together, holding a hairpin in her mouth.

"Huh, can you really wear red with your hair?" Malou looked skeptically at Chamomile, whose beautiful red hair hung loose.

"Yeah, you know people rarely die when I wear red."

Malou rolled her eyes and stuck her head back in the wardrobe.

Kirstine didn't have much to choose from. She hadn't brought a lot with her when she moved to Rosenholm, and she hadn't been home since. She just chose her nicest pants and a clean blouse.

"What about this? With a smokey eye?"

Malou was wearing a tight, black dress of thin wool. The sleeves were long but the dress only just hit mid-thigh.

"You look great," Kirstine said. "But don't you think you'll be freezing?"

"I'll have tights on underneath. And the high boots. And you've gotta suffer a little for beauty, no?"

Chamomile, finally done braiding Kirstine's hair, considered her work critically.

"All set! Having your hair up really suits you."

"Kirstine, if you're done in here could you come with me for a minute?" Victoria asked, getting up from Chamomile's bed.

Kirstine nodded and followed Victoria back to their room. Victoria seemed more relaxed than usual. Kirstine knew she was looking forward to celebrating Christmas with her family.

"I was just wondering if you'd like to borrow something," she said.

"Ohh, no . . . that's really sweet of you," Kirstine could feel herself blushing, "but I don't think your clothes would fit me." Even though Victoria was pretty tall, Kirstine was taller still, and besides, Victoria was quite slender and lacked Kirstine's hips and bust.

"I have something that might fit you. In fact it really doesn't fit me at all. Would you try it on?"

Victoria held out a colorful silk blouse but immediately stuck it back in the wardrobe. "Nope, that just wasn't you. What about this dress?"

It was a dark blue dress in a heavy, luxurious fabric. It had long sleeves, and there was a deep V in front and back.

"You can wear a shawl over it or something. And I have some tights you can borrow too."

"This is way too nice, Victoria, I can't . . ."

"Just try it on, I'm never going to wear it. Oh, and there's a drawstring at the waist."

Victoria helped Kirstine get the dress over her head.

"It's way too tight, it doesn't fit," Kirstine said, looking down at her hips. Her father would die if he saw her like this.

"It's perfect!" Victoria said. "It's meant to be fitted. It's like a tent on me. You look great. And the mid-shin length works on you."

"This is really sweet of you," Kirstine said, "but I really don't think it's me."

"Here's what we'll do . . ." Victoria said. "We'll ask Malou for her honest opinion. You know she never says anything just to be nice. If she says you look good then you keep the dress on, okay?"

Malou stomped into the room in her tall, black boots when Victoria called.

"Chamomile, you can't say anything, only Malou. Malou, what's your honest opinion?" Victoria asked, nodding toward Kirstine.

Malou got a slightly pissed-off expression on her face when she saw Kirstine in the dress. She let her eyes run over her briefly.

"It's perfect," she said acidly, stomping back to her room to finish her makeup.

"See! Now you have to wear it."

"You have to! All the boys will be obsessed," Chamomile smiled. "And maybe if I stand next to you, they'll look at me too."

"Boys?"

Chamomile and Victoria laughed.

"Yeah, you didn't really think we were going to all this effort for Birgit's sake, did you? The party is for all the students—both boys and girls," Chamomile smiled.

"Ready, ladies?" Malou was standing in the door again.

"Wow, you look like a model, Malou," Chamomile said.

"Oh, shut up," Malou said as she turned toward Kirstine. "And remember the plan? You have to wait for Jakob to be good and drunk before you ask him."

Kirstine nodded and swallowed. Then she felt Victoria giving her hand a squeeze. "Let's go."

When they got to the main staircase, they ran into the stream of students all on their way to the main entrance and out to the castle's snow-covered park. The celebration was being held in a large circus-style tent, except without the gaudy colors and flags. The path to the tent was marked with torches, and inside there was a large bonfire. Kirstine leaned her head back and saw that there was a large hole in the ceiling of the tent, so the smoke could get out.

"Come on, this'll be something to see," Malou said, taking Victoria by the hand. Victoria grabbed Chamomile's hand, and Chamomile grabbed Kirstine's. Then they let themselves be carried through the crowd of students to find a place around the bonfire.

Kirstine's thoughts were somewhere else entirely. How would she ever find a way to talk to Jakob in this chaos? Wouldn't it be better to ask him when they were alone?

"Here we are," Malou said when she'd pulled them all the way up to the front so they could feel the heat from the fire and see what was happening.

"Welcome!" Birgit was dressed in a deep-red suit with a cape on top for the occasion. "First, I want to say happy Yule to you all, and now I will give the floor to Thorbjørn, who will preside over this evening's ceremony."

Thorbjørn stepped forward, and Kirstine gasped involuntarily. He was naked from the waist up; his bulging upper arms were covered in tattoos of Viking-style dragons that swooped in and out among each other. Around his upper arms he wore thick gold rings, and his long hair and beard were braided.

"In honor of our roots, the Earth's magic, and the power of History, today we celebrate Yule." His deep voice rang out through the tent, and he seemed looser and less inhibited than he usually did in the classroom. Some of the oldest students cheered.

"We drink to Yule!" More cheering broke out. "Let the cups be dispersed!"

The teachers stepped out from the crowd. Each carried a stack of pewter mugs. Then Thorbjørn reappeared pushing a large vessel on wheels. It was filled with an amber liquid and several large pitchers floated on the surface. Thorbjørn dipped a pitcher into the liquid, filled it, and sent it around so that everyone could fill their cups. When a pitcher was empty, it was sent back to be filled again. Kirstine saw several of the third-year boys fill and empty their cups more than once before Thorbjørn raised his voice again.

"As our forefathers before us, we drink to Yule. First, we drink to our forefathers' gods. To Odin, the king of the gods, to Freja, the god of fertility. Skål!"

Thorbjørn raised his cup, and the tent was silent as everyone drank. Kirstine started coughing. The drink was sweet but also very strong and she wasn't at all used to alcohol.

"Mmmm, delicious!" Chamomile and Malou said in chorus. Then they burst out laughing.

"Now we drink to the slow return of light, to a fruitful and auspicious new year, skål!"

Kirstine carefully sipped her drink again. She felt her cheeks reddening and the warmth spreading through her body. Thorbjørn refilled the pitchers and let them circulate again before raising another toast.

"We drink in honor of our dead, for those we have lost, for those we miss!"

How strong is this stuff? Kirstine already felt a little dizzy.

"And now we sacrifice," Thorbjørn announced. There was silence in the tent. Suddenly they heard a scream from the entrance, and Kirstine jumped. She turned and saw Lisa dragging a pig behind her.

"No, they're not going to sacrifice a real, live animal, right?" Malou asked, staring in disgust as Lisa struggled and strained to get the drag the pig into the middle of the crowd.

"Well, that's what the Vikings did," Victoria remarked.

"Yeah, it seems like they're going all in on traditional Yule," Chamomile whispered.

When the pig was in the center of the tent, Thorbjørn nodded as if he was giving a signal. Then Jakob—Kirstine hadn't noticed him yet—stepped out of the crowd. He was wearing a dark blue shirt, but as he walked toward the bonfire's glow, he slipped it over his head so that he too was bare-chested. Kirstine felt her eyes burning holes in his skin and the bulging muscles of his upper body and abdomen. Blushing, she forced herself to look away. Then she heard a deep, meditative drumbeat spread through the tent. Kirstine turned her head and caught sight of Zlavko. He was also naked from the waist up, and you could clearly see the bizarre scars twisting over his body like snakes in the glow of the fire. His long, black hair hung loose and shining over his shoulders. He was carrying a large, flat drum that he played with one hand. The rhythms rose and fell in strength, but they could not drown out the suckling pig who squealed and shrieked so violently that Kirstine almost couldn't stop herself from sticking her fingers in her ears.

Suddenly, Thorbjørn raised an arm into the air and, all at once, the drumming stopped. His hand held a large knife. Again, he nodded to Jakob, who deftly grabbed hold of the pig so that its throat was exposed, and, with a roar, Thorbjørn bent over the animal and cut its throat. The blood poured out.

"Oh, that's disgusting!" Malou said, and Chamomile closed her eyes. But Kirstine looked on, mesmerized and incapable of tearing her eyes away from the disturbing sight. Once the pig stopped squirming, Lisa rushed over with a large basin to collect the blood. She chanted over it as the blood poured into the basin. Jakob released the animal. His hands were bloody, and when he dried his forehead with the back of his hand, it left a thin stripe of blood on his cheek. Kirstine watched as Thorbjørn dipped a finger into the blood-filled vessel and drew a five-pointed star on Jakob's chest.

Suddenly, she was struck by a powerful wave of nausea. The tent spun around her ominously. She clutched the pendants of her necklaces, both the small silver plow and the gold cross. At that very moment, she locked eyes with Jakob. She couldn't bear looking at him as he stood there, half-naked and smeared in blood. Now the drumming began to sound again, and other teachers joined in on other instruments. Lisa dipped a birch branch in the basin of blood and began to shake it over students and teachers alike.

"Uggh, hell no!" Malou said.

"You can say that again," Chamomile said, "I'm going to need more mead or whatever that was to get through this party."

People around them were refilling their cups, and the other girls began making their way to the large basin of mead, but Kirstine shook her head. She didn't want any more. Both teachers and students started dancing to the music as Thorbjørn butchered the pig. Large pieces of meat were set to roast over the fire. It was hot in the tent now, the air was thick with the smell of blood and sweat and roasting meat.

The music grew louder—there was something hypnotic about it—and Kirstine felt a strange spinning sensation, as though her feet were no longer connected to the earth beneath her. Her eyes found Jakob in the crowd again. The red star of blood shone on his chest, she couldn't take her eyes off it. It seemed to hover in the air in front of her. She squeezed her eyes shut, but the star remained. It shone before her inner gaze and slowly morphed into the bleeding fox they'd seen in the forest. Kirstine shook her head. *What's happening?* She had to get out of that tent. Stumbling, she fought her way to the exit. She kept running into dancing, sweating bodies, then suddenly she was outside. She breathed the ice-cold air down into her lungs and the nausea eased, but she still felt dizzy. What had she had just witnessed? Were they all mad? The snow crunched under her feet as she staggered toward the castle.

"Kirstine!"

Oh no, couldn't he just leave her alone? He was the last person she wanted to see.

"Kirstine!" Jakob caught up with her when she was almost to the castle. "Wait!"

He grabbed her hand, but she pulled it away in disgust, staring at his bloody fingers.

"Don't touch me!"

"It's just blood, see, I can wash it off with the snow." He bent down and drew his hands through the white flakes, which turned red where he'd touched them.

"Why didn't anyone tell us what kind of . . . what kind of sick ritual they were going to do?" she shouted, hearing the shrillness in her voice.

"It's not a sick ritual. That's how the Vikings celebrated Yule. It's to honor our history. The history that gives *you* your powers."

"What powers?" she shouted at him. "I'm starting to think this is all just an excuse to cultivate a disgusting hobby! I do *not* understand why you would want anything to do with those people!"

"Disgusting hobby? Okay, listen, I understand how it might seem a little violent, but you're overreacting. For starters, you would know how the Vikings celebrated Yule if you had read about it like everyone else. Secondly, all they did was slaughter a pig. How do you think they get the ground meat for the meatballs they serve in the dining hall? They slaughter pigs."

Kirstine felt the anger surging through her. What was he saying?

"Don't talk to me like some silly little kid! No, I hadn't read about it because I can't goddamn read, but I come from the country. I'm perfectly well aware of where food comes from!"

"Kirstine, I didn't mean it like that . . ." Jakob reached toward her, but she pulled away.

"Yes, that's exactly what you meant, but you can't shut me up by talking down to me. It's not just an animal being slaughtered. It's a . . . it's a totally barbaric ceremony. The Vikings sacrificed people too. But maybe the human sacrifices don't start until after midnight or something?

"Of course not. But this is our culture, our history. My history. And yours. Whether you like it or not. It sounds like your parents are the ones talking right now. Barbaric? Next thing you'll be calling it sinful? Or Satanic maybe?"

"And what if I did? Half-naked people getting drunk and dancing around a bonfire while they sprinkle each other with blood? And that . . . that star."

She nodded toward the five-pointed star on Jakob's chest.

"This? It's a fertility symbol. It has nothing to do with Satan. Satan is something Christians invented. Not the Vikings. Listen, no actual mage would ever turn it on its head and claim that it's a Satanic symbol. That's the work of blowhards and hucksters. And if you want evidence that you're one of us, just look down . . ."

Kirstine didn't understand what he meant at first. But then she saw it. Dark, wet cobblestones were visible in a circle around her feet. The snow had melted around her. *She* had melted the snow . . .

"Get away from me!" Kirstine held her hands up in front of her and began to back away from Jakob.

"Kirstine, it's nothing to be afraid of . . ." He took a step toward her.

"No!" she shouted. "Just leave me alone! Just stay away!" She turned and ran toward the castle.

"Kirstine!"

Before she slammed the door behind her to run up the stairs, she looked back and saw him standing alone in the empty, snow-covered courtyard.

Chamomile

When she woke up, Chamomile immediately knew that the previous night's buzz had disappeared and left a pounding headache in its place.

"Ohhh, my head, who the hell asked the sun to shine?" Malou buried her face in her pillow. She was still wearing the little black dress, but at least she'd managed to get her boots off. They were in a heap in the middle of the room, together with Chamomile's dress. "Please, Chamomile, can't you close the curtains?"

"No," she moaned, "I don't think I can stand up yet. What did they put in that mead?"

"Never say the word 'mead' to me again. My head feels like it's about to explode." Malou looked up from the pillow. Her makeup was smeared so that she looked like a scrawny panda. A scrawny panda with a massive hangover.

"Okay, I'll try." Chamomile lurched toward the window. The sun shone down on the snow outside, it had to be nearly noon. She closed the curtains and collapsed back into her bed.

"I just need to lie down for a few more minutes. Then I'll make some of my mom's headache tea."

"No! Just the thought of that herbal piss is making me queasy!"

"Malou! There's nothing wrong with herbal tea. You're just not used to it . . . no, okay, you're right. It's disgusting. We need aspirin and a soda—an ice-cold soda."

"How do we get that?"

"No idea. Scream for help?"

"Ha, ha. No one's going to come to our rescue. I bet the entire school is hungover."

"Yeah, except Kirstine. She left early."

"Right, what happened to her? She just disappeared. Did she talk to Jakob?"

"I don't think so."

"Oh hell. It was a stupid idea to let her handle that."

"I don't think Kirstine is used to parties and alcohol," Chamomile said. "Or sacrifices and crazy ladies who spray you with blood."

Malou laughed again. Her voice was hoarse and deep. "What the hell was up with that? Everyone just went nuts. I swear I caught Zlavko and Ingrid having an intimate moment."

"Yeah, and did you see Molly? She was totally making out with one of the third-year boys. That rule about girls and boys clearly doesn't apply when it's Yule."

"Hey, what about you? You were dancing pretty close to that blond guy." Malou raised up on her elbows.

"What?! Was not. Okay, maybe a little. Vitus. He's the one who's friends with Benjamin."

"Yeah, he told me."

"What? You talked to Benjamin?"

Malou just said, "Mmm."

"Were you guys like, 'together'?"

"No, though I think he wanted to be. But Birgit was on patrol and keeping an eye on us. Granted she looked a bit cross-eyed herself. So, we just danced a little. And talked. I think. It's all a little hazy. But Vitus, wasn't that the guy Molly was crushing on?"

"Was she? I remember she said he was cute, but I didn't know she was actually into him. Oh no! What if she like really likes him? Is she going to totally hate me?"

"I don't think you need to panic. If she was really that into him, she wouldn't have been playing suckermouth with someone else, right? Nah, I'm much more interested in whether YOU really like him?"

"Stop it, we were just dancing. And he was really sweet. Cute too."

"Chamomile is in loooooooooovvvvee!" Malou sang.

"Shut your face!" Chamomile said, throwing a pillow at Malou. "He was probably really drunk. When he sees me in daylight and without alcohol in his blood, he probably won't want anything to do with me."

"What are you talking about? Men love women with red hair. And hips and boobs. You're a catch."

"Whoa, did you just give me a compliment? What's happening?"

"No idea," Malou said, letting herself fall back into the pillows, "I must still be drunk."

Chamomile laughed, "That explains it."

"Good morning! I thought I heard your beautiful voices!" Molly was sticking her head in the door. "Oh dear my little first years! I think you two could use some fresh air!" She went over to the window, opened the curtains, and threw the window open.

"Nooo!" Malou and Chamomile moaned in chorus before hiding under their blankets.

"It's almost noon, and I've been tasked with informing you that you have to get up and pack if you're going to make the bus this afternoon."

"Forget it, I'm just going to stay at school over Christmas," Chamomile groaned. "Do you have any Coke?"

"Nope. But Victoria grabbed a pitcher of apple juice from the dining hall. Should I ask her to bring some in?"

"Please!" groaned Malou, "Better than herbal tea at least."

Chamomile stuck her tongue out.

"And now up with you!" Molly said on her way out the door.

"How the hell is she so fresh?" Malou mumbled, letting herself fall back into bed again.

"Good morning," Victoria said as she came into the room with two large glasses of juice.

"Aww, thank you," Chamomile said, drinking half the glass in a single gulp. "When did you leave the party?"

"Around one in the morning, I think. How long did you guys stay?"

Malou shrugged. "No idea."

"Until there wasn't any more mea—any more to drink," Chamomile said. "Where's Kirstine?"

"She went for a walk. She seemed pretty upset. I told her not to feel bad about not getting to talk to Jakob. And I invited her to celebrate Christmas at my house, but she doesn't want to. I think she's going to be the only one from our year staying at school over the holidays."

"Anne is staying too," Malou said. "She was supposed to go skiing with her parents, but the trip was canceled."

"That's too bad for Kirstine," Chamomile said. "I'll tell her that if she changes her mind and wants some company then she can always take the bus out to Mom and me. It's just the two of us and we live nearby."

"What about you, Malou? Are there going to be a lot of people at your place for Christmas?" Victoria asked.

"Nah," said Malou, getting up. "I'm going to shower now. You all can just get in line and wait until I'm done."

"Right," Chamomile said, taking another swig of juice. "We'll do that then."

The sun was already setting over the snow-clad park and the black trees—their bare branches stretched toward the pink sky— as they walked down to the highway to catch the bus. Chamomile would be taking the local bus in about half an hour, so she stood at the side of the road and waved goodbye as the others boarded the first bus. Darkness fell and it was quiet and cold. The temperature was below freezing now. Suddenly she could barely wait to get home to the little half-timbered house. She pictured the lights her mother would have hung on the tree in the courtyard. And her mother always put out homemade birdseed ornaments for the birds too. The house would be filled with the spicy scent of hot apple cider and vanilla and cardamom and anise. Her mother would have decked the whole house with pine boughs and every last ugly, wonky elf Chamomile had ever made in the course of her entire childhood. She smiled to herself. Then she felt her phone vibrate. It was probably her mom.

> Hi Chamomile. I got your number from Molly. Hope that's ok. Just wanted to wish you Merry Christmas. —Vitus

The smile on her lips stretched until Chamomile felt it straining her cheeks. She leaned her head back and looked up at the sky as the first stars appeared.

Kirstine

Kirstine checked her phone again. *No emails. No texts. No calls.*

Neither from her parents nor Jakob. She hadn't heard from him since the Yule celebration, and now he'd gone home for Christmas. Of course she *had* told him to stay away from her. It was probably just as well. She got cold and clammy at the thought of what could have happened. She wasn't herself when she was that angry. *Luckily it only affected the snow this time.*

Kirstine put the phone back in her pocket. She should be relieved he hadn't texted. Then again, she'd promised to talk to him about the spirit. Her fingers fidgeted with the phone, almost unconsciously. Could she let herself text just to ask if he knew about an old murder that had been committed at Rosenholm? Would it be super awkward after what happened on Yule?

Kirstine tossed the phone away and found the blue dress she'd borrowed from Victoria for the ceremonial gathering. She even tried braiding her hair—Chamomile made it looks so easy—but it wasn't working, so she just combed it out and coiled it into a bun at the nape of her neck. Suddenly she heard a noise next door. Someone was in Malou and Chamomile's room. *Who could it be?* She was the only one left in her cluster. Kirstine's heart hammered in her chest.

"Hello?" She knocked on the door.

"Come in," a familiar voice answered, and Kirstine breathed a sigh of relief. Malou was unpacking her old suitcase. Her hair was in a messy bun on top of her head, and loose wisps were haloed around her head.

"Malou, why are you here?"

Malou turned her back to her, pretending to be busy putting a dress on a hanger, but Kirstine could see that her eyes were red and swollen.

"I just changed my mind, okay? Suddenly tons of people were coming for Christmas Eve. I just couldn't handle it." She turned toward Kirstine with a defiant look on her face. A muscle quivered in her cheek.

"Okay," Kirstine said. "Are you coming down to the Christmas Tree Party? Should I wait for you?"

"I need to change. Just go, I'll be there soon."

A half hour later, a better-coiffed Malou stepped into the library where they would be celebrating Christmas Eve. She was wearing a red wrap dress and matching lipstick, and her hair was up in a high ponytail. She smiled broadly at Kirstine, tramped over to her, and gave her a hug, surprising Kirstine so much that she barely managed to return the smile.

"I didn't get a chance to say Merry Christmas," Malou said. "Where should we sit?"

The many round tables that normally filled the library had been replaced with one long table set with a white tablecloth, white napkins, and beautiful porcelain plates. Candles burned in tall, silver candelabras, and pine boughs and small, red apples were arranged down the center of the table. A fire blazed in the fireplace next to a beautiful Christmas tree decorated with lights, stars, Danish hearts, and more red apples.

"Look, there's mulled wine! Let's have a glass," Malou said, dragging her away.

Kirstine felt completely grateful. Before Malou had turned up, she'd just been standing helplessly in the corner not knowing what to do with herself. Anne hadn't arrived yet and, apart from a few teachers, she didn't know anyone there. And she wasn't about to start chatting up the teachers. Over by the fireplace, Zlavko was playing some kind of a board game with a student, and Birgit was engrossed in conversation with Jens and Ingrid. She guessed most of the teachers had gone home to celebrate Christmas with their families.

"Here!" Malou said, putting a glass of mulled wine in Kirstine's hand. "Cheers and Merry Christmas!"

"Hey, you two!" a pair of arms wrapped around them both from behind.

"Molly! You're here?" Malou shouted in surprise.

"Well, I was supposed to be celebrating Christmas with my sister, but I can't stand her husband. He's some total lawyer-type, so I bailed on the get-together. Could you get me a glass of that?" Molly nodded toward the large bowl of mulled wine on the small table in the corner. She was wearing a black knit hat over her dark dreadlocks and her T-shirt featured an elf with a line drawn through it. *Christmas sucks* was written beneath the canceled elf.

"What about your parents?" Malou asked, handing Molly a glass.

"They're diplomats. I think they're in Japan at the moment. Could be Hong Kong, I can't keep track of them."

They found a corner and threw themselves down on a sofa to wait for dinner.

"Okay, Molly, are we finally going to hear about who you were with at the Yule celebration?" Malou lowered her voice so that none of the teachers would overhear them.

"His name is Frédéric, and his parents live in Paris." Molly pronounced the name with an impeccable French accent.

"What about Vitus, weren't you crushing on him?"

"Nah, that was a long time ago. We're just friends."

"Are you and Frédéric together now?" Kirstine asked. She found herself envying Molly's no-nonsense style.

"No, but we might be soon," Molly said, smiling. "I bet I can persuade him that we're the perfect couple before the Spring Ball. I just *have* to go with him."

"Oooh, a ball? When is it?" Malou asked eagerly.

"Sorry, just for third years!" Molly said. "Well, technically the third years invite whoever they want, but normally you go with someone from your own class."

"Uggh, so unfair," Malou said. "Why isn't it for the whole school?"

"That's just how it is," Molly said. "But you'll get something out of it. All the classes have to learn and practice the formal dances before the ball. Especially Les Lanciers. And the first-year girls practice with the third-year boys. In theory the third-year boys are levelheaded enough to handle it. So there's that to look forward to."

"Aren't the teachers afraid the boys and girls will be too close to each other?" Malou asked.

"Actually, the majority of the teachers turn a blind eye toward it. Especially for the third years—and after they've had enough wine—just you wait," Molly said. "They were teenagers once too. Even if that was a like a hundred years ago."

"Here comes Anne," Kirstine said. They all hugged her when she arrived. She was wearing a fancy hairclip with Christmas bells in her freshly trimmed bob, and the bells jingled faintly whenever she moved her head.

"I had a clothing dilemma," she said as she smoothed her burgundy skirt.

"You look so *fancy*," Molly said. "Oh, it's so nice that you're all here. Now I'm extra happy I skipped the lawyer's fascist Christmas."

Suddenly, someone cleared their throat.

"Dear students, dear colleagues. Dinner is served, please be seated," Birgit said.

The main dish was roast goose. Kirstine had never had it before—they always had roast pork on Christmas Eve at home—but the goose and the apples and prunes and brown sauce were delicious. And there was wine to go with each course—every student was allowed one glass of each of the wines—and Malou's cheeks went red as the last traces of sadness disappeared from her face. Afterward, they had almond rice pudding with homemade cherry sauce. Zlavko found the almond in his dish and won a giant marzipan pig for his troubles. He immediately bit the head off the candy animal.

After the food, the Christmas tree was lit and Birgit sat down to the piano that had been moved into the library for the occasion. She started in on some Christmas carols with real spirit, and the rest of them sang along as best they could to the somewhat troublesome notes as they danced around the tree. When they were done, Birgit pulled out a large bag and distributed gifts. Her cheeks had gone red too, and she giggled sheepishly at herself in the role of Santa Claus. Molly got a leather bracelet with a small amber bead that she immediately put on her wrist, Malou got a beautiful notebook with gold embossing and pink roses on the cover, Anne got a nice headband, and Kirstine got a pair of warm wool mittens with a red-and-white-checked pattern. Afterward, stuffed to the brim, they collapsed onto the various sofas. As Molly had predicted, there was more wine and coffee and by then, the teachers had stopped keeping track of how much wine the students were drinking. Kirstine saw Malou and Molly giggling as they smuggled a bottle into a corner.

"Who wants to play the gift exchange dice game?" Birgit called out as she began clearing space on the table and pulling out dice and dice cups. Anne said she was tired and was going to bed, and Kirstine had intended to pass on the game too, but Malou charged over and dragged her off the sofa and toward the table. Soon everyone was caught up in snatching as many little packages for themselves as possible. It was a complicated game, and permissible tactics included bluffing and lying and subterfuge of all kinds. Birgit had just stolen the game's largest gift from Zlavko, and he swore in a language Kirstine didn't recognize, when Molly suddenly burst out: "Oh, here comes Jakob! You're a little late, dude. We've gone and eaten the goose." Malou and Molly collapsed into a fit of giggles, then they tried to steal a gift from a second-year student in the ensuing confusion.

Kirstine turned. Jakob was standing in the doorway in his big winter coat looking like someone who'd gotten the address wrong. Suddenly her pulse was rushing in her ears. Why was he here?

"Coming in?" Birgit asked, her cheeks red and her hair sticking out at odd angles. "Sit down, you can join the gift exchange game."

"What!? Oh, no, I actually just wanted . . . well, I wanted to wish you all a Merry Christmas."

"Seems like a pretty long trip just to wish us Merry Christmas," Zlavko said with raised eyebrows.

"Join us! Come on, sit down!" Birgit pulled a chair up to the table and Jakob took off his coat.

"Have some wine, it'll warm you up!" Birgit clumsily poured a glass of wine and it spilled out onto the tablecloth. Jakob picked up the glass and drank. Then his eyes met Kirstine's. Her cheeks burned and she couldn't quite decipher his expression. Above all he looked incredibly sad.

The game continued for a few more rounds. Malou and Molly were exiled for cheating way too obviously, and Zlavko ultimately ran off with the large package that turned out to be a badminton set. Kirstine didn't know where to look. Every time her eyes met Jakob's, a current ran through her. It was suddenly impossible to remember why she hadn't wanted to see him ever again. The anger and fear disappeared as he sat there looking so miserable. Finally, the game was over, and the group broke up.

Kirstine felt dizzy from the heat and wine, and she had a spinning sensation in her body. She needed some fresh air. She crept out of the library without a word to anyone. Should she have at least said goodnight to Jakob? She could still turn around. But that would probably be super awkward. Instead, she walked through the gallery toward the stairs. The moon lit up the park, creating spectacular images with the bare, black trees against the bright, white snow. She caught a glimpse of a large bird in the form of a black shadow against the white snow, but then it disappeared into the darkness even as she heard its cry ringing through the silence.

"Kirstine." He said her name ever so softly. "Kirstine, wait."

She turned. The moonlight fell in through the windows and washed over him. He looked tired. And tortured.

"Why are you here?" Her words sounded harsher than she'd meant.

He ran a hand through his hair. "Yes, why did I come," he said, turning away from her so that he almost seemed to be talking to himself. "I probably did it to prove once and for all that I'm a complete idiot." He laughed a short, harsh laugh. "It's obvious you think I'm some kind of pervy sinner or something. And even if it wasn't like that—even if you liked me back—then it's still doomed from the start, right? It's all wrong on *so* many levels. You're a first-year student—I'm a goddamned teacher. It's wrong and forbidden and probably dangerous. But here I am. It's been proven conclusively: I am an idiot."

Kirstine moved closer him and laid a hand on Jakob's arm. "I don't think you're an idiot, or a pervy sinner."

"Yes, you do," he said.

"Okay, maybe a *bit* of an idiot."

He laughed and turned toward her. The muscles in his jaw were tensed.

"But not a . . . a pervy sinner," she said.

"Good," he nodded, "that's good. Because when you say everyone here at Rosenholm is wrong or weird, then you're saying you're wrong and weird too, Kirstine. Because you're one of us. But you're so far from wrong. As far from wrong as can be. You're beautiful and brilliant and sweet and funny. And I'm head over heels in love with you."

Kirstine's eyes widened. The moonlit hallway spun around them, and she felt like she was in free fall.

"And if you don't move now," he whispered, "I'm going to kiss you."

Kirstine didn't move. Instead, she closed her eyes and let herself slowly fall into him. His chest felt so hard and strong and different against her body. He gently pressed his mouth against hers. The feeling of his tongue pressed against hers was startling, but she felt safe with his arms wrapped around her. She lost all sense of time and place; the world was only them, bathed in silver-white moonlight, and his burning mouth pressing against hers.

Suddenly the silence and the moment were torn apart by the sound of a horrified shriek. Kirstine stiffened and pulled away from Jakob. His face was serious. Then they heard a pleading cry for help.

"Come on!" Jakob grabbed her hand and they set off.

The scream had come from the upper floors. Jakob took the stairs two at a time, pulling Kirstine along behind him. They raced up to the girls' hall.

"It's coming from in there," Kirstine gasped, out of breath, "from our hall!"

"Stay back," Jakob said. "Is anyone here?!"

"In here!" someone called out. It was coming from Anne and Sofie's room.

They rushed into the room. Kirstine felt her heart skip a beat at the sight. Molly was crouched next to Anne, who lay on the floor between the two beds. Her arms and legs were spread out to either side and her pajamas were slashed to pieces so that her breasts were exposed. Her body was covered in bloody lacerations and scratches.

"She won't wake up!" Molly said, panicked. Anne's head was thrown back and her eyes had rolled up so that only the whites showed.

"Get away from her!" Jakob shouted, and his voice made Molly flinch. "She might be cursed." He murmured a series of runes in a long chant as he knelt by Anne's side to check her pulse.

"She's breathing. We've got to get her to Ingrid immediately." Jakob lifted Anne as if she was a child. Her arms and legs hung limp. "Molly, find Ingrid. Tell the teachers to come too. Kirstine, clear the way for me. Come on, we've got to move fast!"

Malou

Malou was biting her nails. She'd never have long nails; she always wound up biting them to bits. The great hall seemed especially big today. There weren't a lot of students around for the holidays. Then the door to the courtyard swung open and she saw Chamomile hurrying inside. Her tousled red hair and ruddy cheeks made it look as if she had run all the way up the path from the bus stop.

Chamomile quickly found Malou and Kirstine among the students who had silently gathered in the great hall.

"It's ridiculous that you came all this way," Malou said. "I could have told you everything over the phone."

"Oh, stop. I couldn't just sit at home." Chamomile gave first Malou and then Kirstine a hearty hug. She looked like she'd been crying.

"Are you guys okay? I've been worried sick."

"What did your mom say about you going back to school when there's some kind of psychopathic slasher on the loose?" Malou asked as Chamomile squeezed in between them.

"I didn't tell her. I just said you were all here and I didn't want to miss out. I'll go back again tomorrow."

Malou looked around. Chamomile wasn't the only one who'd come back to school for the assembly Birgit had announced just that morning. Malou saw both Benjamin and Vitus, and Sara and Sofie were sitting a few tables away next to Molly. Sofie was Anne's roommate—she was crying quietly with her head on her sister's shoulder.

"Have you heard anything else?" Chamomile slipped off her big winter coat.

"The teachers were busy investigating Anne's room all night. But none of them will talk to us. Jakob came and checked on us this morning, but when I asked if they'd caught the perpetrator, he just said it was complicated. What the hell is that supposed to mean?"

"Shh, she's coming!" Kirstine shushed them and pointed at the door. Birgit had walked in followed by Jens, Zlavko, and Jakob.

Birgit took the floor. "As you all know, a student was badly hurt yesterday evening. I can assure you that Anne is on the mend, and that she regained consciousness this afternoon. She is being transferred to a hospital closer to home this afternoon. Although we expect her to make a full recovery, she will not be in any condition to rejoin us for some time."

Malou breathed in deeply. She hadn't even realized that she'd been holding her breath ever since the teachers walked in. Chamomile squeezed Malou's hand.

"We're still investigating what happened yesterday, but there is every indication that Anne was possessed by a spirit and that the spirit is responsible for the injuries she sustained last night."

What . . . A spirit?

Shocked whispering spread through the hall.

"What does that mean? I've never heard of a spirit that can injure a person like that," Molly asked.

Birgit nodded at Jens. "No, the spirit did not directly inflict Anne with the injuries in question." Jens looked directly at Molly. "The spirit apparently possessed Anne, taking over her body. Anne remembers nothing of what happened, and people sometimes have no memory of events that occurred while they were possessed."

"You mean she cut herself?"

Malou turned toward Kirstine, who had posed the question. She was surprised—Kirstine rarely spoke in large gatherings.

"You could say that, but she wasn't conscious of it. Anne is still too weak for us to talk to her, but my guess is that she was tinkering with some spirit magic and it went wrong."

"I cannot overemphasize how important it is that you all comply with the school rules," added Birgit. "Performing unauthorized magic is strictly prohibited. If you don't have control over it, it can be fatal. Anne's misfortunate accident is clear proof of that." Birgit let her eyes run over the students, and Malou noticed her pulse rise when, for a moment, she made eye contact with the headmistress.

"Are we in danger?"

A second-year student Malou didn't know had asked the question.

"No," Jens answered. "As long as you follow the rules and don't make any foolish attempts to perform spirit magic, you have nothing to worry about."

Several students raised their hands with questions, but after briefly answering a few more, Birgit said that, unfortunately, they were out of time. They had to get back to Anne and continue investigating the case.

The students were unnaturally quiet as they left the hall.

"Do you think it's the same spirit?" Chamomile whispered as they walked up to their suite.

"Not here!" Malou hissed. Once they'd gotten up to their room, and Malou had checked that there were no teachers in the vicinity, they began talking quietly.

"This is unbelievably creepy!" Chamomile said, wrapping her arms around her body as if she was freezing. "Do you think it was a warning from the spirit because we haven't solved her murder yet?"

Malou rubbed her hands over her face. "I don't know."

"I don't understand how she could have done that to herself. Those cuts . . ." Kirstine sat on the bed, staring into space.

"It must have been terrifying to find her like that," Chamomile said, sitting next to Kirstine and putting an arm around her. "Do you want to tell us about it?"

Tears welled up in Kirstine's eyes and she laid her head on Chamomile's shoulder as Malou stared at them.

It hadn't even occurred to her to ask Kirstine about her experience. Malou shrugged off the thought. That was Chamomile's domain anyway—better to let her take care of it.

"She was lying on the floor. The room was so cold—I think the window must have blown open. She was half-naked and there was so much blood. It was very . . . animalistic. Just like the fox . . ." Kirstine sobbed.

"Fox? What fox?" Chamomile looked at Malou questioningly, but Malou just shook her head. She had no idea what Kirstine was talking about.

"A dead fox I saw in the forest. It was lying in the same way. With the limbs spread out to either side so that it formed a pentagram. She was lying the exact same way."

"But why would a spirit possess a fox?" It didn't make any sense.

Kirstine shrugged and looked up at Malou with swollen eyes. "What do we do now?"

Malou pursed her lips. "We have to get a hold of Victoria."

It was not the right girl. But no one suspects a thing. And I can still make it right. I mustn't be careless; I must plan meticulously. Try harder. And the girl. It has to be the right girl this time. The exact right girl.

Hi :)

Geez, it's crazy what happened with Anne. Did you know her well?

Yeah she lives in our hall. It's so creepy :(. . .

Damn. Are you okay?

Yeah. One of the other girls in my cluster was there when they found her. She's a little shaken . . .

Wow. I'm sure . . .

How was your break?

Fine – a little boring.

Mine too. I'm almost looking forward to school starting . . .

we might be seeing a bit more of each other next semester . . .

Why?

Wait and see :)

Victoria

See me . . .

Something had startled Victoria, and she sat straight up in her chair. She must have fallen asleep over her homework. She really wanted to finish the assignment for Spirit Magic before she went back to school again. She sighed deeply and rested her face on her hands. It was getting dark outside, and the light from her desk lamp didn't reach into the corners of the room. *She was so tired.* If she could only sleep, but every time she closed her eyes, the white shadows came back again. She thought being home for the holidays would give her a break, but the white shadows were as insistent as ever.

"Can't you just leave me in peace?" Victoria felt the hot tears rolling down her cheeks as she buried her face in her hands. She was alone in her room, but she was not alone. She felt it. It was as if the dream continued even when she was awake. A sweet scent billowed up around her and the temperature dropped.

"Go away," Victoria whispered. "Please just go away." She didn't want to lift her head, didn't want to see.

A crunching sound, like footsteps in frost, made her tremble.

"No," she begged, digging her clenched fists into her eye sockets. "No . . ."

See me . . .

The whisper was like a breeze. Victoria raised her face from her hands. The white shadow stood before her. But it wasn't a shadow anymore. It was a young girl, her face twisted in a silent scream.

Victoria screamed.

Hey Victoria. Do you have time to talk?

Hey, tried to call you again . . .

Just tried to call again, could you please text or call back?

Are you ok?

Victoria?!!

Victoria

An icy January rain poured down on them as they got off the bus. Victoria already felt chilled to her bones. She pulled the hood further down over her face to shield herself from both the rain and the eyes of the other girls. She'd intentionally returned to school late the night before and gone straight to bed. And, up to this point, she'd been able to dodge the other girls and their questions.

"We'll start by walking through the forest and down to the lake." Thorbjørn's deep voice had no problem getting everyone's attention. All the first-year girls were going on a hike with Thorbjørn and Jakob. They were visiting Tissø. There'd been a settlement there in Viking times, and it had enormous ritual significance. Archaeologists had found remnants of shrines and artifacts that suggested sacrifices had been made on the lakeshore.

"It's freezing! And this mud has completely ruined my boots." Malou scowled at the rain and the gray sky. "Who the hell goes on a hike in weather like this?"

"Don't you have any rubber boots?" Chamomile asked. She was wearing a knit hat, mittens, large rubber boots, and wool socks.

Victoria had been looking straight down at the narrow path covered with wet leaves and mud. She didn't need to turn around to know that the girls from her cluster were exchanging looks behind her back. Their anxious, eager curiosity felt like an annoying and persistent swarm of mosquitoes. She sped up before any of them got a chance to ask her about what they so wanted to know: Had the spirit assaulted Anne? And if so, was it their fault?

The large beech trees of the forest were slowly replaced by small, stunted trees reaching their bare, black branches toward the gray sky. The path wound in and out among the scrawny trees; they had to walk carefully and creatively around the large mud puddles and over the rain-slick trees that had fallen across the path. After a bend, the path ended abruptly, and they found themselves on Tissø's shore. The water was steel gray and blended into the sky. A few lonely water birds squawked, but otherwise it was deserted.

"Charming," mumbled Malou.

"Welcome to Tissø," Thorbjørn said after they'd all reached the lakeshore, "or Tyr's Lake, as the name means. Many weapons were sacrificed here; Tyr was, of course, one of the most important gods of war in Viking times. Now we'll just walk a bit further. The settlement was associated with a number of important shrines where Viking-age people made sacrifices to statues of the gods. This place is rich with history, and those of you with special abilities related to Earth should be able to feel that. But, theoretically, everyone should feel some hint of the rich history in a place like this."

They walked along the lake's shore for about a hundred meters before turning away from the lake and climbing a low hill. A flock of ducks flew low over their heads and continued out over the lake. Victoria tried to sense the place's power, but the only thing she really felt was cold.

"Over here, everyone. Gather round." Thorbjørn motioned to them. "We're standing on the site of a Viking-age shrine. Now please take a good look at this," Thorbjørn took a metal rod out of his backpack, "can anyone tell me what this is?" It had some kind of ornament on one end.

"Yes, Kirstine?"

"Is it a seeress's staff maybe?" Kirstine's voice sounded thin in the fierce wind.

"That is exactly what it is. Though this is a replica, naturally. And what was it used for?" Thorbjørn nodded encouragingly at Kirstine.

"The seeress used it when she conducted seid."

"Precisely. The Danish word *vølve*, or seeress, actually means 'staff-bearer,' and the staff was very important in the practice of seid. *Vølver* were the Vikings' psychic or clairvoyant women. When she—with the help of the staff—seided, a vølve could predict the future, see a man's fate, or curse an enemy. The goddess Freja was a very powerful vølve, and she was—like seeresses generally—known for her powers of seduction.

Chamomile whistled and elbowed Kirstine in the side so that she blushed.

"Now that you've begun your second semester of coursework, you can begin to exercise your practical skills. Up to this point, we have focused on theory, but you will now become acquainted with the power of praxis. Of course, this is not something that can be achieved overnight, but we'll take the first steps now. I want you all to attempt to connect with the power of this place by holding the seeress's staff and focusing. Who wants to try first . . . Kirstine?"

Kirstine stepped forward hesitantly and took the staff from Thorbjørn.

"Focus, be calm, and channel your power through the staff," he instructed her.

Kirstine stood for a moment with her eyes closed, then she opened them and focused on the staff she was holding with an expression of serious concentration on her face. The wind whipped through her hair, and the air around her was charged with energy.

"Look, the staff!" Chamomile pointed. Victoria saw it too. It was changing color; the black metal was turning orange and then it glowed red.

Kirstine dropped the staff with a gasp and it fell sizzling into the wet grass.

"Well done, Kirstine! You really connected to the power here. That was a real breakthrough. Now that you know how it feels, it will be easier for you to achieve connection in future." Thorbjørn patted Kirstine on the back. "Who wants to try next?"

"Oooh, did you burn your hand?" Chamomile asked, when Kirstine took her place again.

"Not at all!" She held up her palm so they could clearly see it was uninjured.

"Wow, Kirstine! You're really getting good," Chamomile said. "You'd almost think you were in love or something."

"What do you mean?" she whispered.

"Well, I mean, that's why we're not supposed to have anything to do with the boys. Being in love can make your powers go off the charts!"

"Please concentrate on what's going on up here!" Thorbjørn thundered. "Who wants to try next?"

After Kirstine's impressive performance, the girls were eager to try, but none of them had half as much success. Victoria would have preferred to pass, but Thorbjørn insisted and so she took her turn. Nothing happened, and after five painful minutes, he urged her to practice connecting to the Earth and releasing control. Afterward, they were told to investigate on their own and take notes for an essay about sacrificial practices during the Viking era and the Late Iron Age. Victoria tried to slip away by herself, but this time Chamomile wouldn't be shaken off.

"Wait, Victoria, let's go together, okay? Then we can talk." Chamomile resolutely stuck her arm under Victoria's and pulled her over to the edge of the forest where no one else was. Malou and Kirstine followed.

"Why won't you answer your phone or text back?" Malou scowled at her, and Victoria felt Malou's hostility prickling against her skin along with the driving rain. She felt them all. Malou's smoldering anger, Chamomile's suffocating sympathy, and Kirstine's nervous anxiety. And she couldn't give them what they wanted. *Absolution.*

"What do you think, Victoria?" asked Chamomile. "Did Trine attack Anne because we haven't solved her murder?"

Victoria felt everything inside her contracting. "You must never pronounce a spirit's name!" she hissed.

"Okay, okay, I didn't know." Chamomile held up her hands as a show of innocence.

"The sound of their name gets a spirit's attention," Victoria said, attempting to control her voice. "I don't think we should talk about it here."

"What's wrong with talking here?" Malou asked. "We're trying to figure out what happened to Anne. But maybe you just don't care?" She took a step closer, her pupils looking like small black stones.

"I'm sorry, but I can't help you."

"What are you talking about?!" Malou exclaimed. "You're the *only* one in contact with the damned spirit. We have nothing else to go on. It's no good asking the teachers after what happened to Anne. We need you to ask the spirit for more leads, for some clues or something."

"I can't . . ." she whispered. *I can't, I can't, I can't.* "I'm sorry Anne got hurt, but it wasn't the spirit's fault."

"Then whose fault was it?" Malou stared at her defiantly. "What are you trying to say?"

Victoria took a step back, then another. Then she turned and ran.

It's my fault. I'm the one that attracted the spirit. I'm the one it was after.

What's up?

Busy . . . ?

Hey, why don't you ever answer?
Pretty rude, really . . .

Just lots of homework

Student rule number 2: Beware of
doing too much homework

Don't think the teachers agree with that one

No—it's a STUDENT rule. An important one.
Don't take it all so seriously . . .

cutie . . .

stop

. . . cranky?

. . . ?

Okay, I get it. I'll stop. Bad day?

New record

Want to go for a walk with me?
Fresh air is good for the brain :)

I don't know . . .

Come on—half an hour—the usual place?

I'm not good company. You'd better stay away.

I'm a big boy. I'll decide for myself
who's good company ;)

Come on

Pleeeeeease . . .

I'm not going to stop until you say ok

uggh . . . ok

:)

Malou

The thin scalpel felt cold in her hand. Malou turned it slowly so that it caught the light. It wasn't the pain that scared her, or the sight of blood. No, it was more that the feeling of the sharp knife in her hand made her feel oddly confident. Was that normal? Even for a blood mage? Or was she a total freak like their Blood Magic teacher, Zlavko, who was in the middle of yet another temper tantrum?

"We are talking about the world's smallest incision in a fingertip," Zlavko sneered. "A few drops of blood—this isn't the chainsaw massacre! So, please suppress your pathetic whimpering. Please, at least *pretend* to be the promising next generation of mages rather than a whining mass of spoiled children!"

Malou let her eyes wander around the class. The girls sat two to a desk. Each had been provided with a scalpel and a glass of water. Their task was to cut a finger and let a few drops of blood drip into the water. They'd experimented with pricking their fingers with a needle before the holidays, but even that had been difficult for many of the girls. Today was the first time they were trying with the scalpels.

Malou watched as Kirstine, whose face was white as a sheet,

drew the scalpel over the pad of her index finger. Apparently, she couldn't will herself to press the blade into her finger enough to cut. Blood magic was everyone's least-favorite subject. Hers too. But not because she couldn't handle it.

"Malou?" Zlavko bent over her invasively. Why did the man have such a hard time respecting other people's personal space? She sighed audibly and flicked the scalpel over her index finger. It was so sharp she almost didn't feel it. The blood welled up in the little cut and she hurried to let the blood drop into the glass of water. At first, her blood was visible as small, reddish clouds in the water, but soon it dissolved and disappeared. Malou observed the glass with disappointment. Nothing happened. What had she expected? *Not nothing.*

"Hold the glass." Zlavko stood so close that she could feel his breath on her cheek. Malou closed her hand around the glass. The finger with the cut made a bloody print on the outside of the glass.

"Your blood is part of you," whispered Zlavko. "You are part of the water. It will feel you now. It will reflect you. How are you feeling Malou?"

Malou closed her eyes and attempted to ignore the teacher standing way too close to her as well as the other girls who were either complaining, moaning, or nervously giggling. How was she feeling? She felt . . . hot? Yes, she was sweating under Zlavko's oppressive gaze, but it wasn't just that. She felt as if her insides were burning. Why would that idiot Zlavko torture her like this? He clearly knew how much she hated it. Why was she the only one with abilities in Blood magic? Why couldn't she have it easy for once? Hadn't she drawn enough short straws already?

Malou felt the glass vibrate between her hands. When she

opened her eyes, she saw tiny bubbles forming at the bottom and then rising slowly to the surface and popping. The water had begun to boil. Startled, she let go of the glass.

"What the hell, Malou!" Zlavko shouted, and the sound of his voice, loud and sharp, made her flinch. "Why did you stop? What are you afraid of?"

Then he was distracted by the sight of Sofie holding a bleeding hand and looking like she was about to faint.

"I said a *small* cut!" Zlavko snapped. "Hold your hand above your heart." Before he walked over to staunch the bleeding, he bent over Malou again. "You're betraying your own potential, Malou. We need to have a chat about that. Stay back when class is over."

"I'm very disappointed in your performance."

Malou didn't answer. Just looked him in the eye. Didn't want him to think he could scare her.

"I actually had high expectations for you." For once Zlavko's face lacked even the shadow of his usual condescending smile.

That was totally unfair. Not one of the other girls had gotten the water to react! But she was the one sitting here. Everyone else had been allowed to escape. He was always giving her a hard time. But her next thought made her sweat even more than the scalpel had: She was the only one with a teardrop-shaped pendant hanging from her neck.

"You need to ask yourself if you actually want to be here. And if you do, what are you afraid of?"

She looked at her feet. What was she afraid of? The sight of the bubbling water had filled her with an amazing sense of being in control. Of power. It felt good, but then she'd cut off the feeling. Why? She'd performed blood magic far above her level, she'd saved a damned life! She hadn't hesitated when Victoria was dying. She'd known instinctively that her blood would save Victoria. It'd felt so right, but every time Zlavko bent over her, her confidence dissolved. And now, when it was so important to look strong, Malou felt her eyes were filling with tears. *Damn it! Pull yourself together!*

"I know why you don't perform as well as you could," he hissed. "As you *should*. You still need to recognize what you are. Like all the other silly little girls in your class, you're afraid of the dark side of magic. The side that can give. That dares to take. To sacrifice. The magic of blood. But you disappoint me, Malou. I actually thought you were different. I thought you knew something of the dark side of life."

"And I thought black magic was forbidden at Rosenholm." Malou looked defiantly and directly into his eyes and hoped that he didn't notice her shining eyes.

"Black magic, white magic." Zlavko laughed contemptuously. "Only fools talk like that. Nothing is purely black or white. Everything is black *and* white. No mage performs only white magic. Anyone who says otherwise is either stupid or lying."

"And does Birgit agree with that?"

Zlavko scoffed but said no more. Apparently, she'd hit a nerve.

"I'm going to give you some advice, Malou. Concentrate on your own education instead of worrying your pretty little head over speculations about whether or not I always agree with the rest of the faculty." Zlavko stood up, irritated, and nodded toward the door as a sign that she should go. "I'll expect you to turn in twice as many pages on Friday. Maybe that will help clarify certain things for you."

Malou walked through the room and slammed the door after her so that it echoed in the hallway.

Asshole!

She walked without noticing where she was going. She just wanted to get away from Zlavko's classroom. Suddenly she found herself somewhere other students rarely went. But she had been there before. On the day of the entrance exams. It was the hallway behind the library where the old class portraits hung. Malou's eyes wandered over the black-and-white photos. The worst part was that he was right. She wasn't doing nearly as well as she ought to be. She'd always been the best in the class. But not at Rosenholm. And if she wanted to figure out this murder, she'd need to smarten up quick. Victoria refused to talk to them about Trine, so Malou would have to handle it herself. It was her fault anyway. She was the one who'd suggested the seance in the first place.

"Um, are you okay?"

She hadn't heard anyone come in. How had he walked down the hall without making a sound? She turned away from him and quickly dried her eyes. Why did she have to run into him just now? *Another awesome day at Rosenholm!* The universe was clearly out to get her.

"I'm fine." Malou wiped under her eyes, hoping her mascara hadn't run.

Benjamin turned toward the photos on the wall and acted as though he found them very intriguing. "So, come here often?"

"What do you mean?"

"Well, this is the second time we've met here. Or rather, the last time was in the library, but you'd come from this direction."

Malou shook her head. "I haven't been here since."

"It's strange, with all the students who walked here before us. Maybe in a hundred years or so two students will be standing here looking at pictures of us."

"It's only the class portraits of third-year students here, right? So, it's not likely I'll ever make the cut for this hallway." She'd meant to say something funny, but it came out sounding bitter.

"Maybe it'll work out in the end? If you take things too seriously at Rosenholm, you'll go mad. It's important to have a little fun too."

He took a step closer to her, still looking toward the old photographs. He made her nervous. People generally assumed she had loads of experience with boys, and she let them. But the truth was that few boys ever got close enough. Maybe they were afraid of her? But not Benjamin.

He turned toward her. She returned his gaze. If this had been a movie, he would have kissed her now. The thought occurred to her, but suddenly the door at the end of the hall opened.

"Don't you have somewhere to be right now?"

Birgit. Had she been watching them?

Benjamin turned away from Malou and toward the window. His eyes wandered as if he was looking for something.

"Birgit's right, I'm late. I need to get going." A slight smile pulled at the corners of his mouth. *A bitter smile.* Was he tired of being interrupted?

"Remember what I said," he mumbled low enough that Birgit wouldn't hear, "try to have a little fun now and then." Already moving back down the hall, he winked at her. When Birgit closed the door after him, it occurred to Malou that his footsteps hadn't made the slightest sound on the castle's creaky, old floorboards.

Kirstine

Kirstine looked warily into her cauldron where a gray-green mass bubbled merrily. The garlic was potent. Lisa, their teacher in Nature Magic, walked around between the tables to see how their flu remedy, their task for today's lesson, was coming along. Very fitting. A third of the students were now laid up. Kirstine had chosen garlic and nettles as the base for her potion, but who would want to take this?

Chamomile's cauldron was another matter. It was full of a dark purple liquid that smelled of elderberry and basil. Lisa had avoided Kirstine's cauldron, but she stuck her nose right over Chamomile's.

"Elderberry has been used against influenza for centuries. And basil acts as an expectorant," Chamomile explained. "And then I added a little echinacea to strengthen the immune response."

Lisa nodded smiling. "Sounds like an effective blend," she said, "and it smells lovely. Remember," she said, addressing the whole class now, "greater well-being is the ultimate goal of nature magic. So it's important to please all the senses as much as possible."

Kirstine looked down into her cauldron and sighed. Nature magic was not her strong suit. Chamomile, on the other hand, had a clear knack for it. Not only did she know the plants much better, but her instincts helped her make good choices when they had to make healing draughts or use their powers to heal an injured animal or a sick person.

Luckily Kirstine was doing well in Norse magic. The other day she'd toppled a stack of books purely by casting a runic spell— something none of the others had been able to do yet. In Norse Studies she was the best in the class. In her wildest dreams, she'd never imagined she'd be able to say she was the best in a class.

After class, she hung back and took her time cleaning the smelly mass out of the cauldron. She had to talk to someone. The sight of Anne, laying bloody and lifeless with her limbs spread out to the sides haunted her dreams. Was it really the work of a spirit? She couldn't forget the horrific scene, and when she slept, the images of the bleeding Anne melded with those of the murdered fox she'd seen in the woods, and the bloody star on Jakob's chest.

She'd tried to talk to Jakob, but he brushed her off, and she hadn't brought it up again. Time moved so quickly when they were together. Kirstine felt a tiny smile spread over her face as she rinsed the cauldron one last time and dried it with a dishtowel. She knew what they were doing was strictly forbidden at Rosenholm, and if anyone found out about them she'd be kicked out and Jakob would lose the job he'd fought so hard for. But for some reason, she wasn't worried about it. For some reason, the ever-anxious, ever-virtuous, ever-worried Kirstine had disappeared for the time being. She simply didn't care. She wanted to be with him. *Is this what being in love feels like?*

"Oh, are you still here, Kirstine?" The sound of Lisa's voice startled her. Their Nature Magic teacher's black eyes looked at her curiously. Kirstine took a deep breath and asked her question.

"A pentagram? You mean a five-pointed star?" Lisa said, surprised, when Kirstine told her what was on her mind. "I thought you were going to have a question about today's lesson," she said, and Kirstine sensed a twinkle in her eyes.

"I came across the symbol the other day. And since then, I've been seeing it everywhere," Kirstine said.

"I'd believe that," Lisa said. "The five-pointed star is a very old pagan symbol. In ancient times it was used as a fertility symbol, and in antiquity the star was a symbol of health and happiness. In Christianity, the five-pointed star is said to symbolize Jesus's five wounds, while in tarot cards it stands for the element of Earth." Lisa paused and gazed steadily at Kirstine. "Does any of this make sense in terms of the pentagrams you've seen?"

Kirstine shrugged. "Does it have any connection to spirits?" she asked.

Lisa smiled. "Everything is connected. If you take only one thing from my classes, then let it be that. But yes, the five-pointed star is connected to spirit magic. Many traditions have believed the five-pointed star could protect against, invoke, and bind spirits. You can see that in the various names it has. I prefer *Druidsfoot*, but in folk belief, the five-pointed star has often been called a *mare-cross*. Do you know what a *mare* is?"

Kirstine shook her head.

"The *mare* is an often female and erotic dream-creature that torments sleeping people by riding them. Accordingly, it is also called a mare-ride, or a nightmare, a bad dream. A clear example of the historical anxiety around female sexuality in our part of the world, if you ask me."

"And the mare-cross could keep the mare away?" Kirstine asked.

"Yes—or bind it, if that was what you wanted to do."

"What would a spirit even get out of using the pentagram?"

"What do you mean?" Lisa's eyes searched Kirstine's face. A bit like her mother's did when she was questioning Kirstine's motives. "Is there something specific you're thinking of?"

Kirstine shook her head. "No, it was just a thought I had."

"You should talk to Jens, if you want to know more about spirit magic," Lisa said, closing her old leather bag. "He has a much better understanding of it."

"Okay, thanks for your help." As Kirstine hurried out of the door, she felt a scrutinizing look on her back that suddenly gave her a strange sense of homesickness mixed with skin-crawling claustrophobia.

Victoria

Victoria surveyed her gifts. She'd gotten a new iPhone from her parents, but the old one worked just fine. She briefly considered packing it back into the box but dropped it on her bed instead. Her grandparents had gotten her a purse that was really not her taste, and the girls had bought her a set of long underwear because she was always freezing. Victoria put the long underwear on under her clothes and grabbed her jacket.

"I'm going to take a walk," she said to Kirstine who'd settled in with her books on medicinal plants.

"Want me to come with?"

"No thanks, I just need some fresh air. And Kirstine? Thanks for the birthday pastries and everything."

"My pleasure. Sixteen—it's a big day."

Victoria walked down the stairs and out into the courtyard as her phone vibrated in her pocket. There was snow on the ground, the air was sparkling clear, and the sun was shining. The snow squeaked under her shoes.

> **Happy birthday sweetheart. Sweet sixteen, huh? Hope you've had a good morning?**

> **Thanks. It was fine.**

> **Want to go for a walk?**

> **With the girls just now. Maybe later**

> **Okay, just write if you want to**

Victoria put the phone back in her pocket and looked around. She saw something move out of the corner of her eye. Maybe it was just a bird. Or maybe it was the lack of sleep driving her crazy. She was terrified of lying down to sleep, and when she eventually gave in to exhaustion, the white shadows were there immediately. She took a deep breath and walked into the forest.

The snow lay almost untouched here, and it was easy for her to see an animal's tracks. A large dog, or maybe a badger, had been here, and she followed the tracks without thinking. They led her away from the path and toward the bluff. Beneath it ran a small brook, not yet frozen over—the water's babbling filled the still winter air. Suddenly, the tracks stopped. The snow was scraped away in a kind of circle, and tiny splashes of blood were clearly visible against the white snow. Maybe the animal had attacked another animal? Chamomile would probably have been able to see through what had happened here, she was so good at that sort of thing.

Victoria's eye caught something brownish in the snow, and she picked it up. A feather. It was big, probably from a larger bird of prey, maybe an osprey? A hawk? Why would a dog attack a hawk? Or had they been fighting over the same kill? A chill ran through her body. It was as if the temperature had fallen further, then she was suddenly enveloped by that smell. *Strong and light at the same time. Refined and perfumed.* Now she recognized it. *Violets.* But violets don't bloom in winter when snow covers everything. *No, not now . . .* It couldn't be. The white shadows were never visible in the middle of the day.

"Why?" she whispered. "Why can't you let me be?"

See me, rustled the poplars. And then she knew what she had to do. It was no use fighting it, Trine would catch up with her sooner or later. Victoria dropped to her knees and then lay down in the snow surrounded by the heavy-light scent of violets.

"I'm here now, Trine. I'm here now. Show me."

The blue sky disappeared. It became dark, and the air was filled with the rustling of the silver poplars and the scent of the violets. The frayed, blurry dream vision was without color or sound, except for the unsettling rise and fall of the rustling poplars. The man carried the young girl into the forest, down to the brook, where he laid her on the forest floor. She could not move, but she was conscious, her eyes wide open, full of fear. He moved her arms and legs, straightened her dress, spread her hair out, stroked her cheek, whispered things in her ear. He kissed her throat, let his hands move down her body. Victoria did not want to see. "Stop it, stop it!" she begged, but Trine would not let her go now. She had to watch it all. And Victoria watched the man lay on the young girl as tears streamed down her cheeks. And she watched, at the end, as he kissed her mouth and laid his hands around her throat and squeezed and squeezed and squeezed until the sky turned black and there was no more.

Chamomile

"Victoria!" Chamomile could tell from the shrill tone of her own voice that she was getting really worried. It was quiet outside. Darkness had fallen and all she could hear was the snow squeaking with every step she took. "When did you last see her?"

"Before lunch," Kirstine said, walking behind her. "She just wanted to go for a walk."

"Victoria!" Malou's voice made Chamomile flinch. She couldn't see her in the dark, but she heard Malou's footsteps up ahead. It was very cold now, and Chamomile was shivering. She dialed Victoria again, but no answer. Instead, she used her phone to light the way as they headed into the forest. The snow was deep here, and an animal had made clear tracks in the bright white carpet.

"Here! She's here!" Malou's yell resounded through the forest. It was coming from the brook. They both started running, but Chamomile stumbled in the snow, and Kirstine's long strides quickly overtook her.

Malou knelt by the side of a figure lying in the snow. "Victoria!"

"Let me!" Chamomile laid her hands on her forehead. She could feel her, she wasn't gone yet. But she was very cold. "We have to get her inside immediately!"

Kirstine slipped off her jacket and wrapped it around Victoria, then lifted her thin body up in her arms with a panicked but steely look on her face, like a mother with an injured child.

"I'll run ahead and wake Ingrid," Malou said before taking off.

Chamomile walked ahead of Kirstine to light the way and murmured an old charm. It was a simple protection spell her mother had taught her when she was little, but it was the only thing she could think of now, and, if nothing else, it was comforting.

Kirstine groaned from the exertion, but she refused to stop or let Chamomile help.

When they had almost reached the castle, Malou came running to meet them. "I can't get to Ingrid. Her room's locked, and she isn't answering the door!"

They stopped and Chamomile let the light shine on Victoria's face. Relief streamed through her like a warm river: Victoria's eyelids were twitching.

"She's coming to! Come on, let's just get her inside. Can you handle the last bit, Kirstine?"

Kirstine nodded and began the trek up the stairs. Between clenched teeth she murmured the name of the Uruz rune. Chamomile knew it would give Kirstine the last bit of power she needed.

"Turn up the heat, and wrap her in blankets," Chamomile commanded when they had gotten up to the tower. "Kirstine, lay your hands on her like this, and visualize the sun rune with your inner eye. Malou, boil some water!"

Meanwhile, Chamomile ran into her room and rummaged in her stash. All students had the most common herbs for use in nature magic, but Chamomile gathered and dried other plants she'd foraged from the forests and fields around Rosenholm. She crushed bay leaves, verbena, and yarrow in a large cup.

"Malou, is the water ready?" She poured it over the herbs. "It just needs to steep a moment." Chamomile sat by Victoria's side and laid her hands on her. The warm prickling began, and soon she felt the power flowing from her hands and into Victoria. Her energy was growing stronger.

"She's waking up now," Malou said, and Chamomile, who'd been sitting with her eyes closed, opened them again.

Victoria's dark eyes were shiny with fever.

"Here, drink, it helps with the cold and will bring the fever down," Chamomile said. She supported Victoria and encouraged her to drink the hot liquid in small sips. "You should drink it all."

"Thanks," Victoria whispered hoarsely when the cup was empty. "I feel better now." A tremor ran through her body.

"What happened?" Kirstine whispered as large tears ran freely down her cheeks.

"Trine showed me how she was killed. That was what she wanted me to see the whole time," Victoria whispered.

"Could you see who did it?" asked Malou.

"No, he was just a dark figure without a face. If Trine could see him, then she would have shown me. I couldn't see his face, because . . . because she couldn't see it either . . ."

"So, she didn't recognize him?"

"No . . . it wasn't that she didn't recognize him. She couldn't *see* him. That's how it felt."

"Did she hurt you?" Kirstine asked.

"No, it wasn't like that. I must have fainted afterward, but it wasn't Trine's fault. She just wants us to know how she was killed. And warn us . . ."

"About what?" Chamomile whispered.

"I don't know," Victoria said, her teeth still chattering.

"Maybe it wasn't Trine who possessed Anne," Kirstine said. "It doesn't add up. Why else would she warn us?"

"We can ask her," Malou said.

Chamomile looked at Malou in horror. "You don't mean that. Don't say things like that."

"I think Malou's right," Victoria said quietly.

"Victoria, you're way too weak, it won't work," Chamomile said. "Remember what happened last time."

"I don't think she meant to hurt me, she was just desperate. And we promised to discover her murderer. As long as we don't ask about her killer, then I don't think anything will happen to us. And she doesn't need to possess me like last time, she can talk to us another way."

There was something in the way she talked about the spirit that made Chamomile uncomfortable.

"You're speaking as if you know her," she said.

"In a way, I do. Ever since I first came Rosenholm she's been near me. I just haven't wanted to admit it."

"Would you be able to make contact with her again?" Malou asked.

"Easily. I can already feel her here. Malou, get your mirror, the round one. And close the curtains."

"Victoria . . . please. Shouldn't we get hold of Ingrid so she can see if you're okay?"

"Trust me," she said, squeezing Chamomile's hand. "I'm fine. Come on, help me down to sit on the floor."

Kirstine lit a candle and set it beside the mirror resting on the floor between them.

"Turn off the overhead light. And let me do the talking. We must not stress her out, okay?" Victoria found Malou with her eyes, and her expression was no longer distant, but insistent and sharp.

They took each other by the hand. Victoria's hand still felt very cold in Chamomile's. This time only a few seconds passed before the candle began flickering despite the lack of wind, and the room became ice cold. Chamomile tried to suppress a shiver.

"Is that you, Trine?" Victoria whispered, her breath was visible. It was quiet, none of them moved.

"Look at the mirror!" Malou whispered suddenly.

The mirror's surface fogged up as if someone was breathing on it in the cold air. Slowly, an invisible finger wrote in the fogged-over surface. The line shook and trembled as if each letter required great effort to write.

YES

"Thank you, Trine. Can you tell us when you died?"

They sat with their eyes glued to the mirror, but nothing happened. The seconds dragged by. Suddenly the flame flickered again. Was she gone?

"It's okay, Trine, if you don't . . ."

"Look!" Kirstine whispered.

Slowly, very slowly, the numbers appeared on the mirror's surface, one by one.

1989

"Did you attack Anne?"

No

"Do you know who did?"

YES

The word appeared quickly this time.

"Can you tell us who did it?"

No

"Is it the same person who killed you?"

No

They sat quietly for a moment as the word faded away. Victoria said nothing. Maybe she wasn't sure what to ask next. It had to be a simple question.

"Which branch of magic is he?" Victoria asked.

A single line was drawn in the fog, but then nothing happened. As if the spirit was hesitating. Then the words came.

GROWTH
BLOOD
EARTH
DEATH

Victoria looked doubtfully at the words as they appeared and disappeared again. "What should we do?" she whispered.

The light flickered, the spirit was going to leave, but then another word came, written fumbling and uncertain.

THE BALL

"Will he attack again?" Victoria's voice was so low it was almost inaudible.

This time the letters appeared on the mirror's surface quickly, clumsily, like they were written in haste.

YES!!!

A loud sound made them all flinch, and the candle went out. When they turned on the lamp, they saw that the mirror was cracked down the middle.

Kirstine

"She's sleeping now." Kirstine had sat by Victoria's bed until she finally fell asleep.

"She was completely exhausted, but she had a hard time falling asleep. She was still shivering."

Kirstine dropped down next to Chamomile, who was curled up at the end of Malou's bed. While she was soothing Victoria, she'd been surprisingly calm, but now the disquiet came creeping back to her again.

"What the hell are we dealing with here? What *should* we do?" Chamomile, who usually seemed so upbeat, now sounded desperate and defeated. Maybe she was just as afraid as Kirstine felt.

"Isn't it obvious?" Malou got up and stood on the floor. "The teachers were wrong, we were wrong. It wasn't a spirit who possessed Anne. It wasn't Trine. It revolves around two cases: an old murder and a new attack. And it means there's probably some sick slasher roaming the school right now. For some reason, Trine can't tell us who it is. So we have to put the pieces together ourselves."

"What pieces, Malou? We don't have any pieces. We know *nothing*," Chamomile interjected.

213

"That's not true. We know plenty. Come on, help me go through it all."

"Malou, we haven't accomplished anything in the last hour. We're not getting anywhere. You're obsessed with finding a pattern, but what if they're all just unrelated coincidences that don't prove crap?"

Chamomile's rant silenced Malou for a moment. Then she seemed to pull herself together.

"You're tired, we all are, but we haven't gone over everything with Kirstine. Maybe she'll see something we overlooked."

"Fine, Malou. You're just going to do whatever suits you anyway," Chamomile muttered, pulling the blanket tighter around herself.

"Great," Malou said, ignoring Chamomile's last comment. "So we know Trine was killed in 1989. That gives us something to go on with regards to finding her killer. We know Trine's killer is not the same as Anne's attacker, but they're still connected. We know the psychopath will attack again, and that he possesses power in all the branches of magic."

"That's not a thing," Chamomile said. "All mages can do magic within other branches, but you're always strongest in one branch."

"But that's what Trine said."

"Maybe she just didn't know which branch he has. Maybe that's what she meant?" Kirstine suggested.

"Which again means that we have no pieces!" Chamomile snapped.

"We know he was at school on Christmas Eve," Malou continued stubbornly. "We know he attacked Anne, that he cut her."

"And the star," Kirstine said. "I think the star is meaningful. He positioned her in a pentagram-shape."

"What does the pentagram symbolize?" Malou asked.

"I don't know," Kirstine said, "but maybe it's connected to Trine or another spirit. Maybe it was to keep spirits away. Lisa told me about it. The five-pointed star is also called the mare-cross, and you use it to scare away spirits."

"And the ball," Malou added. "When Victoria asked what we should do Trine wrote, 'the ball.' What does that mean?"

"The Spring Ball," Kirstine whispered.

"What?" Chamomile looked at them.

"Molly told us about it," Kirstine said. "It's for the third-years."

"Of course," Malou said. "The Spring Ball. Somehow, we need to go to that ball. And we have to figure out who attacked Anne. Before it happens again."

Trine . . .

Trine . . . ?

Why did you leave me? Why did you come to me only to leave me again? After everything I did for you? After I solved the riddle you gave me? I can't feel you, can't hear you, but I know you hear me. High above all the worthless, little human lives I soar. And I am screaming. I am screaming at you. But you are silent, and your silence forces my hand. You're forcing me to do it, Trine.

PART 4
SPRING

On the last day I took her
where the wild roses grow
And she lay on the bank
the wind light as a thief
As I kissed her goodbye, I said,
'All beauty must die'
And lent down and planted
a rose between her teeth

From *Where the Wild Roses Grow* by Nick Cave.
From the album *Murder Ballads*, 1996.

I found the girl. Now I know who it must be. With her I can make it all right again. But I must be careful, I must gain her trust, not scare her away. And this time I will wait until the perfect moment. The violets will be in bloom. Just like back then. And the poplars will rustle in the wind. Just like back then. And the girl will die. Just like back then . . .

Spring Dance Lessons

The dance lessons for girls from
the first year will begin on
March 14th at 3:00 p.m. in the great hall.
Attendance is mandatory.

Attire: skirts, preferably long.

Chamomile

"Where's Victoria?" Chamomile said, tugging at the yellow summer dress she'd chosen for the first lesson. It was pretty wrinkled; she'd found it all the way at the back of the wardrobe.

"She probably just doesn't want to practice with us amateurs. I'm sure Miss Upper Crust has been dancing Les Lanciers since kindergarten," Malou said tartly.

"Malou, come on, stop being such a hater." Chamomile gave Malou one of her mother's now-really looks. Malou rolled her eyes but didn't say anything else.

Once Chamomile had gotten to know Malou better, she'd realized she was good at heart. That good heart was just buried deep, deep down. Sometimes she thought it might be buried as deep down as hell itself.

"I think she's coming," Kirstine said. "She told me she doesn't know this dance. See, there she is . . ."

"Hi!" Victoria waved as she appeared in a black, floor-length skirt that looked as though it had been made for dancing.

The great hall was cleared of tables and chairs. The floor was open, apart from the large group of third-year boys hanging around at the far end of the room.

"Well this is pretty damned exciting," Malou said, squeezing Chamomile's arm so tightly she winced.

Some of the boys craned their necks, not even trying to hide the fact that they were shamelessly surveying the girls; others acted as though they were above this sort of nonsense. Chamomile found Vitus's blond curls in the crowd. He turned and looked straight at her for a brief moment and smiled. Chamomile got so flustered she could barely smile back.

Then she noticed Birgit had taken the floor. She clapped her hands and called them to attention.

"Good afternoon. Today we'll embark on your dance lessons. Every student at Rosenholm must learn the classical dances. The third-year boys dance with the first-year girls, and in the second year you will dance with students from your own class. We mix the students across the classes because we expect the oldest students to behave responsibly and maturely as they, by virtue of their age and experience, have better control of their powers and won't get carried away. Any erratic behavior may lead to a ban from taking part in the Spring Ball. Is that understood?"

Birgit, looking over the top of her glasses, scanned the group of boys. Not too many of them nodded.

"You will be assigned a dance partner momentarily. Thereafter, we'll start learning the dances. The most important is Les Lanciers, but we will also try our hand at the waltz once you have gotten a handle on the steps," Birgit said. She pulled out a piece of paper. "And now I will read off the couples: Adrian and Sofie, please come stand over here. Bertil and Yasmin . . ."

Kirstine's dance partner, Tobias, was about half a head shorter than her. She blushed intensely when he gallantly took her hand and led her toward the other couples. Victoria's dance partner was Frédéric—Molly's beau. He bowed to Victoria and doffed an invisible cap before offering his arm as if they were in an old, silent movie.

"Vitus . . ." Chamomile's heart skipped a beat " . . . and Chamomile." She couldn't help smiling broadly when Malou rather indiscreetly stuck two thumbs into the air to congratulate her.

"Didn't I say we'd be seeing more of each other?" Vitus whispered in her ear as he took her hand.

"What? How did you know . . . ?" Chamomile whispered back, but Vitus just smiled and winked.

"Benjamin and Malou."

Malou had a bit more luck controlling her facial expression. She nodded calmly and smiled at Benjamin as he bent over her hand and gave it a fleeting kiss before leading her to the line of couples. The last couple was announced—Sara got someone named William—and then they were ready.

Birgit asked Frédéric to help her demonstrate the steps. Chamomile almost didn't dare blink for fear of missing something.

"Okay, so I think you've all got the basic idea. Go ahead and form quadrilles," Birgit ordered.

"What!" Chamomile wailed. "I most certainly have not gotten the basic idea!"

"Just relax, we'll take it as it comes," Vitus said, wrapping an arm around her waist as he took her hand as Birgit and Frédéric had demonstrated. "Besides, you've got me. It's my third year, and I've done this before, so I ought to be able to remember some of it." He smiled at her, and Chamomile felt her stomach fill with butterflies. *Goddammit. Relax.*

Birgit turned on a giant boombox that had been set up for the dance lesson and the music began.

"Okay, please bow!" she called out.

Chamomile was not the only one who really didn't have the basic idea. They laughed and stumbled into each other when they couldn't remember who was supposed to step forward, but Vitus was good at leading her with a firm hand around her waist, so Chamomile was pretty satisfied with herself when Birgit announced the day's lesson was over. It didn't go quite so well for Kirstine, who looked absolutely miserable after the dance lesson.

"Thank you for the dance," Vitus said, bowing slightly to Chamomile in farewell. "See you next week."

"Ha, that was ridiculous!" Malou whispered on the way up the stairs. "I would die to go to the ball!"

Chamomile gave her a wry look. "Uh, have you forgotten why going to the ball is so important?"

"Of course not, but surely we're still allowed to enjoy it? Hey, no one's taking this more seriously than me."

"I know." Malou had spent countless evenings at the library, but even though they now knew Trine's death-year, they still couldn't find her in the yearbooks or on the school rosters. There was simply no Trine, not anywhere.

"I can't get over the fact that the two of us just danced with Benjamin and Vitus," Malou said.

"I think Vitus might have had something to do with this," Chamomile said. "I didn't understand it at the time, but over the holidays he told me we would be seeing more of each other this semester . . ."

"Oh, of course! They fixed it!" Malou said.

"Well, I don't know about Benjamin . . ."

"It makes total sense. Otherwise, it would be quite the coincidence, no? I mean, I talked to Benjamin at the Yule celebration, and you talked to Vitus. This is perfect!"

"What do you mean?"

"The third years can invite whoever they want. And they already have an eye on us, otherwise they wouldn't have fixed it so that we would be their dance partners. Now it's just a matter of being so charming they wouldn't dream of inviting anyone else— and *voila*—we'll have official invitations to the ball."

"Are you sure that's a good idea?' They'd walked into their kitchenette, and Chamomile hadn't even noticed Kirstine standing by the counter. "What if they don't invite you? What do we do then? And what if they do end up inviting you? Are you in danger? We're looking for an extremely dangerous person, don't forget that. And we don't know who it is. It could be anyone. In theory, it could be Benjamin."

"Oh, come on," Malou said. "Besides, Benjamin wasn't at school on Christmas Eve. We should be focusing on one of those people. Where's the list?"

They'd made a list of all the students who were at Rosenholm on Christmas Eve. Next to each name they had noted whether the person in question had been in the library the whole evening or might have had an opportunity to follow Anne when she went up to her room.

"Who do you think we should focus on?" Malou found the list and set it on the kitchen table. "My money is still on Zlavko. He's capable of something like that."

"But he was in the library," Kirstine objected.

"We *think* he was in the library. Can you be one hundred percent sure he didn't sneak out and then rush back?"

"What about Jakob?" Chamomile asked, placing a finger on his name. "It says he arrived late and left shortly after."

"It's not him," Kirstine said.

"How do you know? You said it yourself: In theory it could be anyone."

"I saw him right before we found her," Kirstine said.

"But he could have done it before you saw him? Maybe that was why he came so late."

"It wasn't him!" Kirstine's voice was low but smoldered dangerously with anger.

"Okay, okay!" Chamomile said. "Don't be mad!"

But Kirstine had already walked out. The door slammed after her.

"Did you see that?" Chamomile whispered to Malou.

"Yep. Suddenly the expression 'like a thunderstorm' makes complete sense," Malou answered. She ran her hand over her hair and it crackled with static electricity. The air around them was still charged.

Rules and Regulations
of Rosenholm Academy

3. Students are strictly prohibited from engaging in any sexual, romantic, or intimate contact with other persons at Rosenholm Academy.

Kirstine

"Break," Jakob whispered hoarsely, rolling away from her and onto his back. "I need a little break."

Kirstine sat up and looked down at him as he lay on the forest floor in the sharp spring sun surrounded by white anemones.

"Is something wrong?"

"No, nothing's wrong. I just . . . You're just too lovely, that's all."

She smiled in relief and lay down beside him again. The leaves of the trees weren't completely out yet, but the sun was warm today. Soon the forest would be green again.

"Are you tired of kissing me?" she asked teasingly.

"I will never be tired of kissing you," he answered, finding her mouth again. He kissed her intensely as his fingers stroked her jawline, throat, and earlobe with featherlight movements. This time she was the one to roll away.

"You said we were going for a walk in the forest," she laughed. "You said you wanted to show me the forest lake. Are you coming or what?"

He raised up and sat on the forest floor for a moment before shaking his head. Then he sprang after her into the forest.

He caught up with her a little ways up the path. "Come here for a second."

"No, I want to see the lake," she protested, but she let herself be caught.

"It's in there, between the trees," he mumbled as he let a series of tiny kisses rain down over her throat. "Isn't this nice?"

"Stop, it tickles. By the way, this is terrible for my grades. You're supposed to be telling me about rune magic—we have to write an essay! We have this super mean teacher who gives us way too much homework, you know."

He laughed and lifted her up only to lay her down on the forest floor again.

"It's good for your grades in the practical subjects," he said, burying his face in her hair.

"What do you mean?" she asked, pushing him away half-heartedly.

"That's why it's suddenly so easy for you to connect to your power. Because you're maybe a tiny bit in love? And because you're getting to know yourself and your sexuality."

"Ew, Jakob, gross!" She wrestled herself free and got to her feet.

He looked up at her teasingly as he shaded himself from the sun with a hand over his eyes. "Then tell me, Miss Jensen, what exactly do you think is going on here?"

"We're looking at forest lakes!" she said, assuming an offended expression. "Now show me where it is."

They continued through the forest without saying anything more for a few minutes. A starling sang in a treetop.

"What is it with sexuality and magical abilities being so closely connected anyway?" she asked Jakob after they'd walked around the small forest lake.

"Sexuality contains an enormous amount of power; it releases tons of energy. It can be used and abused, and if you don't know what you're doing it can end badly."

"How badly?"

"Relax my little Valkyrie, I'll watch out for the both of us. Don't worry about it. Unbridled magic can be dangerous, but that is precisely why one goes to Rosenholm, isn't it? So you can learn to direct your energy, so you don't lose it." He smiled at her reassuringly.

"Have you ever done that? Lost it?"

"Yes, I have, when I was younger," he answered, laughing suddenly. "My brothers are quite a bit older than me. I was a late surprise, and they used to tease me a lot, but then one time I got so angry that something happened. When I was fourteen, I shattered all the windows on the first floor of our house. My parents were furious. Mostly at my brothers, luckily."

"You shattered the windows? How?"

"I don't really know. I was so enraged I can't remember. My brothers love that story, they still tell it at family gatherings. According to them, I said some kind of curse that busted all the panes. I didn't really know rune magic back then, but I still managed to do quite a bit of damage."

"What about your parents?" she asked. "What did they say?"

"Yeah, they chewed us out alright. And then we had to mow the grass and paint the shed and that sort of thing for the rest of the summer. My parents are mages, of course. I'm sure it would have been harder to explain that sort of thing if they weren't . . ."

They stopped. Jakob looked at her meaningfully, but she avoided his eyes. Instead, she stared at the button at the top of his shirt.

"My parents believed I was possessed by Satan," Kirstine whispered. "They were afraid of me."

"Come over here." Jakob took her hand and pulled her down to sit on a fallen tree trunk lying on the forest floor. "Tell me what happened."

"It was about six months before the entrance exams. My parents took me to a priest who thought he could help me with my problems. He was so creepy. This old, gaunt man. His face was like a skull, and he had such thin hair lying over his sweaty forehead. He kept saying he could feel the sin in me. He kept saying I needed to confess. Needed to tell him all my sinful thoughts. Confess! Confess! He kept shouting it. Right in my face." Kirstine paused for a moment. The memory of it suddenly brought back the feeling. She felt her stomach contract into a hard knot and her pulse quicken.

"I just wanted it to stop, you know? That was all I wanted. For him to shut up and leave me alone. I didn't even notice until it was too late. It was as if the air became electric and suddenly the gross, old armchair he was sitting on went up in flames. He jumped up and screamed to high heaven. Nothing happened to him, but he kept screaming, saying I was possessed by Satan and he would never see me again."

"You set him on fire?" Jakob sputtered. "You just set him on fire? Baller!"

"You think it's funny?" Here she was revealing her deepest secret to him, and he was laughing. Kirstine looked at him. And suddenly the knot in her stomach loosened. Suddenly, she couldn't help laughing either.

"So, you did get the old fool to shut his damned mouth," Jakob laughed. "I guess that was really the only thing to do."

Kirstine felt her smile fade. She shook her head. "My parents didn't think so. After that everything got worse. They were afraid to let me do anything. They monitored me twenty-four seven."

"That must have been really hard." Jakob put an arm around her and pulled her close. "But it's good you're here now."

"After what happened with Anne, I'm not sure I made the right choice," Kirstine said. "To think that something like that could happen here."

"Of course Rosenholm is the right place for you! Try to put that thing with Anne behind you. Besides, this should be the best year of your life, Kirstine! You're young, you're beautiful, you're going to a fantastically exciting school, you have a fantastic lover—enjoy it!"

Kirstine laughed and let him pull her into a hug.

"Back when I went to school, we didn't think about things like that, serious things. All I ever wanted was a fantastic lover."

Kirstine shook her head. "Nothing like that ever happened when you were a student at Rosenholm?"

"Nah. The most sinister part of my schooldays was the caramel pudding they always served on Sundays."

"Can you remember if there was ever talk of a girl who'd been killed at Rosenholm?"

"What? No. Thank heavens. When would that have been?"

"In 1989 or thereabouts."

"Hey, how old do you think I am, missy? I'm only five years older than you."

"Six."

"Okay, six years older. But I wasn't even born yet in 1989."

"But maybe it was something people talked about?"

"I've never heard anything like that. Where did you get this?"

"It was just something we were talking about in Spirit Magic the other day. We got some . . . evidence to suggest a young girl was killed back then."

You must not lie. Kirstine tried to push the thought away.

"Ah, spirit magic," Jakob scoffed. "Spirits are wildly unreliable. They can even be dangerous. But as a rule they're just full of lies. They'll say anything to stoke a little drama or get some attention. It's clearly crazy boring to be dead. There's nothing happening and so they wind up entertaining themselves by telling us these scintillating stories." He took hold of her shoulder again and pushed her back a bit so that their eyes met. "Remember, spirits are just the souls of dead humans. And humans in general are wildly unreliable. Apart from me, of course," he said, kissing her lightly on the nose.

"Are you reliable?" Kirstine asked.

"Very," he said, bending down to meet her lips.

"Then tell me what *you* think happened to Anne."

"Ughh, not again, Kirstine," Jakob sighed tiredly. "Like Birgit says, it was her own fault for playing necromancer."

"I don't think so. I don't think it was a spirit. You saw her too. Did you think it looked like a possession?"

Jakob frowned. "I don't actually know what I thought just then. It happened so fast. It was Birgit who suggested the spirit. After she and Jens had investigated. That's two of the best mages in the country we're talking about. Leave it to them and try to stop thinking about it."

"But maybe they overlooked something?" Kirstine refused to drop the subject. "Do all the teachers agree that that's what happened?"

Jakob's eyes flickered ever so briefly, but she'd seen it.

"Jakob . . . ?" Kirstine pulled away from him.

"I shouldn't talk about it . . . it really only concerns the teachers."

"Say it."

"Okay, but you have to promise not to tell anyone else."

Kirstine nodded. "Of course."

"Lisa didn't think Anne had been possessed. Of course, spirit magic isn't her specialty, she's a nature mage—everything is very hands-on for her."

"So what did she think happened?"

"I don't know, but she said she thought blood magic was involved."

"Blood magic?"

"Yes, but she also said the scratches looked like something caused by an animal. That just goes to show she doesn't know what she's talking about. Put your money on Birgit's assessment. That's what I'm doing." He took hold of both her shoulders and tried to pull her into his embrace, but Kirstine wrenched herself away and got up.

"Kirstine, what now? You're leaving?"

Kirstine jogged through the forest's carpet of white anemones. "I'm sorry but I just remembered something."

Malou

"It all fits. Zlavko was at school on Christmas Eve, he's a blood mage, he's a teacher, so he knows all branches of magic—maybe that's what Trine was trying to tell us: Anne was attacked by a teacher."

"But you really think Zlavko is capable of attacking a student? I know he's obnoxious, but still . . ." Kirstine said.

"Listen," Malou said, "blood mages are pretty rare. There aren't that many of us at Rosenholm, right? And on Christmas Eve, when the majority of students had gone home, there were only two blood mages here. I was one of them. Can you guess who the other one was?"

"But a teacher . . ." Victoria said.

"You don't know him like I do. One afternoon when he was angrier than usual, he started talking to me about all sorts of crap after class when the rest of you had left. About dark magic. About taking. About sacrificing. And I don't think he was talking about sacrificing his own blood. He sounded like a total psycho."

"What? He really talked about dark magic as a good thing?" Chamomile asked.

Malou nodded.

"But it's not allowed at Rosenholm," Victoria objected, "it's completely forbidden."

"I think Zlavko's pretty numb to the rules," Malou said. "And hey, even that thing with the star fits. Don't you remember the first class where Zlavko made us all sit there and stare at his half-naked body?"

"A pentagram!" Kirstine whispered. "He had a pentagram scratched into his side. I remember it because the wound was so fresh. It was still bloody."

"Exactly," Malou nodded.

"Damn, what are we going to do if it's really him?" Chamomile asked.

"It *is* him," Malou insisted. "It all fits."

"What should we do?" Kirstine asked.

"We need to tell someone," Chamomile said, "but who? We have no evidence, and I don't want to think about what Birgit would say if we showed up and told her not only that she's made a mistake but also accuse one of her teachers of attacking students."

"What about Lisa?" Victoria suggested. "Maybe she even thought about it when she realized there was evidence of blood magic."

"We can't tell Lisa," Kirstine said quietly. "We can't say anything to any of the teachers. Jakob would be fired if they found out he was talking to students about this."

"So what if they fire him?" Malou asked. She stared at Kirstine, who seemed be trying to make herself invisible by hunching over as much as possible. *This doesn't add up*. "Why did Jakob tell you all this in the first place? Why would he do that?"

"I asked him . . ." Kirstine said. Her cheeks were bright red, and she looked at her hands.

"You've got something going with him, don't you!?"

Kirstine bit her lip and continued staring down at her hands.

"What the hell, you do! Naughty girl!"

"Malou!" Chamomile said, putting an arm around Kirstine. "That's enough!"

"What? Here we are, thinking Kirstine is this little, holy virgin, and then she scored with our teacher!"

"Geez, Malou, you're about as sensitive as a jackhammer," Chamomile snapped. "Can't you see that she's getting upset?"

"Hey, I'm just trying to say it was a good score. It's not like you committed a crime or anything, right?" Malou put her hands up in innocence, but Chamomile just shook her head.

"We have to be able to use this for something," Malou thought aloud.

"What do you mean?" Chamomile asked.

"We need a teacher we can talk to, right? If only one of us had a special relationship with one of the teachers. A more intimate relationship. Or maybe just, you know . . . a relationship?"

Kirstine looked up and dried her eyes.

"Malou, I can't, I promised Jakob not to tell anyone about this . . ." She looked at Chamomile and Victoria in a desperate bid for support, but this time they weren't coming to her aid.

"You don't have to say you told us about it," Victoria said. "It can just be something you've figured out for yourself."

"You have to," Malou said. "But you can't say anything about Trine."

Chamomile grabbed her hand and gave it a squeeze. "I'm sorry, but I think Malou's right. Jakob may be our best chance to get a teacher to talk. I mean, what if it is Zlavko? What if he does it again?"

Kirstine

The castle was dark and quiet, and the hallways were deserted when Kirstine crept toward the teachers' quarters. They'd agreed on her cover story: If she was stopped by a teacher, she'd say she was looking for Ingrid for a remedy for a seriously upset stomach. "Nothing makes people keep their distance like the threat of explosive diarrhea," Chamomile had said.

Kirstine breathed in deeply. There was, thank God, no activity in the teachers' wing either. She crept toward Jakob's door with her phone. She knew where he lived, but she'd never been there before. At first, she knocked ever so softly, but when no one answered, she knocked harder. It sounded like a thunderbolt in the silent hallway.

"Yes, yes, I'm coming, just a minute."

His voice sounded distant. He must have gone to bed already, but then again, it was after midnight.

She could hear him moving around by the door and finally it opened. Kirstine slipped into the room immediately. "Shh," she whispered and closed the door. "It's just me."

"Kirstine? What are you doing here?"

The room was almost completely dark, a single shaft of light fell out of a door that opened onto the next room. His bedroom? Of course the teachers would have more than just a bedroom, they probably had a sort of apartment. Jakob fumbled at the wall and switched on the light. His hair was disheveled, and he was wearing boxer shorts and a T-shirt that looked like he'd only just pulled it over his head.

"Are you okay?" He looked at her, surprised and a little confused, but then his expression changed, his pupils became larger, and a little smile played at the corners of his mouth. Suddenly it hit Kirstine that he might think she'd come for something else.

"I'm fine," she said hurriedly. "Sorry to wake you, but I need to talk to you about something you told me. About the thing with Anne."

Her explanation did not lessen the confusion on his face, but he hurried to clear a place for her on the small, plaid sofa in the middle of his living room.

"Uh, okay. Sit down, it's a bit messy. I was just taking care of some laundry . . . and preparing some lessons . . ."

Kirstine looked around. It was really very messy in the little living room. Laundry was hanging to dry over every chairback and there were open books and stacks of paper everywhere, but it was also pretty cozy. A collection of strange-looking cactuses was arranged on the broad windowsill.

"Do you want something to drink? I have tap water?"

Kirstine shook her head. "I need to tell you something."

Jakob sat beside her on the sofa. Kirstine took a deep breath and did her best to tell him everything quietly and calmly. He let her speak without interrupting. When she finally stopped, he ran a hand through his hair and took her hand.

"Kirstine, Zlavko didn't attack Anne. Maybe you're right, maybe it wasn't a spirit that hurt her, who knows? But it wasn't Zlavko. And I'm sorry if what I said scared you, I shouldn't have said anything." He rubbed his face with his hands. "Listen, I know Zlavko, and he would never do something like that. I know his demeanor is a bit different and not many students like him, but he actually is a really good guy."

"And what if you're wrong?"

"I'm not, Kirstine. You don't need to worry about Zlavko. Trust me."

Chamomile

Chamomile held her breath as Malou and Benjamin swept past them in a waltz. They were hands down the most beautiful couple in the great hall. Malou held her head up proudly, and Chamomile felt a pang of envy. They looked like a prince and princess. No matter how many times she and Vitus practiced the waltz, they would never look like that.

After everyone pretty much had a handle on Les Lanciers, they'd begun learning the waltz. It was much more difficult, not that you could tell from Malou and Benjamin. They looked as if they'd been born to waltz. When the music stopped, Benjamin bent over Malou's hand and kissed it, and the look he gave her made her blush. It suited her.

"Your turn," Malou smiled giddily as one half of the students left the dance floor so the rest of the couples could give it a try.

"Is the fair maiden ready?" Vitus asked as he led Chamomile out onto the floor. His friendly green eyes were turned attentively toward her, but she couldn't help staring down at her feet. She didn't have any nice shoes and wearing a long dress with worn-out sneakers just looked so stupid. So, today, she'd gone with bare feet. *Bare feet don't go terribly well with pointed, patent-leather shoes either.* Vitus let his eyes follow hers.

"That . . . that is a damned good idea," he said. "I'm getting blisters from these stupid shoes." He bent down and pulled off his shoes and socks as the music started. "Whoops, now we're behind."

The dance lesson was over all too soon. It was the last one before the Spring Ball.

"Thank you, dance partner," Vitus said, giving her a quick hug while Birgit was busy with something. "I hope we get a chance to dance together again soon."

Chamomile noticed a silly grin spread over her face as she nodded way too eagerly. Luckily, he couldn't see how fast her heart was beating.

"Take a look at this text from Molly." Malou pulled her discreetly by the arm as they headed up the stairs. When the other girls had slipped past them, Malou stuck her phone up to her face.

> Okay you didn't hear it from me,
> but Benjamin says he's going to invite
> a girl from the first year to the ball . . .
> I think we're gonna party together!!!!

> Vitus btw has also set his sights on
> a first year ;) Isn't that just too much?!

> Might as well go to the ball I guess ;)

> Oh stop playing hard to get Malou—you know you want to—admit it!

Malou grabbed her phone, keeping Chamomile from reading any more messages.

"The invitations will be distributed tomorrow," Malou said. "Then we'll know if we've succeeded."

"And what is the point of going to the ball?"

"To dance Les Lanciers!" Malou said, winking.

"Malou!"

"Yes, and also to keep a damned close eye on Zlavko. If he thinks he's going to get a chance to sneak away, he'd better think again."

"And you think we can stop him?"

"I'm not afraid of him."

"I am," Chamomile admitted.

"Relax, I'll look after you. You'd better start worrying about something else."

"What?"

"What we're going to wear!"

Malou

Ehwaz, the horse rune. Again. *Can symbolize death, ecstasy, travel to other worlds, change.*

Malou wrote it down and Victoria put the symbol back in the bag. As part of their classes on clairvoyance, they were doing a unit on rune magic, but Malou had trouble collecting her thoughts, and the runes she drew seemed to point in every direction. Jens had watched her, but after a moment he just shook his head in despair. Victoria, on the other hand, kept drawing the horse rune.

"And how would you interpret that, Victoria?" Jens asked. "What have you learned of rune magic?"

"The horse rune is associated with Odin's horse, Sleipnir, who carries him between worlds. It can bring people into ecstasy and connect them with other people and other worlds," Victoria answered. "And it can also be a portent of death."

"It's true that the horse rune can portend death, but, as with all signs, we have to use our reason to read them correctly. I do not see death, but I would interpret this as a sign that your mind is still too open to applications from the world of the dead. It is essential that you continue with your extra lessons," he said seriously and low enough that only Malou and Victoria could hear. "You can't start squandering your powers."

Malou looked questioningly at Victoria once Jens had moved on to the next desk, but Victoria avoided her gaze and concentrated on writing Jens's interpretation in her notebook.

It felt like the class on clairvoyance would never end, but finally Jens let them go. The four of them had only just gotten to the kitchen when Molly came bursting in, out of breath after having raced up the stairs.

"Here are the invitations, girls! I got permission to deliver yours—all the third-year students have gotten theirs, and I'm going with *mon amour!*"

"Congrats," Kirstine said. "I'm so happy for you!"

"Thanks! Well, I figured he wanted to, but it's still fabulous to actually have the invitation. And Birgit asked me to bring these two invitations up for you two. Let's see . . ." Molly opened a large, white envelope and pulled out a smaller one. "This one is for Chamomile, and this one is . . ." Molly stopped as if someone had found her off switch. Then a look of disbelief spread over her face. Chamomile, who'd been tearing open her envelope, paused too. Malou could feel her pulse hammering against her eardrums.

"What is it, Molly?" she asked.

"I'm really sorry, Malou . . ." Molly said quietly. "I must have misunderstood something. This one is for Victoria."

"Malou? Malou, open up."

To hell with Chamomile! Couldn't she leave her alone for five minutes? And to hell with this idiotic school where you don't even get your own room.

"Please just go away!" Malou shouted.

"Please open the door. It's just me. You can't stay locked in the bathroom all night."

"Leave me alone! What do you want? To gloat?"

"What? No! Oh, Malou, you're such an idiot sometimes. I want to make sure that you're okay. I'm worried about you, alright!?!"

"I don't need you. Or your worry. Just go away!"

"I mean it. Either you come out, or I'm going to get someone. You have one minute."

"Ugggh! You are so annoying! Okay, okay. I'll come out in a minute." She got up from the bathroom floor and bent over the sink to splash cold water on her face. The mirror reflected a pale face, and her mascara had run down her cheeks in black stripes. Her eyes were red and swollen.

"Idiot," she whispered to herself in the mirror. "Stupid, stupid idiot." Why had she been so sure Benjamin would invite her? And now the others were going to see her like this . . . she felt the tears welling up in her eyes again. Why had he chosen Victoria over her? "Get it together!" she hissed at her reflection as she bit hard into her lower lip. "Get it together, get it together, get it together." She bent over the sink and splashed more water on her face. The she coiled her hair into a tight bun and frowned into the mirror.

"Malou . . . ?"

"I'm coming! I'm coming!" She opened the door and looked at Chamomile defiantly. "Happy?"

"I'm really sorry . . ."

"Don't mention it. I'm just annoyed. All our plans are down the drain. Could I possibly get permission to go to my room and have some privacy? Oh, of course not, you'll be there too."

Chamomile looked at her with a mix of pity and fear.

"Stop . . ."

But Malou was already stomping into their room. Then she slammed the door and threw herself down on the bed. She heard the door open again. Couldn't they let her have any damned privacy?

"Malou, now you're going to listen to me, whether you want to or not." Chamomile's voice was sharp, as if she'd come to a decision and would not be brushed off. "Everyone else is terrified of saying the wrong thing to you. You always have to be such a badass, don't you? Kirstine is, of course, almost dying from fear that you're going to flip out, but Victoria is freaking out too . . ."

"I hate her . . ." Malou sobbed into her pillow.

"What? Victoria?"

"Yes, I hate her. She has everything. Have you seen pictures of the house her family lives in? She's rich and beautiful and clever, and thinner than I will ever be even if I stopped eating from here on out. Her parents aren't even divorced. And now she's got Benjamin too? I hate her!"

"You don't hate her . . ."

"Yes I do!"

"No, you don't," Chamomile sighed, and, sitting on the bed, she cautiously stroked Malou's hair. "You're just seeing everything you want. But you're forgetting the fact that Victoria's life isn't all rainbows and butterflies. First with Trine, and then the thing with Anne . . . Kirstine says she never sleeps, just paces around restlessly."

"She's clearly fresh enough to turn Benjamin's head. Why did he invite her, do they even know each other?"

Chamomile sighed. "Yes, well . . . she just told us while you were . . . away. He was evidently kept overnight in the infirmary the same night she was, but she promised not to tell anyone he was there. They talked a bit, and ever since they've been texting and going for walks . . ."

Malou buried her face in the pillow, no longer trying to hide the fact that she was crying.

"Why didn't she say anything? She probably wanted to make me look like a total idiot when it came out that he wanted to invite her the whole time."

"Don't be so paranoid. I don't know why she didn't say anything, but I know she wasn't trying to hurt you. She was just as surprised by the invitation as the rest of us. I know you really wanted to go to the ball, and not only because you wanted to keep an eye on Zlavko. But honestly, do you really truly care about Benjamin?"

"Why are you being so mean! Can't you just leave me alone? Do you absolutely have to make me feel worse?"

"I'm saying this because I'm your friend. Not to be mean. I've just heard you talk about Benjamin as if you really like him. Do you?"

Did she? Have strong feelings for him?

"I don't know. Not anymore. Now I just think he's a giant idiot."

"Exactly. Not worth crying over."

"It's not him I'm crying over. And if you tell anyone I was crying I will absolutely flip out on you!"

"Relax, you don't need to be such a tough cookie all the time. Everyone makes a fool of themselves or is let down or gets sad. You don't have to be so super cool and super perfect all the time."

"Yes, I do."

"Why? No one else is perfect, why do you have to be?"

"Because . . . otherwise people will realize I'm actually a giant loser."

"You're not a loser, Malou. You're beautiful and smart and brave. You're strong and you're a fighter. But that's not even what I like best about you. Do you know when I like you best?"

"Nah."

"It's when you're sleeping. Did you know you sleep with your mouth a bit open? And that you snore a little? And sometimes you drool, too."

"I do not." Chamomile sure was annoying to listen to sometimes.

"Yes, you do. And you lie there and grunt in your sleep like a sweet little hamster with messy hair, and no makeup, and drool on your chin. That's what I like best about you. Not because you're cool or clever. But because you're my sweet little hamster."

"Shut up!" Malou mumbled into her pillow, but she couldn't help smiling a tiny bit. "And if you tell a single living soul I snore you'll never see the light of day again!"

"Understood!" Chamomile said. She arranged the comforter over Malou as if she was tucking in a little child, and Malou let her do it. "I promise not to tell. Cross my heart, my little hamster."

Did you get my invitation?

Yeah, thanks, I got it

So, ummmmm, should I count on you coming?

I don't know. Malou got really upset.
But you must have known that.

What? No . . . ?

Why?

She thought you wanted to invite her.
Everyone thought so

But I didn't, I wanted to invite you

But didn't you fix it so that you
would be dancing with Malou?

for the lessons?

What! No?

Where did you get that?

Malou

Malou must have misunderstood something! I'm sorry but I wanted to invite you the whole time! Didn't you know?

You've been flirting with her a lot

I have not! I've been nice to her. We were dance partners . . .

She's really disappointed

Yeah maybe, but that's not my fault . . . She'll get over it

Hey . . . Victoria

You can't punish me because Malou misunderstood something. That's not fair!

Sweetheart . . . ?

Remember student rule number . . .
I don't remember what we're up to—but it goes like this: Say yes when a nice guy invites you out!

Are you a nice guy?

I am. Promise.

Ok. I'll come

Chamomile

"Ready?"

Chamomile nodded. "Thanks for helping me. Doing this alone seemed sad, and I didn't want to ask Malou, you know . . . that would be awkward . . ."

"Of course—anytime, it'll be fun," Victoria said with an encouraging smile.

"What are you going to wear?" Chamomile asked as they walked down the stairs and then through a long hallway that ran parallel to the teachers' hall.

"Oh, we went to a wedding held at a castle last year and I had a fancy dress made. My mother sent it to me. It's red."

"I'm sure it's gorgeous." Chamomile returned the smile and looked seriously at Victoria's pale face. "Are you really up for all this? The ball? Malou was counting on it being her and me who would . . ."

"Somehow it makes sense that it's me, I think. Trine came to me. We promised her we'd find out who killed her. And she said we should go to the ball. I choose to trust that this is the right thing to do."

Chamomile nodded. "That sounds a little *fulfill your destiny.*"

Victoria smiled. "Well, maybe that's how I feel. How's Malou doing?"

"She's okay. She just thought Benjamin was going to invite her."

"I can understand why," Victoria said. "I thought so, too."

"Malou's a good person, you know, she's just a little intense sometimes. She's convinced Zlavko's behind it all, and she's completely obsessed with finding evidence against him. It's like it's somehow become her sole responsibility."

"I know," Victoria said.

"Hey, I think this is it," Chamomile said, pointing at a door. "The storage room beside the supply closet. I have permission to borrow the key for exactly one hour, then I have to get it back to Birgit." She fumbled with the lock. "I wonder if there's even anything left. The third years have already gone through it all."

"I'm sure we'll find something."

Chamomile finally got the door open. The long, narrow room had a high ceiling. The air was stale and dusty, and there were curtains drawn over a single, large window opposite the door. In front of the window, two enormous, full-length mirrors with carved gilt frames stood across from each other, and the walls were covered in racks of dresses spanning the whole length of the room.

"There must be hundreds! Wild!" Chamomile whispered. "But where do we start?"

"Have you thought about a color?" Victoria asked as she slowly walked along the line of dresses, letting her hand run over the different fabrics.

"Green, maybe? And preferably a bit princess-y. I've always wanted to try a dress like that."

"Go stand by the mirror and take your clothes off. I'll bring over some dresses."

Chamomile kicked off her pants and slipped the shirt over her head.

"Socks too," Victoria said, unable to conceal a smile, "ball gowns and Minnie Mouse socks just don't go. Here, try this one."

Chamomile pulled her socks off as Victoria walked toward her carrying a light green dress with pearls and sequins on both the bodice and the flared skirt.

"Here, I'll help you." Victoria pulled it down over Chamomile's head and zipped up the back. Then she opened the curtains so the light poured in and turned to look at Chamomile in the mirror.

"Hmm . . ."

"I look like a bridesmaid from an American movie," Chamomile observed. "The kind where they have to wear a hideous dress so the bride looks nicer. It looks awful."

The dress was too much: too pale green, too many sequins, too puffy.

"This isn't the one. Off with it," Victoria said, unzipping the back.

The next was a bottle-green bodycon dress with a glittering sash at the waist. The color worked better, but it was nearly two feet too long and had a slit that went nearly up to Chamomile's navel. The third dress was seven sizes too big, while the fourth was strapless with a giant skirt in a blue-green, nautical theme. Victoria struggled with the zipper, but even though Chamomile tried not to breathe, it was impossible to get it zipped.

"Rejected!" Victoria said, laughing. "This *is* actually pretty fun!"

"Not as much fun as I imagined," Chamomile sighed as she took in her reflection. Her face was flushed and her hair had gotten messed up from pulling dresses on and off over her head. "Come on, Sunshine, chin up!" she told her reflection, blowing a whisp of hair out of her face.

"I think we should look for something simpler," Victoria said. "And does it *have* to be green?"

"Nah, it doesn't have to be," Chamomile said. "I'll be happy if we can just find something that fits."

"This one's pretty!" Victoria said. "Try it on."

Chamomile pulled it over her head and Victoria zipped it up.

"*Now* you look like a princess!"

Chamomile looked at her reflection. The dress was made of a light, flowy fabric and the color reminded her of the dried lavender her mother had given her so she'd always have the scent of home nearby. The bodice fit tightly, and the cut was revealing. It made her throat look long and gave her nice cleavage. Otherwise, the dress was very simple, with cap sleeves and a long, billowing skirt consisting of several layers of thin, light fabric in the same dusty, pale-purple color.

"This one's really nice. You look beautiful. And if you put your hair up, your neck will look even longer." Victoria gathered Chamomile's hair and held it up so that she could see. Chamomile nodded.

"This *is* really nice. It's even the right length," Chamomile said, looking down at her bare toes just peeking out from the dress's edge.

"Let's get the rest of these hung up again before Birgit starts wondering what happened to us."

When Chamomile got back to their room, Malou was sitting on her bed surrounded by her Blood Magic homework.

"Oh, I thought you were still at the library," Chamomile said, tripping over her rubber boots as she tried to discreetly tuck the ball gown into the large wardrobe without Malou seeing it. Fortunately, Malou was staring determinedly at her book.

"We still haven't found anything," she said. "Kirstine searched the all the yearbooks from the class of 1987 up—just in case. Still no Trine in '87, '88, '89, or '90."

"Oh," Chamomile said, closing the wardrobe doors and sitting down on her own bed. "Did you call that other library?"

"The *royal* library," Malou said. "Yes, at first they wouldn't help me at all. They said I was welcome to come in and look through the newspapers from 1989. Of course they have every newspaper all the way back to prehistoric times lying around in old film canisters or something. Eventually I got reassigned to a young librarian and he promised he would help me figure out if a young girl named Trine was found murdered in 1989. But he said it'll take some time because he'll have to look through all the papers from the entire year."

"Wow, how did you get him to help you?" Chamomile asked, impressed.

"I have reasonably good powers of persuasion," Malou said simply as she turned a page in her textbook.

"Shouldn't he get something for that?"

"Well, he got my number," Malou said with a wink.

"Oh, Malou, you're brutal," Chamomile laughed. "So what, he thinks you're his girlfriend now?"

"I never said anything about that," Malou said. "But he probably hopes it'll help him get a date."

"And he hasn't even seen you. Well done."

Malou shrugged. "Hey, what size shoe do you wear?"

"Why?"

"You can't wear your Jesus sandals with that purple ball gown. Or maybe you were going to wear the rubber boots?"

Chamomile felt her face get hot. "Five or five and a half," she said.

"I wear size six, but they'll probably work. Can you walk in heels?"

Chamomile shook her head. "At least not stilettos."

"Yeah, I thought so. I have some white sandals with a low heel. You'll probably be able to walk in them easily enough. Otherwise, you'll just have to practice. Try them on."

Malou walked over to the wardrobe and rooted around until she found the shoes.

"Thanks, Malou, this is really nice of you. Are you sure you're okay with . . . with everything?"

Malou shrugged. "Mostly."

"It's not Victoria's fault, you know," Chamomile said.

"I know." Malou held up a lock of Chamomile's red hair. "What are you going to do with your hair?"

"I was wondering if you would do it for me?"

"Of course I will. We're gonna make you look so fancy your Vitus will never be able to think of slipping off with another girl right under your nose. Not like his friend Benjamin. I just don't understand why he would flirt with me like that if he wasn't interested."

"Aww, what about you and that librarian," Chamomile teased. "It'll break his heart when he finds out you're only interested in old ghosts!"

"That's not the same thing!" Malou chided, but she couldn't help laughing. "Sit down, we'll practice your updo."

Malou let the brush glide through her hair, and it reminded Chamomile so much of her mother that she felt tears in her eyes.

"Malou?"

"Mmm."

"I'm afraid of tomorrow."

Malou laid her hand on Chamomile's shoulder and gave it a squeeze. "I know. But you and Victoria will have each other. And all the teachers will be there too. And Kirstine and I will be nearby. We'll have our phones on the whole time. Besides, I have a plan . . ."

"Not another plan! What now?"

"Nothing to worry about—I've got it all under control. Now sit still or this will never look right."

Malou

Maybe seeking out Zlavko late at night to accuse him of a crime—by herself—wasn't a smart thing to do. Maybe the other girls would have tried to talk her out of it. But that was why she'd decided not to tell them. Because there was nothing else to do. Malou didn't want to let Chamomile go to the party tomorrow when she couldn't go with her to keep an eye on him. And Victoria? Who knew how much she could really handle? No, Malou needed to confront him tonight. Besides, he probably wasn't stupid enough to attack her in his own room with other teachers sleeping right next door.

Malou walked down the teachers' hall. Zlavko's name was on the second to last door.

She hesitated. Should she just leave? No, no she had to do this. She knocked on the door. Loudly. The door opened immediately.

"You?!" Zlavko stuck his head out and looked at her furiously. He had pants on, but his upper body was bare, and his usually well-kept hair was gathered into a messy topknot. Tufts of hair hung around his face scraggily, making him look even crazier than usual. "Why are you here?"

She stiffened. "I have to ask you about something. It's important."

"Ha! Yes, this is exactly what I need. Come on in!" He opened the door for her with exaggerated swagger.

The small apartment was in a state of total chaos. All the lights were on, and clothes, books, and papers were scattered all over the place. In the middle of the room stood several large suitcases.

"I was packing," he said into her ear. He was standing behind her. *And, as per usual, way too close.* She suppressed a shudder, and, jerking a little, stepped away. He wasn't going to get the pleasure of knowing how much he scared her.

"Are you going somewhere?"

"I've resigned. I'm leaving the school. So now you're free of me," he hissed bitterly, picking a book up from the floor and tossing it in a suitcase.

"Why?"

"Disagreements with management. Isn't that how it's said?"

"Birgit?"

"We don't agree on how best to command respect as a teacher," he mumbled and picked up another book. "Or how best to ensure the students' safety."

She narrowed her eyes. "Birgit has seen right through you. Maybe she knows about what happened with Anne?"

"What are you talking about?" His eyes bored through her. "Tell me why the hell you're really here?"

"I came to ask why you attacked Anne. I know. I know it wasn't a spirit. It was blood magic. It was you."

She held her breath. Zlavko's face was a mask of fury. Then it broke into a slightly maniacal laugh.

"You're a real piece of work. You think *I* attacked Anne?"

"I know it was you." Blood rushed into her ears so quickly she almost couldn't hear her own voice.

Zlavko let go of the book he was holding. Slowly he walked toward her.

"Do you think I need to avail myself of simple violence to get what I want?" He scoffed. "It's almost alarming how little you actually know about blood magic. People *give* me what I want. I don't even have to ask."

He stood right in front of her. She felt paralyzed. She wanted to get away from him, but her legs felt frozen in place. Zlavko took her by the chin and forced her face upward so that her eyes met his.

"Do you understand?" he whispered.

Malou felt a stabbing pain between her eyes and sensed something running from her nostrils. She wanted to pull away, but she couldn't move. Zlavko let his thumb glide lightly over her lips and held it up in front of her. *Blood.* He'd given her a nosebleed. Without even touching her. She trembled.

"Do you understand?" he whispered again. Malou nodded.

"DO YOU UNDERSTAND?!" he shouted.

"Yes, yes, I understand," she cried.

"Good," he nodded, letting go of her. "I'm glad. Now get out."

She backed away from him, almost tripping over a pile of clothes, and stumbled to the door.

Her legs shook beneath her as she ran.

Chamomile

"Is it too much? Is the dress too low-cut? Maybe you shouldn't have used so much eyeliner."

"You look beautiful, now stay still."

Chamomile closed her eyes and tried to be patient while Malou finished her hair. It had taken more than an hour. She'd been made up and straightened and blow-dried like never before.

"Now you have to promise to enjoy yourself. But keep an eye on each other, okay? Just because Zlavko's left Rosenholm doesn't mean you don't need to be careful. You never know."

"I can't believe you went to his room in the middle of the night, Malou. You're crazy. Anything could have happened."

"Well, luckily nothing did. And thanks to Birgit I could have saved myself the trip. The point is he isn't here anymore. Okay, you can look now."

Malou had insisted that Chamomile not look until she was done, and she was afraid she was going to look like a clown after everything Malou had put on her. Slowly she opened her eyes and looked into the mirror Malou was holding up.

"Wow!" she whispered. It wasn't too much. The warm brown shades of the eyeshadow made her blue eyes seem larger and deeper in color. Her skin was smooth and even, and her hair gleamed. Half of it was done up while a long, waving lock hung down along her neck and curled softly over her shoulder.

"You really can work magic, Malou."

"Yes, but this is all thanks to my trusty makeup case. You'll outshine everyone tonight!"

Chamomile suspected when Malou said "everyone" she was thinking primarily of Victoria.

"Thanks, roomie. What would I have done without you."

"You would have been completely lost. And wearing rubber boots. Put the shoes on, you can't let your prince wait too long. And NOW I'm going to the bathroom!"

Chamomile fastened the clasp of the shoes. The heels felt a little weird, but she'd manage. Then she bent over her bed and took a small box from under her pillow. Chamomile clutched the box and read the card for at least the twentieth time. It had been lying on her bed when she got back to her room last night. Molly had probably played courier again, because the boys weren't allowed into the girls' rooms under any circumstances. The handwriting looked like a boy's, with beautiful, flowing letters.

Since I can't give you heaven,
you'll have to settle for this small gift.
(Corny, I know!)

264

The box contained a necklace. Chamomile studied it as she fingered the little silver leaf already hanging from her neck. The symbol of Growth. Vitus wore the same leaf on a leather cord. To think that he'd actually given her a piece of jewelry! It was the first time Chamomile had gotten something like that from a guy, and she hadn't told anyone. Malou and Victoria were probably used to getting gifts from boys who were head-over-heels about them, and Kirstine had a boyfriend or whatever you were supposed to call it. But this was new and special for Chamomile.

She heard Malou's purposeful steps out in the kitchen and she quickly took the new chain out of the box, hung it around her neck and closed the clasp.

"Ready, babe? You can't go until I've taken pictures," Malou said when she came back into the room.

"Malou? I wish you were coming too . . ."

"Well shucks, you'll just have to remember to miss me. Now smile for the camera! And don't worry, Kirstine and I are going to be too busy to feel bitter," Malou said as she stuck her phone in Chamomile's face for a closeup.

"What are you going to do?"

"I talked her into going through the yearbooks one more time. A wild Saturday night, I know."

"Ugh, Malou, can't you take just one night off?"

"Of course, but not tonight. We promised Trine, right? Come on!" she said, pulling Chamomile toward the kitchen.

"Are we ready?"

Chamomile turned and saw Victoria standing in the middle of the small kitchen.

"Oh wow!" Chamomile whispered. All Malou's efforts to make her outshine Victoria had been in vain. Victoria looked like a real-life Disney Princess. She was dressed in a deep red ball gown with a tight, sleeveless bodice that highlighted her slender figure and narrow waist. The skirt spread in a perfect A-line all the way down to the floor. Victoria's skin was snow white and flawless, her hair was combed back softly and almost looked black. A silver, leaf-shaped barrette with sparkling gems glinted in her dark hair, but otherwise she wore no jewelry. Her makeup was simple too, her large, deep brown eyes were just highlighted a bit, and her lips were peach colored.

"You look like a million bucks," Chamomile said, and Victoria smiled a smile that didn't quite reach her beautiful eyes.

"Thank you," she said, giving Chamomile a cautious hug to keep from ruining her makeup. "You look gorgeous in that dress."

"Ooh, wait, you can't go yet," Kirstine said from inside the room. "Not until I've seen you. Ooh! You look so fancy! And you have your phones?"

"Yes!"

"With the batteries charged?"

"Plenty of battery," Chamomile assured her.

"Keep an eye on each other the whole time," Malou added. "Call if anything happens. We'll be right around the corner."

"And Jakob will be there too," Kirstine said.

"Yeah, if you think you can trust a teacher who seduces his students," Malou commented.

"He had no choice," Kirstine said. "I seduced him."

"Oh, Kirstine!" Chamomile shrieked. "Malou was right, you are a naughty one!"

Kirstine just shrugged.

"Okay, we'd better get going," Chamomile said, turning to Victoria.

"Yes, I just wanted to say . . . Malou? I'm sorry I didn't tell you about Benjamin. It was stupid of me."

Malou stood in the door with her arms crossed over her chest. Chamomile held her breath. *Come on, Malou!*

"It's fine," she said measuredly.

"Oh, I'm so proud of you!" Chamomile whispered, throwing her arms around Malou's neck to give her a bear hug.

"Watch your hair!" Malou scolded, frowning at her. "And get going!"

Tonight the violets bloom. After tonight we will never be parted.

Victoria

Remember what you promised, the wind whistled outside the castle's large windows.

I haven't forgotten, Trine.

Victoria felt light and at ease as she walked down to the great hall, arm in arm with Chamomile. Her flowing skirt rustled with every step, and nervous expectation hummed through her whole body. Why shouldn't she get to party a little for once? Be carefree and young for a change? Tonight, she'd just let herself feel like everyone else. Chamomile smiled and gave Victoria's arm a squeeze.

"Welcome, ladies. May I see your invitations?" After they'd handed Jakob their invitation, he bowed deeply and threw open the double doors into the great hall. He wore a tuxedo with a bow tie he'd evidently struggled to tie. "Enjoy yourselves! And don't do anything I wouldn't do," he said with a wink as they walked in.

"I guess that means relationships between students and teachers are okay," Chamomile whispered, giggling, after Jakob had closed the door behind them.

The great hall was beautifully decorated—it was festooned with green beech boughs, and candles burned in large, silver candelabras. Long tables covered with white tablecloths and decked with enormous platters of all kinds of hors d'oeuvres and slender champagne flutes with bubbly contents were arranged along the walls. At the end of the hall a string quartet played on a small stage set up for the occasion.

"Not to worry! I'm going to DJ later!"

They turned and saw Molly; she was laughing and had an arm around Frédéric. Frédéric was wearing a dark red velvet suit with matching bow tie. Molly was dressed in a black dress that she seemed to have abused in every imaginable way. The skirt was ripped to reveal her legs and shredded stockings, and she'd pulled a sheer top, similarly ripped, over the tight bodice of the gown. Her long dreadlocks were piled high up on her head and her makeup was even bolder than usual. Her bright red lipstick was already pretty smudged, and Victoria noticed that Frédéric seemed to be wearing a similar color on his own lips.

"Molly!" Chamomile squealed before practically falling on her. "This is wild, all of it, I've never seen anything like it. I feel like royalty. Awesome dress!"

"I know, right?" Molly said, spinning around so they could see it from every angle. "You look pretty good yourselves. But where are your dates?"

"We just got here," Victoria said.

"I saw Vitus a minute ago, over by the champagne. Typical of him to be pre-gaming! Come on, we can get a glass too."

Molly dragged Chamomile and her escort off, leaving Victoria alone.

Victoria nodded to Birgit as she walked by in an elegant, high-necked aubergine dress. She didn't recognize many of the other faces, especially when they were decked out in ball gowns, shiny tuxedoes, and fluttering feelings.

"Hi, sweetheart." The voice was so close to her ear that it gave her goosebumps. "Did you miss me?"

Victoria turned around and saw Benjamin holding a glass of champagne in each hand. The stylish suit made him more attractive than she cared to admit. His incredibly blue eyes bored into her as they clinked glasses.

"I was beginning to be afraid you'd backed out," he said.

"I almost did," Victoria replied. She felt like the alcohol had hit her bloodstream as soon as the bubbles hit her tongue.

"I'm glad you chose to come. You look beautiful."

Victoria couldn't think of anything else to say, but luckily someone started clinking a knife against a glass at that moment.

"We welcome you to the Spring Ball . . ." Birgit's voice cut through the dense cacophony of chattering and laughing students, ". . . with a dance. Please assemble into quadrilles and prepare for Les Lanciers."

Oh, this is happening already? Victoria looked around in confusion. How did you know which couple you were supposed to dance with? The students pushed and shoved their way through each other, and total chaos erupted as they all attempted to form quadrilles.

"Come on," Benjamin whispered as he grabbed her hand. She let herself be led through the crowd of giggling third-year students.

"Can we dance here?" Benjamin asked, swinging Victoria

elegantly up beside himself as if the dance had already begun. He clearly wasn't waiting for an answer.

"We're still missing a couple," said a tall girl with blond ringlets. Victoria didn't know any of the others.

"Wait for us!" Giggling, Vitus and Chamomile ran toward them and got set up just as the music started. It occurred to Victoria that Chamomile and Vitus had been dancing together every week for over a month. They were used to having each other as partners. But this was the first time she and Benjamin would be dancing together.

"We got this," he said encouragingly as he wrapped an arm around her waist.

The first steps felt awkward, but soon she began to relax and feel the music. Benjamin's hand on her waist gave her stomach butterflies, which mixed with all the other students' sparkling expectations for the evening so that soon she couldn't tell where her own feelings ended and others' feelings began. During the gentlemen's mill, Benjamin swung her around so that her feet almost didn't touch the earth, and she heard herself shriek giddily in chorus with Chamomile. At the end of the dance, he grabbed her around the waist with both hands and lifted her high up in the air. Then the music stopped, and everyone clapped. It was already over.

"Thank you for the dance," Benjamin whispered into her ear. A shiver ran over her skin like a wildfire.

"I think I need a drink," she said. Benjamin took her hand and led her off the dance floor as the other students prepared to dance a waltz.

Victoria caught a glimpse of Chamomile, who smiled and winked as she laid a hand on Vitus's arm as the waltz was about to begin. During Les Lanciers, a few wisps of hair had worked their way free from the fancy hairstyle Malou had arranged. Chamomile looked beautiful and so happy as Vitus, smiling, put his arm around her waist.

Rules and Regulations
of Rosenholm Academy

4. The practice of dark magic is strictly prohibited at Rosenholm Academy.

Malou

"Kirstine, are you coming?"

They were walking through the empty hallways and up to the library together. The students who weren't going to the party had a free weekend, and most had gone home the day before. It was never something they talked about, but Kirstine and Malou were often some of the only students left at school on free weekends and holidays.

They were quiet as they walked. This suited Malou perfectly, even though she'd gradually gotten used to Chamomile's constant chatter. At first her roommate had driven her crazy, but it sometimes felt a little too quiet in their room when Chamomile was home visiting her mother. Still, she appreciated Kirstine's quietness. Malou stopped. Something had caught her attention.

"What is it?" Kirstine asked.

"Do you smell something?" No, *smell* was the wrong word. It was more an impression, a sensation. She could feel it. *Blood.*

"Look!" Kirstine grabbed her hand. "Over there, on the wall!"

Malou followed her gaze. "What the hell is that?!"

Kirstine recoiled, but Malou walked closer. Hung on the wall in the narrow hallway that led to the library was an animal. It was a black cat. And it was dead. Someone had nailed it to the wall; its four legs were spread to either side. The soft fur of its belly was ripped to shreds and its blood had run down the wall and pooled on the floor. Using the blood, someone had drawn a star around the cat and written a message on the wall.

TONIGHT WE'RE GONNA PARTY LIKE IT'S 1989

"A pentagram," Kirstine gasped. "And the year! What does this mean?"

Malou shook her head in disbelief. "1989. The year Trine was killed." She let her finger slide over the cat's beautiful fur. "It can't be a coincidence . . . He knew about Trine. He knew when she was killed. She said she knew him. But he knows her, too."

"But she died so many years ago . . ." Kirstine whispered.

"Maybe he knows her as a spirit? Just like we do? I think . . ." Malou's voice faltered and disappeared in the darkness of the silent hallway, ". . . I think this means he's going to kill tonight. At the party."

"You mean Zlavko? Is he back at the castle?"

"Maybe . . ."

Something didn't add up, though. It was so violent. So inelegant. Not something you would expect from a blood mage . . . Malou couldn't tear her eyes away from the cat.

"An animal must have killed this cat. Or something . . . animalistic. Like whatever mauled Anne," she mumbled.

"But an animal wouldn't nail its prey to a wall," Kirstine whispered.

"No, but what if this was done by a cross between an animal

and a human? Something in the middle. I'm beginning to think I was wrong about Zlavko . . ."

Malou's thoughts swirled around her head. *The bloody gashes, the dead cat, Lisa, who talked about animals, soundless steps over old, creaky floorboards . . . What had he been doing in the empty hallway behind the library, where students never go? And didn't Birgit seem nervous when she spoke to him? Maybe even afraid? What was it Molly had said about the rumors their first day?*

"Malou, I don't understand what you're talking about," Kirstine's voice was shrill, and she tugged at Malou's sleeve to drag her back to reality.

Malou turned to her. "Maybe Jakob is right, maybe this has nothing to do with Zlavko. Maybe someone else is behind it all. Do you remember what Molly told us about Benjamin? That some people say he's a shapeshifter."

"A shapeshifter? Benjamin?!"

"Maybe it's been him the whole time."

"But, but . . . Victoria?!"

"Yes, we've got to warn her. *You* have to warn her. She could be in danger. Call her, and if she doesn't pick up, run down to the great hall and explain everything to Birgit. Get her to stop the party. There's something I have to check." Malou turned and ran off.

"Wait!" Kirstine called after her. "How do I explain it all . . . ?"

"Just do it!" Malou called over her shoulder without slowing down. "Take a picture with your phone and show them the cat. You've got this! Hurry!"

Kirstine

Kirstine ran down the deserted hallway with her phone clutched in her hand. Neither Victoria nor Chamomile were picking up. It didn't necessarily mean anything had happened to them. They probably couldn't hear their phones over the music.

"Please, let me find Jakob first," she murmured to herself as she took the stairs down to the great hall. As she stepped out of the stairwell, she saw the large double doors that led into the hall. There he was, Jakob, but he wasn't alone. Jens was keeping him company. Kirstine ran the last bit as the stitch in her side burned.

"Kirstine, what's wrong?" Jakob asked.

"You have to stop the party," she gasped, panting for breath. "Victoria's in danger. He might kill her!"

"What are you talking about?" Jens asked.

"You have to stop the party. He's going to kill tonight. See for yourself!" Kirstine held her phone up in front of them, turning the brightness all the way up so they could see the cat, the blood, and the sinister message.

Jens took a pair of reading glasses out of his pocket and studied the screen.

"Looks like an unauthorized sacrifice," he said, turning to Jakob and handing him the phone. "Listen, what's all this about somebody wanting to kill Victoria?"

"1989," Kirstine said, "a girl was killed at Rosenholm in 1989. And now someone wants to do it again. Maybe it's Benjamin."

"Benjamin!? Kirstine . . ." Jakob looked at her with utter incredulity.

At that moment the door opened, and Birgit came out.

"I need a break, Jens. Would you take my place . . . what's going on?"

Jens and Jakob looked at each other without saying anything.

"You have to stop the party!" Kirstine repeated desperately.

"Someone's evidently made an unauthorized sacrifice in one of the hallways upstairs," Jens said, showing her the phone.

"How horrid," Birgit said. "That's completely unacceptable."

"Yes, and it's scared some of the students. But I don't understand the rest at all."

"The students are in danger," Kirstine tried again. "Someone wants to try to kill a student. It might be Benjamin. We have to warn Victoria because she's his date!"

"Victoria? No, now you're talking nonsense, Kirstine."

"Someone attacked Anne and now he's after a new victim. We think it could be Benjamin because . . . because he's a shapeshifter." The last words came out as something between a whimper and a sob. Why couldn't they just believe her?

Birgit's eyes widened and she looked at Jens, who returned her knowing look.

"Listen, you're obviously upset and don't know what you're saying," Birgit said, putting an arm around Kirstine. "I can assure you that I just saw Victoria myself. Less than a minute ago. She's dancing a very impressive waltz, surrounded by other students. She was definitely not in danger and looked to be enjoying herself splendidly. Nothing has happened to your friend, and I can assure you that Benjamin—regardless of what he may or may not be—is perfectly harmless." Birgit patted Kirstine's arm a bit awkwardly. "Unfortunately we see such things from time to time. That cat looks like a clumsy attempt at some sort of love magic. Now you'd better go up to bed. We'll talk it all through tomorrow, but in the meantime you can rest easy. The school's teachers are here to make sure that nothing happens to either you or Victoria." Birgit gently pushed her toward the stairs.

Kirstine took a few steps. Everything Birgit said had made sense. Except . . .

"Like you took care of Anne?" Kirstine asked, turning back toward them.

"What do you mean?" Birgit asked, the sympathy fading from her voice.

"Anne was attacked. While you were all here. Someone used Anne in some sort of sick ritual right under your noses. You can't afford to not take this seriously."

"Where on earth did you get such an idea?" Birgit snarled. "Anne was possessed by a spirit. It was very unfortunate, but it was her own fault. We cannot stop students from acting foolishly."

Kirstine felt Jakob staring at her, his blazing eyes locked firmly on hers and he slowly shook his head, begging her not to say another word. But Kirstine tore her eyes away and looked Birgit in the eyes.

"I don't believe it," she said. "And neither does Lisa. She said Anne's wounds looked like they were made by an animal. By claws. Like a cat's. Wouldn't a shapeshifter have claws?"

"And who told you what Lisa said?" Birgit kept her voice steady, but large, red patches on her throat revealed how angry she really was.

Kirstine's eyes shifted from Birgit's piercing eyes to Jakob, who was now avoiding her gaze.

Birgit stared at her for a moment before turning toward Jakob. "You?! Did you tell her that? A student? But . . ."

Birgit blinked a few times, looking as if she wanted to say more. But she swallowed the rest of her words. Jakob didn't say anything either. Birgit took a deep breath. "Go up to your room. I'm not going to listen to any more nonsense from you tonight. Jakob, we'll discuss this later. Right now I want you to help me find the cat so that we can figure out who did this. Jens, stay by the door. Don't let anyone in until I get back, okay?"

Without waiting for an answer Birgit headed for the stairs, followed closely by Jakob. The look he gave Kirstine as he walked past felt more painful than if he'd punched her in the face.

Where are you?

The gallery

Stay where you are, I'm coming!

"Hey, watch out!"

"Whoa, she's wasted."

The voices merged with the music's booming bass into a strange blanket of sound that reminded her of being deep under water. She was thirsty and her throat was dry, but when she tried to take a drink from the glass in her hand, she missed and barely noticed as the liquid ran down her dress instead of into her mouth. The room hummed around her, and the lights drew long tails in front of her eyes whenever her head moved.

"Come on," he laid a protective arm around her, "you'll feel better with some fresh air."

Malou

She'd been wrong. Zlavko hadn't attacked Anne. And Victoria wasn't the intended victim.

Malou's feet smacked again the castle's old floorboards and echoed through the empty hallways. The class portraits. Why hadn't she thought of them before? Most people didn't know they were hanging in the deserted hallway behind the library, but she'd been there before. Twice before. They'd scoured everything—old student rosters, yearbooks, every record they could find—except the class portraits. It wasn't until she'd started thinking about Benjamin that she thought of the portraits.

She sprinted around the corner and into the gallery. Kirstine stood like a statue in the deserted hallway.

"Come on!" Malou grabbed her wrist and pulled her back toward the great hall downstairs. The music thundering from the party below.

"It's no good, they won't listen to us."

"We *have* to get in," Malou said, "before it's too late."

"Birgit says Victoria's fine," Kirstine gasped as she ran.

"It's not Victoria," she said, stopping for a moment. "I made a

284

mistake. Look, I took a picture of Trine's old class portrait, class of 1989." She zoomed in on the names under the picture. "It's right there."

Rose Katrine Severinsen (Trine)

Kirstine's eyes widened. "Trine was her *nickname* . . . That's why we couldn't find her on the rosters!"

"And look." Malou zoomed in on the students instead. On the far left stood a young girl with apple cheeks, smiling. Her red hair fell softly around her face.

Kirstine looked at Malou. ". . . Chamomile?!"

"We have to find her," Malou said, "They look just like each other!" She swiped back one picture. Chamomile laughing in her party dress and with her hair done up. The resemblance to Trine was uncanny. Malou started to put the phone in her pocket, but Kirstine grabbed her hand.

"Wait!" She studied the picture closely. "What's that?" Kirstine's voice was only a whisper.

Malou zoomed in. "Erm . . . her necklace? No, there are two necklaces?! I've never seen that one before. The pendant is a sun, a moon . . . and a star."

"A five-pointed star! He's marked her—that's a mare-cross!"

"A what?"

"A mare-cross. But he isn't using it to keep spirits away. He wants to bind her soul to him!"

"What are you talking about?"

"I'll explain later, but you're right! Chamomile's in danger, and Jens is standing in front of the door and won't let anyone in!"

"Damn . . ." Malou looked helplessly around the empty hallway, searching desperately for a solution. "Hey, how's the food supposed to be served—it wouldn't come in through the main doors, right? We have to find the kitchen!"

Kirstine

Kirstine looked around in confusion. The great hall was dark, the music was deafening, and it was impossible to hear anything else. Malou had led them through the kitchen, which was deserted apart from a single, amorous couple looking for a bit of privacy.

"Have you seen her?" Malou put her mouth right up to Kirstine's ear and shouted. Normally that would have made her wince, but now the words only just came through. Kirstine shook her head.

"We have to split up. I can see Molly up at the DJ's table. I'll ask her while you check the dance floor. Keep an eye on your phone. I'll text as soon as I find her, okay?"

Kirstine nodded. Malou let go of her arm and disappeared into the crowd of dancing, sweating teenagers. Kirstine attempted to cross the dance floor, but it was impossible to move forward, and she couldn't see anything in the darkness, which was broken only by strobing party lights. If she could get to the side of the room then maybe she could find a chair to stand on and get a better view.

"Kirstine!" A hand grabbed her wrist and spun her around. The familiar movement briefly reminded her of a walk in the

287

forest, but the sight of Jakob's face contorted in anger told her that the sentiment was completely different now. "What are you doing? You can't be here!" He pulled her to the side of the hall and in through a door she hadn't noticed before. When it closed behind them the darkness was complete. The light from her phone revealed it to be some sort of utility closet.

"We have to find Chamomile! She's in danger," Kirstine said. "You've got to help us."

The screen's greenish light make Jakob look ill. His eyes were in shadow, and she couldn't read his facial expression.

"What? Ten minutes ago it was Victoria, but now it's Chamomile?" His voice sounded cold. "And is it still Benjamin that's the suspect? Or Zlavko? Or maybe it'll be me next time?"

He stared at her, and, for a moment, Kirstine didn't know what to say. She shook her head. Jakob grabbed her arm, and his voice shook with barely suppressed rage.

"You have to stop this and get back to your room before any of the other teachers discover you here. You sound like you're losing it."

"Jakob, we have to find her! If you won't help, then fine, but I'm staying until we know she's okay!" Kirstine tore herself free.

"Are you trying to ruin everything for me?" he shouted. "Are you aware of what will happen if Birgit finds the two of us together after what you told her? Do you think she can't figure it out? I've sacrificed so much to get this position. It isn't exactly easy for someone my age to get a job here. And now I've screwed it all up. I should never . . ."

He stopped, but he didn't need to say anything more. Kirstine understood. He should never have talked to her at the deserted train station that summer morning, or sat beside her on a bench in the fall breeze, or offered to tutor her so she could keep up with her classes, and he should never, ever have kissed her in the moonlight on Christmas Eve.

She pulled away from him, left him with his mouth forming her name, opened the door, and, taking just one step back, let herself be swallowed up again by the dancing mass of bodies.

Victoria

Victoria could feel the hammering bass in her body. Standing in a crowd of humans in the dark gave her a sense of being part of a large, sweating animal without head or tail. But she needed her head, her eyes. She felt the champagne. *Where are they?*

"Victoria!" She was caught off guard when Malou hugged her hard. *She's afraid . . .*

"What's going on?" Victoria asked, but the music drowned out her voice.

"Where's Chamomile?!" Malou shouted, pulling at her arm to get away from the dance floor.

"I don't know!" Victoria shouted. "I can't find her."

"What about Benjamin?"

"He's gone, too. He said he needed some air," Victoria said once they'd gotten away from the speakers.

Malou showed Victoria her phone, the light from the screen seemed cold and sharp in the dark hall. Victoria saw a bloody animal, maybe a cat, and a message, written in blood . . .

Malou swiped a finger across the screen so the dead cat was replaced by a new picture. "That's Trine. Her real name was Rose *Katrine . . .*"

Victoria stared at the picture. She could see that it was Trine. The real Trine and not the white shadow of her. But suddenly she could also see how much Trine looked like Chamomile! Why hadn't she recognized it before? The simple explanation dawned on her. Victoria's visions consisted of flickering glimpses in black and white; the class portrait was in color. She'd never known Trine had red hair.

"Chamomile . . ." *Where has he taken you?* Victoria closed her eyes for a moment, ignoring Malou's hectic energy and the loud music. *The poplars rustle, the violets bloom . . .*

"Come on, we have to go!" she shouted at Malou, who nodded and pointed toward the back wall. They moved behind the stage and down to the corner at the very back of the hall where Kirstine was waiting for them. Victoria opened an unlocked door that led them down a flight of stairs and out through the dark kitchen.

"Where are we going?" Malou asked as they raced along the counters, stovetops, and cabinets.

"Out. Down to the brook," Victoria answered.

"Was that where Trine . . ." asked Kirstine.

Victoria nodded.

"Come on, there's an exit here!" Malou said, opening a door to the courtyard.

The evening was still, the birds' song clearly audible, and the dark-blue sky still glowed even though the sun had set. It wasn't as late as Victoria had thought. She felt the chill of the night air against her shoulders and bare arms, but she wasn't cold.

"Show the way," Malou urged her.

I see you . . .

As they ran away toward the forest and the little brook—she was there. Victoria was there in her high-heeled dancing shoes and her red ball gown with Malou on the one side and Kirstine on the other—but at the same time she was with Trine. Trine who was carried, her eyes open, but her arms and legs hanging limp, as the man without a face carried her down to the bluff where the violets bloomed.

I see you, Trine.

Chamomile

Glimmers of light flickered in front of her eyes; she had trouble focusing. Where was she? It was dark, and her naked back rested against a cold, hard surface. She faintly registered a pain somewhere in her body but couldn't hold onto the sensation long enough to decipher where it was coming from. The world spun around her and the darkness closed in again.

Malou

They ran. Victoria stumbled in the dark in her heels, and Malou pulled her up again as Kirstine lagged behind. *Keep going!*

"Come on! Come on! Before it's too late!" Malou hurried them on as they approached the forest.

"This way!" Victoria whispered, leading them away from the path. They tripped over tree roots and sank into the mud, but Victoria insisted it was the right way and suddenly they were there.

The bluff, the brook, a sea of blooming violets. And they weren't alone. Malou put a finger to her lips, but none of the others even breathed. All was silent around them as twilight fell. A figure stood on the bluff. Twisted and stooped. It sniffed deeply, its face buried in the grass. It was searching for something. With a jerk, the creature straightened up and looked in their direction. Even though they were still in the shelter of the overhanging leaves, even though none of them had made a sound, it *sensed* them. It knew they were there. And the sight of the ice-blue eyes in the distorted face turned Malou's stomach. *Uggh, it was hideous.*

"Benjamin! Where is she?" The sound of Malou's voice startled Kirstine, who was trying to hold her back, but Malou stepped forward.

This bizarre version of Benjamin was the most disgusting creature she had ever seen. It stood on two legs, but it was misshapen, neither fully man nor beast. Muscular and lean, but deformed, as if the parts had been put together wrong. The jaw was massive, the eyes glowed. He growled. Maybe he couldn't do more than growl in this form. *Maybe it was like with an aggressive dog*, thought Malou. *You could never let your fear show.*

"If you've done anything to her, I'll kill you!" she shouted.

A deep sound came from his throat, maybe a laugh or a warning, and he bared his teeth. She forced herself to stand tall and look him straight in the eyes. Why hadn't she at least grabbed a branch or something? If he lunged at her, she'd have no way to defend herself.

"Benjamin . . ." Victoria's voice sounded so gentle, as if she was trying to soothe a distraught child. He turned away from Malou and toward Victoria as she stepped forward in the dusk. The blood-red dress, the white neck. The deep growling rose in strength, and Malou saw his muscles tense.

"Victoria, get away from it!" Malou screamed, but instead of tackling her, Benjamin suddenly turned and lunged back in the direction of the castle.

"Hey! What have you done with her, you monster!" Malou screamed after him.

"Search the bluff!" Victoria said. "She *has* to be here somewhere."

"Chamomile! Chamomile!" Malou's panicked eyes darted around, but there was nothing to see.

"Ugh, what's that?" Kirstine squatted in the grass, where the wolf-like version of Benjamin had stood. Malou let her phone's light fall on Kirstine's hand.

"It's blood." Malou turned toward Victoria. "She isn't here. Where else could he have taken her? Can we ask Trine?"

"I can't feel her," Victoria said falteringly. "I don't think Trine is here."

Kirstine let out a stifled sob and slumped into the grass.

"Come on, let's hold hands, we have to try to summon her!" Malou grabbed Kirstine's bloody hand and hoisted her up.

"Trine, help us!" Victoria said, closing her eyes. Malou did the same. She could feel the energy from Victoria's cold hand, the blood from Kirstine's. Night had fallen, the birds were no longer singing, there was silence around them, but then a rustling sound arose. Like thousands upon thousands of leaves shaking in the wind despite the stillness of the air.

"I know where she is," Victoria said, and they all opened their eyes at the same time.

Victoria

Of course. That was where she'd first felt Trine. The very first day she'd set foot in the castle. Victoria had had no idea what was going on, she'd just noticed the strong scent of violets, felt the cold, and heard the strange song. It was only now that she realized what it was. She knew it well. The last verse was: *For roses and violets shall never be parted.* The man without a face had sung it for Trine down in the dark room. Before he carried her to the bluff. Before he killed her.

You are my flower, and you will be my mare.

Kirstine

"We have to get back to the castle!" Victoria shouted as they ran. The moon was rising, large and red-orange over the park. "This way." She led them over the courtyard and in through a door which, via a staircase, led down into the basement. Suddenly Kirstine knew where they were. They'd been here on the day of the entrance exams. Victoria gestured for them to creep forward. Here was the wooden door down to the oldest part of the basement, the cellar where they'd been shut in by turns. Victoria put her ear against the door but shook her head. Then she carefully pushed it; it was unlocked. Soundlessly, the door opened, and Victoria stepped through.

The basement was dark, and there was no sound in the large room. The silence suggested they were alone. In the darkness, Kirstine felt a hand on her arm; Victoria pointed to the left. Back in the basement's furthest corner they could see flickering candles. Slowly, they snuck closer. When they passed the last sandstone column, Kirstine gasped.

On the floor lay Chamomile, naked, her eyes closed, her legs and arms spread to either side. And a five-pointed star had been drawn around her. Her hair was spread out on the floor around her head and she was surrounded by a circle of lit candles. Runes, either scratched or cut into her skin, shone red with blood all over her body.

"How did you find us?"

Malou

Next to Chamomile, in the middle of the circle of flickering candles, crouched Vitus. He was naked too. In one hand he held a large knife, probably what he'd used to scratch the many runes into Chamomile's paralyzed body. Now he pressed the blade of the knife into her throat, his eyes fixed on them. An ice-cold feeling spread through Malou's bones. *He's really going to kill her.*

"Just stay where you are, or I might lose control of the knife." His voice was low, measured, but Malou could feel the rage just beneath the surface. "And now, please be so kind as to tell me how you found us."

"Trine told us everything," Victoria answered, looking at him searchingly. Malou saw it too. A spasm passed over his face, making him look momentarily insane before he regained his composure. *She's testing him.*

"You . . . know her name?"

"Trine has told me many things," Victoria replied. "I know her well."

"Ha, sure, maybe you think you do," he hissed. "Maybe she made you think so. But no one knows her like I do."

He looked at Victoria for a moment. Malou looked at her too, and suddenly she knew what Victoria was doing. As long as Vitus was looking at Victoria, he was not looking at Malou.

"Maybe I should have taken you instead, if you're such good friends with Trine?" He leered at Victoria, but then looked down at Chamomile. A shudder, an involuntary convulsion, ran through her body. She was still alive.

"But no," he said, letting the knife caress her cheek, "I think she's perfect. Maybe she isn't as beautiful as you, but she looks like Trine. It wasn't until I thought to look at the class portrait that I was sure who I should choose. Her real name is Rose, you know? He had his Rose, I have my Chamomile. Poetic, no?" He laughed.

"And Anne?" Victoria asked.

Malou's eyes searched the room, she needed a weapon, a stick, a pole, a bottle she could break—anything.

"Ah, yes. I'm not proud of that. Didn't prepare properly, but I'd spotted an opportunity and I took a chance. Improvised you might say. That was a close one, but the girl was good-for-nothing. A total fiasco.

"But you weren't at school on Christmas Eve?"

He laughed curtly. "Let's just say I'm pretty good at quickly getting from place to place," he said, keeping his eyes fixed on Chamomile. He slowly slid the knife down her throat and over the carotid artery pulsing beneath the skin. "And actually, she is beautiful, lying here like this. I have made her beautiful. I think she'd appreciate that."

Malou took advantage of his distraction to take a step closer to the back wall of the basement. She caught Victoria's eye and nodded at her.

"Trine and you are close . . . ?" Victoria asked as Malou retreated further into the shadows.

"She came to me the very first night I was at school," he said. "She was my mare. At first I was afraid of her. I thought she was haunting me, showing me all sorts of things, it terrified me because I didn't understand. No matter where I went, she was there, I was never alone, never free. But then I decided to get to know her. I began to understand her as no one had understood her before. We understood each other. And then one day, she disappeared."

"And that's why . . ."

"She forced me to find someone else. To create my own mare."

"Do you know who killed Trine?"

"You don't?" He looked up at Victoria triumphantly, as if he was holding the trump card in a card game. "Trine hasn't told you. She can't, in fact. That was a stroke of genius, on his part. He bound her tongue with blood magic, in life and death. She can never reveal her murderer. And she couldn't reveal him to me either. A perfect plan. Which you've destroyed. Now I'll have to improvise again. No matter. Things never go exactly to plan, do they?"

"So, no one knows Trine's killer?" Victoria asked. His eyes were only on her.

Just one step further . . .

"That's not what I said, was it?" he sneered, moving the knife away from Chamomile's throat. "I said Trine can't reveal her murderer. But I figured out who it was. It took me a long time, but I figured it out. I solved the riddle she gave me. And how did she reward me? By leaving me."

"Who is he?" Victoria asked, but he shook his head and laughed.

"You think I'm going to tell you? No, that's my and Trine's little secret. It binds us together, whether she wants it to or not. But I think he'd be proud of me, if he saw what . . ."

At that moment, Malou kicked him in the back. She didn't have room to kick as hard as she could have, but because he was crouched so awkwardly, he fell forward and onto all fours. Quick as lightning, he was standing again, the knife still in his hand.

"Oh, you want to play, huh?" he screamed. "This should be fun!" He stood with his back to Malou, but before she could react, he spun around gracefully and lunged at her with the knife. Malou only just managed to shield her face with her arms; she felt the knife's blade cut a long gash in her arm and the pain hit her like an electric shock. He laughed out loud and raised the knife again.

"*Isaz!*" Kirstine screamed, and the rune-curse's power made the air in the room tremble. The ice rune could freeze an enemy and block his attack. It gave Malou just enough time to pull away before the knife came hissing down again. Vitus shook his head as if to shake off the curse. Malou felt hot blood running from the gash and down her arm. *Sacrifice is your source of power.* The words resounded in her head. When Vitus raised his hand to cut her again, she grabbed his wrist and pulled him close to her. For a moment his eyes widened in surprise. There was a rushing in her ears, and she felt a tidal wave of power washing away all resistance. It was a feeling of pure energy. Vitus moaned with exertion, the blood magic gave her intense strength, and his face contorted with pain as his right arm made a cracking sound. She'd broken it.

Vitus screamed in pain and rage, but suddenly she knew that, despite the broken arm, he was becoming stronger. She wasn't the only one drawing power from the red blood—it was nourishing his power too. He was like a parasite that would ultimately kill its host.

"*Hagalaz!*" Kirstine sent the hail rune and the power of the curse hit him on the shoulder of his knife arm so that he was pushed into Malou. With a clattering sound the knife fell to the ground, and Malou kicked it away. Out of the corner of her eye she saw Kirstine lunge toward it as Victoria stooped over Chamomile, attempting to drag her away.

"*Thuriaz!*" Vitus roared over his shoulder and the rune for chaotic power knocked Kirstine to the ground like a fist.

Kirstine's attack had pushed Vitus up against Malou and when she tried to back away, she realized there was nowhere to go. Her back was pressed against the cold brick wall. Before Vitus could lunge for the knife, which had fallen from Kirstine's hand when she was knocked out, Malou rammed her knee into his crotch with all her might. At first, he didn't react at all, and she wasn't sure whether she had actually hit him, but then he crumpled.

"You little whore!" he hissed, but instead of pulling away, he grabbed her, pressed her against the wall and pulled her down with him as he moaned in pain and rage. His face was less than an inch from hers, his naked body lay heavy over hers, holding her down. His powers were still being nourished by her blood. He smiled. He pressed her shoulders into the floor with his hands and suddenly he performed a freakishly agile maneuver so that his feet now rested on her thighs. Slowly he rose to all fours on top of her.

Then Malou felt a sharp pain in both thighs and looked down at her legs. It was no longer Vitus's feet holding her legs against the floor. It was claws. Shiny, black claws boring into her thigh muscles so that blood ran. With a sudden movement he pulled her upper body away from the floor and up against his own before slamming her head back onto the floor.

Victoria

"No!"

Victoria screamed when Vitus, with a thwacking sound, slammed Malou's head down into the floor and her body collapsed, unmoving. Blood flowed from her head and pooled on the stone floor.

Victoria instinctively laid herself over Chamomile. She'd dragged her toward the door. It seemed imperative that she get Chamomile outside the circle of candles, but she was still unconscious, and Victoria's frantic attempts to murmur healing spells over her had no effect. And now it was too late.

Vitus stared at Malou, the same deranged smile still on his mouth, before he turned toward Victoria and Chamomile, and even though she had never seen it before, Victoria knew what she was seeing. A total transformation. A shapeshifter. Not partial and grotesque like Benjamin, but a complete and perfect metamorphosis. Before her stood a man-sized eagle with wings outspread. Beautiful and terrifying. It opened its beak and screamed at her. Then it flapped its enormous wings, one hung crookedly, and the wingbeats—not quite strong enough to lift him into the air—allowed him to jump several feet. Victoria's head felt empty, there was nothing more to do, and she laid down over Chamomile, hid her face in her loose hair, and waited for the eagle's claws to pierce them both.

At that moment it screamed again, and she lifted her head just in time to see a figure jump over them and lunge straight at the eagle so that it fell to the floor on its back. The wolf-like figure bit into a wing and shook, but the eagle soon wrenched itself free and snapped at its opponent with its beak, hitting him in the chest. A long, deep gash opened in the wolf's chest, and, roaring in rage, it lunged at the eagle again. They rolled around on the floor in the circle of flickering candles. Some of the candles tipped over and the molten wax ran out and mixed with the blood from the two animal's wounds while the sound of the wolf's snarling and the eagle's cry reverberated under the vaulted ceiling of the cellar. For a moment the eagle had the advantage. It flapped its enormous wings, and Victoria felt the wave as the candles sputtered and nearly went out. With a furious cry, it planted its razor-sharp claws in the wolf's chest, and, with another flap of its wings, lifted from the floor and rose up to the basement's ceiling before throwing the wolf's body to the floor.

"Benjamin!" Victoria screamed, but the wolf lay unmoving.

The eagle screamed in triumph and landed on the floor beside its victim. She discovered it before the eagle did. The sparks flying in the air had ignited the spilled wax, and suddenly flames shot up between its black claws. The bird tried to take off again, it flapped its wings, but that only made the flames shoot higher. Finally, the eagle was airborne. It flapped up to the ceiling's vaults and screamed desperately. For a moment it just hovered above Victoria. Then it flew toward the door and disappeared.

The fire spread rapidly in the molten wax that had run out over the floor, then it took hold in some boxes stacked in a corner. Victoria dragged Chamomile. She swore, coughed, and sobbed as the tears ran down her cheeks. She wanted, impossibly, to get them all out. A wall of flame had arisen between her and Malou and the smoke had already made it difficult to breathe. With a scream of effort, she heaved Chamomile out through the door and went back for Kirstine, but the tall girl was too heavy, and Victoria collapsed, sobbing beside her.

Kirstine

It was delightfully hot . . . No, it was *too* hot. *Way too hot*. It roared and crackled around her. Kirstine opened her eyes. At first, she didn't understand what she was seeing. *Dark and light. Flames. It's burning.*

She pushed herself up to sit, her eyes felt like they'd been filled with sand, and the movement made her nauseous. She'd hit her head. *He* had hit her. Where was he now?

Kirstine realized there was a figure next to her, collapsed, leaning forward. Victoria. Was she dead? She looked around. Everything was burning. They had to get out. A movement to her right caught her eye, and she turned. Unbelievable pain cut through her head, and she screamed. The wolf was dragging a lifeless body across the floor. *Malou*. The sight made her sick. Then she heard Victoria moan next to her. She was crying. She wasn't dead. They had to get out.

Kirstine struggled to her hands and knees and shook Victoria. "We have to get out!" The sound of her voice disappeared into the roar of the flames.

They half crawled, half dragged themselves to the door. Kirstine's head felt like it would explode from the pain. When they had gotten to the hall, she heaved herself up to stand so she could close the door behind them. The narrow stairwell was lit by scattered lamps, and the smoke created a surreal fog around them. Chamomile lay on the floor, naked and unconscious. Beside her lay Malou, bleeding from a large wound on the back of her head. And bent over her was the wolf, its jaws terrifyingly close to her throat.

Kirstine wanted to scream at it, attack it, get it away, but no sound came. The wolf nudged Malou with its snout, then stood and looked at her. Its expression was expectant, a question. It wasn't trying to eat Malou or kill her, it had saved her from the fire.

"Find him," she whispered, and her voice rose to a shout. "Find him—run!"

The wolf didn't hesitate but turned and bounded away on all fours. Kirstine bent down, and the movement made her see stars.

"Victoria, are you okay?" Victoria lifted her face and nodded. "I'll get help."

Kirstine leaned against the wall as she walked. The few steps up to the outer door made her vomit, but after that the nausea eased. A white light lay over everything. She'd expected it to be dark, but the moon was shining from a cloudless sky. Far in the distance she could hear the party raging on; it seemed bizarre that anyone could dance while others lay dying nearby. Kirstine staggered over the courtyard, and suddenly the door swung open. It was Thorbjørn.

"What happened?"

"The basement," moaned Kirstine. "It's on fire."

He ran past her. She could faintly hear him roar the name of the water rune. *Laguz*. Why hadn't she thought of that?

Kirstine staggered on, but a sound made her stop. A scream. Like from a wounded animal. The wolf must have found him. He hadn't gotten far. Maybe the eagle was wounded too. She changed direction and walked toward the sound instead of the castle. The scream had come from the forest.

Kirstine's vision was blurred from the blow to her temple and she walked on half blind. The black tree trunks were wet and smooth, and they formed an impenetrable labyrinth. The branches tripped her, and a shallow pool swallowed one of her feet without warning so that suddenly she was knee-deep in water. She sobbed with anger and pulled her leg out. The effort threatened to make her lose consciousness again. She heard another scream from deeper in the forest. She had to keep going.

Suddenly the forest opened to her as if it finally had found her worthy. The ancient oak tree stood in the middle of the clearing, illuminated by the moon's beams, and there she saw them. The wolf. And the eagle. So he was an eagle. An eagle who could hover high above them, watching and waiting. An eagle who could take off through an open window. An eagle who could rip its victim to bloody shreds with its claws.

They were fighting, tearing, and biting at each other, screaming from pain and loathing. The beautiful eagle and the gruesome wolf, they were fighting to the death. The wolf bled from several long gashes, its fur singed in various places. It was more wolf than man in appearance now, but she could still see Benjamin inside. It lunged at the eagle and bit and bit. The eagle flapped desperately, it had a broken wing and was struggling to fly, but suddenly the wolf collapsed with a howl. The eagle's claws had struck its flank. The wolf tried to get up but collapsed again. The eagle flapped its wings. Slowly and shakily it rose into the air and hovered over the wolf's body.

Kirstine screamed. She screamed like they did—inarticulately, like an animal. The wolf looked toward her. Then the eagle struck again, planting its claws in the wolf's body, which moved no more. The eagle released its prey and half flew, half hopped toward her. Then it spread its wings and screeched in triumph. One wing hung crookedly from its side, and it bled from numerous wounds. The moon's light made the eagle's feathers, soaked with blood and melted wax, gleam like silver.

She loathed that bird. Kirstine felt anger wash through her like a storm of fire, and the air around her trembled. Behind the eagle stood the massive oak tree, illuminated by a pulsing light that came not from the moon but from within the tree itself, and she felt as if she too had roots. Roots that reached deep, deep under the ground, as if the earth's primordial powers flowed through her, and she was conducting its energy.

"Now you must die," she whispered. She extended her arm toward the man-size bird and screamed the torch rune, the all-destroying primordial fire. "KAUNAN! KAUNAAAAN!"

A thick ray of fire flew from her hand and took hold immediately. The bird was instantly engulfed in flames. It screamed in astonishment and beat its wings as if it could escape the fire. Then it screamed again, and this time it was from pain, and the screaming became a gruesome wheezing, a wail, a whimper. Then it was quiet, and she saw the silhouette of a boy, engulfed in flames, fall to the ground at the foot of the ancient tree.

Chamomile

The next time she woke up, her mother was still sitting in the chair beside her bed in the infirmary, wearing the same clothes she'd arrived in forty-eight hours earlier. The sun shone through the white curtains and the open window let in a sweet spring breeze. Chamomile carefully rose to a sitting position, trying to not wake her mother. She felt much stronger now than the last time she'd woken up. She was dressed in a hospital gown and, under the blanket, bandages almost completely covered her body, covered all the places where he'd cut into her. Ingrid had smeared the wounds with Lisa's special healing salve. The school's healer didn't think Chamomile would scar. She listened, but she couldn't hear anything. Malou was probably still asleep. They'd had to designate both the exam room and the adjoining rooms as makeshift hospital rooms so that there was space for them all. Victoria and Kirstine had been kept for observation the first night for smoke inhalation, but they'd both been discharged. Malou was a bit worse off—she had a skull fracture and a mild concussion. Benjamin was in Ingrid's office. He'd lost a good deal of blood from his various, deep wounds, one of his lungs was punctured, and he had some serious burns on his upper body. When she wasn't wandering, tightlipped and worried, between the other rooms, she was sitting at his bedside.

Cautiously, Chamomile swung her legs over the edge of the tall bed and gingerly put weight on her feet. The dizziness she'd had yesterday seemed to be gone. She crept silently across the floor. Her mother probably hadn't slept in nearly two days—there was no reason to wake her now.

Out in the hall she could hear a low hum of voices coming from the room next door. She carefully pushed the door open. Malou lay in bed. She looked pale, with dark circles under her eyes and a large dressing on her head. Victoria was sitting on the edge of the bed and Kirstine stood beside it. When Malou saw Chamomile walk in, she greeted her with a broad smile.

"Chamomile! You're awake!" Kirstine looked like herself apart from a large bruise over her cheekbone.

Malou tried to sit up, but Victoria pressed her gently but firmly down again.

"Ingrid said you have to lie down. You know she'll go nuts if you don't do as she says." Victoria got up from the edge of the bed and waved Chamomile over. "You can sit here, Chamomile. I'll get us all something to drink."

Chamomile sat on the edge of the bed and took Malou's hand.

"You look better than the last time I saw you," Malou said, her voice hoarse.

"You don't. That's some bandage," Chamomile said.

"You don't think it's a good look for me?" Malou asked. "And we're supposed to have our pictures taken for the yearbook this week! But Ingrid promised I could wait to have mine taken until the bandages comes off."

Chamomile couldn't help smiling. Despite everything that had happened, Malou still had bandwidth to worry about how her yearbook pictures would come out.

"Any news . . . ?" Chamomile looked at Kirstine questioningly.

Kirstine shook her head. "We haven't heard anything. Birgit refuses to speak to us, she runs away every time we catch sight of her. This afternoon we cornered her in the gallery, but she just said she knew she owed us some answers but that we couldn't have them yet."

"And what have the other students been told?" Chamomile asked as Victoria came in with a tray loaded with glasses and a large pitcher of strawberry lemonade.

"Nothing," she answered, pouring them each a glass. "And that, of course, is why the wildest rumors are flying around."

"None as wild as the truth," Kirstine added. "Birgit begged us not to say anything, and, up to this point, we've done as she asked."

Chamomile shook her head.

"I don't understand everything that happened. Lisa says Vitus put a mixture of mandrake root and henbane in my drink before he led me down to the basement. Listen . . . I don't know how you're supposed to say something like this, but . . . thank you for saving my life."

Victoria put an arm around her and Malou gave her hand a squeeze.

"Any time," she said, "but you'll have to thank Benjamin, too. If he hadn't sniffed us out—literally . . ." Malou sniffed like a curious bloodhound, and Chamomile couldn't help laughing again.

"So corny, Malou. Have you spoken to him?"

Victoria shook her head. "Ingrid won't let us. But she says he's improving."

"And who would have thought Kirstine was such a warrior princess?" Malou said.

Kirstine shrugged. "I just did *not* like that bird."

"How did you figure out the thing with the star? What did you call it?" Chamomile asked.

"A mare-cross," Kirstine answered. "Lisa told me about it, but I didn't think much of it at the time. The five-pointed star is sometimes called a *mare-cross* and they say it can keep mares—that is, spirits that torment people at night—away. But it can also bind them. And that was what Vitus wanted. To create his own mare, because Trine wouldn't come to him anymore."

"Sick freak," Malou sighed. "Trine really chose the completely wrong person to confide in."

"And when she realized how wrong she was, she tried to warn me," Victoria said, her voice shaking slightly. "She scared me. Like she scared Vitus at first. In many ways we had the same experience, Vitus and I . . . it's strange to think of . . ."

"Whoa," Malou said, sitting up in bed, "you have nothing in common with that psycho. If it wasn't for the fact that he's already dead, I would kill him. It was all his fault. And Birgit's because she wouldn't listen to us. There's nothing wrong with you. Trine contacted you because you're a spirit mage. It's as simple as that."

"Wow, Malou, you're singing a new tune," Chamomile said.

"What can I say, the dark weirdos of magic have to stick together, right?"

Victoria smiled and squeezed Malou's hand.

"Weirdos forever," she laughed. "And now you'd better lie down again. Ingrid says it's important for you to be surrounded by peace and quiet."

"Yes, she does," Ingrid said as she walked in. She looked, if possible, even paler than Malou. "And this is against my better judgment," she continued, "but Birgit wants to meet with you all this afternoon. All five of you. I said that neither Malou nor Benjamin are ready, but Birgit wants to talk to you before she explains the situation to the whole school. So Malou will have to rest, and Benjamin and Chamomile will need their bandages changed. And you two will have to find something better to do than disturb my patients." With those words she herded Victoria, Kirstine, and Chamomile out the door; directed Chamomile to her bed; and ushered Victoria and Kirstine out of the infirmary.

Back in her room, Chamomile's mother still sat sleeping in what looked like a very uncomfortable position. Chamomile took a blanket from the cabinet and laid it over her mother before curling up under her own comforter again.

Victoria

Benjamin was the last one to come into the patients room, limping and with an arm around Ingrid, who was supporting him. He looked completely worn out, and Victoria felt a twinge of his pain as he hobbled past without looking at her.

"So, we're all here," Birgit said; unlike the rest of those assembled, she stood. She was dressed in a black suit, and her expression was even more stern than usual. She hid it well, but Victoria could tell she was nervous. Jens Andersen, earnestly staring at his folded hands, sat next to her.

"First, I would like to say that we are, naturally, very happy to see you all on your feet again. We're delighted to see you all recovering so quickly, in spite of everything. And it's clear that we—that I—owe you an explanation. And an apology," Birgit began in a professional tone devoid of feeling. "I regret that the necessary precautions were not taken when you attempted to inform us of an imminent danger. An internal evaluation has shown, however, that we could not have acted otherwise on the basis of the available information. Therefore . . ."

"That sounds like bullshit," Malou interrupted, and Victoria noticed, to her surprise, how Malou's outburst made her smile a bit. That was precisely what it was. *A giant load of bull-shit.*

"An internal investigation?" Malou continued. "So you investigated yourselves and discovered that you did everything perfectly? Oh, that's good to know, but also a bit strange that a student was then assaulted and that the five of us here today were nearly killed by a sixth student who ended up suffering the same fate as a marshmallow in a bonfire."

"Malou, you need to calm down!" Ingrid scolded. "Otherwise, it's back to bed. Sorry, Birgit, please continue."

Birgit looked annoyed at having been interrupted, but she took a deep breath and continued: "The investigation did not show that everything was perfect, no, but we could not have foreseen what would happen."

"But we warned you," Kirstine objected.

"You told us Victoria was in danger because Benjamin wanted to kill her. That's not exactly what happened, is it!" Birgit snapped. She lost control for a moment, but Birgit's calm facade was quickly restored. "You cast mistaken suspicion on Benjamin and, given that both he and Victoria were fine, I saw no occasion to investigate the matter further."

"But you knew Vitus could be dangerous. Otherwise you wouldn't have asked me to keep an eye on him." Benjamin, who'd been sitting with his eyes fixed on the floor, turned his ice-blue eyes to Birgit.

"You said it yourself—you owe us an explanation," Chamomile said quietly.

"Very well," Birgit said, and only the red patches on her throat revealed how agitated she really was. "When Vitus began here at Rosenholm almost three years ago, it became clear that he was a special student. He demonstrated exceptional abilities in every branch of magic. That is the first time I witnessed the tree unable to produce a singular answer. And he could shapeshift, as you yourselves saw. Most often he transformed into an eagle, but he could—if he wanted—also assume the shape of other animals. It was highly unusual. Shapeshifters are rare, and when you find one, they can generally only transform into one specific animal. It was really quite extraordinary."

Birgit paused, as if she'd said too much.

"We were, of course, also aware that it can become problematic when someone has considerable abilities in every branch of magic," she continued, and the professional tone was back. "We didn't know how powerful Vitus would become and when. On the basis of his abilities as a shapeshifter, he was so clearly talented within Growth, we chose to let him develop in that direction. Vitus thrived at Rosenholm, and everything seemed to be going well. He focused on his studies in Growth and did not seem particularly talented in the other branches. We all took that as a good sign."

"He played you," Malou interrupted, but her voice was now more declarative than accusatory. "He had no problem performing magic in any of the other branches, Earth, Blood, or Death. He was better than us at it all."

"Yes, I can imagine. It's very unfortunate that we didn't discover that earlier. But he seemed to be doing so well. After some initial struggles, he developed like a completely normal student. The only thing that concerned us was his marked ability as a shapeshifter. He could transform effortlessly, and we had no idea where he was—either physically or mentally. When one of his classmates also began to exhibit abilities as a shapeshifter, we saw it as an opportunity to have someone keep a bit of an eye on him. And maybe keep him from getting hurt."

A snort escaped Benjamin. "As I recall, *I* was the one who was always getting hurt."

Birgit ignored his comment and continued. "Benjamin could follow Vitus when he was in animal form. Even though Benjamin's transformation is not yet complete and effortless, Vitus accepted Benjamin as a sort of companion. From time to time they disagreed, but Benjamin always got him back safe and sound. We believed that everything was still going according to plan."

"And Anne?" Chamomile asked. "Why didn't you suspect Vitus when Anne was attacked? You knew he could change into an eagle and easily fly up to her window."

"To be sure, we questioned him," Birgit answered, "but he had an alibi for the whole evening—he'd celebrated Christmas with his family. I had no reason to suspect him at that time."

Victoria felt it. It was faint, but definitely there. The combination of creativity, fear, and a feeling of superiority. *Lying.*

"You're lying," she said quietly. "It's not true that no one suspected Vitus."

Malou rose up again. "You covered for him, didn't you?" Her hands were clenched in anger. "But of course, it would have ruined your little experiment with the super genius, if it had come out that he was flying around and tearing other students to shreds!"

"Sit down, Malou!" Ingrid scolded.

"I won't stand for these sorts of ridiculous accusations. If no one has anything reasonable to say, then I will terminate this meeting," Birgit hissed. "Tomorrow I will inform the school of . . .

parts of what we have discussed. It will not be necessary to tell them all the details."

"I'd bet big money that you leave out the details of your gigantic screwups. And how you exposed students to unnecessary danger," Malou said, her arms crossed over her chest.

"I know you believe the worst of me, Malou, and it may well be asking too much for your simplistic understanding of the world to comprehend that it is not for my sake but for the sake of the students that they not be burdened with this knowledge. There is no reason to spread fear and terror."

"And that has absolutely nothing to do with that fact that you want to protect yourself and your position at the school?" Malou asked pointedly, raising an eyebrow that disappeared under her bandages.

"I can promise you that it does not," Birgit said with a small, harsh laugh. "I have spared the board of the hassle and embarrassment by, this very morning, submitting my letter of resignation. From next year onward I will no longer be headmistress here at Rosenholm. Jens will be interim headmaster until a suitable replacement is found."

This announcement succeeded, at last, in shutting Malou up. Actually, no one else said anything, and Birgit was the first to leave the room. She walked out without another word, as if she was already an outsider at the school.

Ingrid started to put an arm around Benjamin to help him back to his bed, but he asked her to wait a moment and hobbled over to Victoria. His nearness made her quiver.

"I'm sorry our first date went down the drain like that," he said low enough that only Victoria could hear. "I just want to say, in my defense, that I don't usually behave quite so . . .

animalistically." He gave her a searching look, and it occurred to her that he was nervous about her reaction.

"It's okay," she said. "I wanted to ask you about something. Why did you leave the party? We saw you on the bluff, I don't know if you remember . . ."

"I remember, even though I wasn't myself at the time . . ." He paused, it was probably difficult to explain to someone who'd never experienced it. He let his eyes rest on his hands as he continued. "It was just the first place I ran when I realized Vitus had disappeared. I had a bad feeling and thought he might have transformed. That place was special for him, I don't know why. He often went there when he had transformed. He was fond of devouring animals he'd caught in that spot. And he'd been there earlier that day. There was blood, I could smell it, probably from that cat he nailed to the wall."

Victoria met his eyes when he finally raised his head. He was pale, his cheeks hollow, the cheekbones clearly visible beneath the skin. But despite the fact that he looked as if he'd only just survived a severe illness, he was so incredibly beautiful she almost forgot what she'd been asking about. He was the complete opposite of the vile creature they'd seen on the bluff that night.

"We never talked about what happened when we were both in our animal forms. It was as if we'd agreed not to discuss it when we were ourselves again. People thought we were friends. But we didn't know each other particularly well. I swear I had no idea what he was capable of . . ." His voice broke and Victoria suddenly wanted to hold his hand.

"Benjamin?"

"Yes?"

"Until it all went to hell, I was having a really nice time."

He laughed hoarsely. "Maybe I could ask you out for a second date?"

Victoria nodded. "That would be permissible," she smiled. "On one condition. You have to stop calling me sweetheart."

"It's a deal."

Kirstine

Kirstine felt a drop of sweat run down her neck.

"Anyone want more sunscreen?" Chamomile held out the bottle. Her wounds had healed just fine, but she was still very dedicated about smearing them in SPF 100 so they wouldn't scar.

"Take it easy with the sunscreen. The fact that we've been lying here sweating for almost an hour should show," Malou mumbled as she turned over on the flowered blanket they had spread in the grass in front of the white walls of the castle. It was hot outside. Kirstine felt heavy and drowsy and had nearly fallen asleep with the smell of grass and sun-warmed skin in her nose.

"I don't understand how you can stand it," Chamomile groaned from the blanket she'd dragged further into the shade beside Victoria. Victoria was sitting under the branches of the large copper beech. "Kirstine, you should get into the shade too, your shoulders are going to burn."

Kirstine continued lying there a few seconds longer before she sighed and got up to move.

"Remember the day we moved in? It was super hot then too. I almost couldn't carry all my luggage. And now the school year's over, and I have to pack it all up again," Chamomile said before taking a swig from her water bottle.

Kirstine remembered that day perfectly. Not to mention the day of the entrance exams. So much had happened since then. If she'd known what the first year at Rosenholm would involve, would she have turned on her heel and gone home immediately? Or would she still have chosen to come? It wasn't an easy question to answer.

"What a year we've had," Victoria said, as though her thoughts had ended up in the same place as Kirstine's. She leaned her head against the trunk and looked up at the tree's crown.

"You can say that again," Chamomile said. "I'm hoping for a slightly more peaceful second year."

"But not too peaceful," Malou mumbled, her face in the blanket.

"Seriously?" Chamomile asked.

"Look at us!" Malou said. "Four old maids! For my part, I'd welcome a little more action next year."

"Malou, you nut!" Chamomile said, but she couldn't help laughing.

"Do you think it's all over, Victoria?" Kirstine asked, and even though the question was so vaguely formulated, Victoria understood it well.

"With Trine?" Victoria was still sitting with her face turned toward the tree's branches. She shook her head. "No, it's not over yet. Not until we've fulfilled our promise. Not until we've revealed Trine's killer."

They were all quiet for a moment. They hadn't really talked about what had happened at the Spring Ball. Once in a while, one of them brought something up or made an allusion, but generally it seemed that they were all enjoying being back to normal. While the third years were prepping for their exams and studying in the library all night, the first years had begun to relax. Most of the teachers were busy with exams too. Only Jakob still had the bandwidth to give them homework. Kirstine felt the familiar sting in her heart every time her thoughts fell on their Norse Studies teacher, and she hurried to move them elsewhere.

"I'll keep trying to figure out who did it," Chamomile said. "Not only because of the promise. But because I owe it to her personally. She warned us, and without her, Victoria wouldn't have known where to look for me."

"Of course," Malou said, "of course we'll keep trying—did we ever stop? I've been researching where she came from. Maybe knowing more about her will lead us to her murderer."

Kirstine shuddered. Suddenly she felt the sweat, cold and clammy, against her skin. She nodded anyway. Of course they would keep trying. Trine's killer could still be walking around out there somewhere.

"You're the best friends in the world," Chamomile said. "Old maids or not."

"I have good news by the way," Victoria said, finally tearing her eyes away from the dark-red beech leaves fluttering against the backdrop of blue sky.

"What? You're saying we should cut you from the old maids' team?" Malou asked teasingly. "Is there something more between *Wolf Boy* and you than we know?"

"No, you know everything worth knowing," Victoria smiled. "But I heard Anne's coming back to school next year."

"Really? That's great!" Chamomile said.

"Awesome!" Malou said.

"Yes, I think it was important to her that they found out who'd attacked her. And that he'll never do it again. But she'll have to repeat the first year because she got so far behind."

"Aw, but that's still really great," Kirstine said.

"And do you know who else is coming back?" Chamomile said.

"Uggh, don't remind me," Malou groaned. "It turned out that Zlavko wasn't the biggest idiot at the school after all. Who would have thought?"

"You owe him an apology, Malou."

"That's a problem for future-Malou," Malou said as she pulled the straps of her top down so that they wouldn't ruin her tan. "The man is still a stupid pig. He shouldn't be allowed to torture me."

"Can you believe we won't be the young ones next year?" Kirstine asked.

"I know! And Molly won't be here. I'm going to miss her," Chamomile said. "And what about Benjamin, he'll be done too?"

"Yeah," Victoria said. "We'll have to see what happens. Maybe we can still see each other from time to time. Maybe it won't come to anything."

"But they say love conquers all," Chamomile said, patting her hand.

"And speaking of love," Malou said, raising up to her elbows, "look who's here."

"Jakob," Victoria said. "Maybe we should just . . ."

"You know, I'd say we've gotten enough sun for the day. Come on Malou, let's split. Kirstine will join us later."

"What? I want to see what happens," Malou protested, but she let herself be pulled up from her blanket by a very insistent Chamomile.

A moment later, they'd packed everything up and were waving and giggling at Jakob as he started to mumble helplessly about an assignment he needed to discuss with Kirstine.

"Ah, so they know," he said as the other girls disappeared.

"For the most part," Kirstine nodded.

"Can I sit down?" He let himself sink into the grass beside her without waiting for an answer. "I ought to apologize for disturbing you when you were sitting with your friends, it's not exactly cool but . . . you refuse to answer my messages or meet with me in general." He plucked a blade of grass and began meticulously pulling it apart in long threads.

"I've needed to be with my friends," she said.

"And what about me?" he asked, grimacing as if he immediately regretted the words. "I'm sorry I didn't believe you, Kirstine. I was horrified when I found out what had happened, and I've written to you thousands of times to apologize. I don't know what more I can do. I really am sorry."

Kirstine nodded. "So am I."

"I didn't mean what I said. About regretting things. I don't regret it. No matter what happens. I just wanted you to know that."

She nodded. "Thanks, I'm glad to hear you say that. I don't regret it either."

"Can you forgive me?" He turned toward her, but she turned away.

"I don't know, Jakob. I really feel you deserted me. You couldn't know what would happen, but that doesn't change the fact that you weren't there when I needed you most. I don't think I can ever forget that," she said.

It was as if she could feel him slump beside her, as if the wind had been knocked out of him.

330

"I was afraid you'd say something along those lines," he whispered. "Everything will be different now. You seem different. Did you take off your necklace?"

Kirstine nodded. She knew he was referring to the cross.

"It doesn't feel right to wear it anymore." She had it still, would always keep it, but she wouldn't wear it. Jakob was right. She was not the same. She had saved a life. And taken one. *That sort of thing takes its toll.*

"So now what?" he asked.

"Now life goes on, I assume. Soon it will be summer break. I've going to try to visit my family. Maybe they'll let me in, maybe not. Either way, I'll go to Victoria's afterward. They have an extra room where I can stay on breaks. Victoria says it's not a problem. And otherwise, I can live at school. In a way it's become my home now. For better or worse."

Jakob stood up and reached out a hand to pull her up.

"Can I at least give you a hug goodbye?" he asked. She nodded, but regretted it when she felt his arms around her. Why did he insist on smelling so good? It made her promise to herself a thousand times harder to keep.

For a brief moment, he held her tight.

"If I ever get another chance, I promise I won't desert you," he whispered hoarsely in her ear.

"Goodbye, Jakob," she said, pulling away. Then she turned so he wouldn't see that she was crying and walked back toward the white walls of Rosenholm.

Are you all packed Mile-Mouse?

I'm so looking forward to your coming home

we have a whole summer in front of us

Listen—I've been thinking about something, what with everything that happened at school. Maybe you're right. Maybe you're ready to know who your father is . . .

What? Mom?

Moooom . . . ??????

EPILOGUE

He still dreams of it from time to time. More often after all that happened recently. The beauty in those moments will always be crystal clear for him, until the day he dies, of that he is sure.

The pulse moving just under her skin—like the infinitely soft beating of a bird's wings—his fingers gliding along her white throat. The red-gold, silky smooth locks spread out between the blooming violets. The girl's pleading gaze. The rustling of the silver poplars. Her glowing skin in the twilight. He sings for her. He loves her. Then. And now.

The mystery and drama continues …

Gry Kappel Jensen
Forget Me Not
On sale Fall 2024
ISBN 978-1-64690-013-8

The four friends are back at Rosenholm for their second year and they find themselves digging deeper into the mystery of Trine's killer. They learn that Trine's sister, Leah, still lives nearby and may have information that could help the girls. But as a powerful blood mage, Leah's power and internal struggles may be too much for them to handle.

As they try to fulfill their promise to Trine, they continue to put themselves at risk. Will they push their luck too far?